BETTING ON A DUKE

Widows of Mayfair, Book 4

Christine Donovan

ARE YOU SIGNED UP FOR DRAGONBLADE'S BLOG?

You'll get the latest news and information on exclusive giveaways, exclusive excerpts, coming releases, sales, free books, cover reveals and more.

Check out our complete list of authors, too!

No spam, no junk. That's a promise!

Sign Up Here

www.dragonbladepublishing.com

Dearest Reader;

Thank you for your support of a small press. At Dragonblade Publishing, we strive to bring you the highest quality Historical Romance from some of the best authors in the business. Without your support, there is no 'us', so we sincerely hope you adore these stories and find some new favorite authors along the way.

Happy Reading!

CEO, Dragonblade Publishing

Additional Dragonblade books by Author Christine Donovan

Widows of Mayfair Series
Loving an Earl (Book 1)
Pursuing a Duke (Book 2)
Marrying a Marquess (Book 3)
Betting on a Duke (Book 4)

Dedication

This book is dedicated to all the readers who took a chance on me as a new author with Dragonblade Publishing. Thank you from the bottom of my heart!

CHAPTER ONE

1810

"I DARE YOU to come in," teased Samuel Radcliff as he splashed lake water with his arms toward where Clarice Dawson stood on the shoreline, gawking at him. His mischievous behavior caused her to jump back to avoid the flying water.

"Stop! You're getting my dress wet," she huffed at the same time she giggled. Some of the tension eased from her body as she wondered what her father, the Earl of Portsmouth, and Samuel's father, the Duke of Stanton, were discussing behind the duke's closed study door. Could she hope it was what she wished for? Was a marriage contract between her and Samuel being negotiated and signed at this very moment? Nothing in her entire life would bring her greater joy.

When she decided to take a walk down to the lake on the duke's country estate, hoping to dip her feet in the cool water, she hadn't expected to find Samuel there. Last she saw him, he had been heading to the stables. Clarice had wanted to sneak off and have some time away from the constant chatter between their mothers. They were already discussing the wedding plans between her and Samuel. It wasn't that she was uninterested in those arrangements, but shouldn't the betrothal happen first? Until it did, she didn't feel comfortable getting her hopes and dreams up.

So here she stood lakeside, shocked to see Samuel nearly

naked and dripping wet, to the point that she wished to lick the droplets of water off his skin. Where had that thought come from? Did people do such a thing? Her mind was in such a muddle today.

Samuel, young and handsome and the second son to the duke, had been her best friend for as long as her memory served. He was three years older than her own eighteen years, and still attending university. As he strolled toward the shore, his bare chest and shoulder muscles rippling beneath the sun as the water glistened across his skin had her insides melting, and she struggled to keep her mouth closed. She'd always known Samuel was handsome and had a healthy physique—riding and training his horses helped with that—but she wasn't prepared for seeing him naked from the waist up. Tingles encompassed her entire being. He held out his hand, and her eyes widened as they were drawn to the line of dark hair that disappeared down inside his water-logged breeches, clinging obscenely to his thighs and what lay between them. What would he look like without his breeches?

When she didn't take his hand, he chuckled, pulling her out of her indecent, wayward thoughts. "Stop staring at me." He flexed his arms and laughed again. "If you can stare at me, I get to stare at you. Strip and join me."

A gasp escaped her lips. Was it from shock or excitement at the idea of frolicking in the water with Samuel? "We are hardly children anymore. If we are caught, I will be ruined."

"Who is there to catch us? This is my father's property, and no one would dare trespass. Besides, aren't our fathers discussing our marriage contract at this very moment? We are practically married already." He stood before her, stealing her breath and causing her heart to race with his words and handsome features. As his fingers gripped the hem of her day dress, she shivered in the most delicious way. He easily slipped it over her head without unbuttoning it. He made quick work of her corset until she stood in nothing but her linen chemise. He was a total gentleman and kept his eyes on her face as he took her hand and tugged her into the lake.

A loud gasp exploded from her throat. "It's freezing."

"You'll get used to it, I promise," he said with a twinkle in his dark-gray eyes and a lopsided roguish grin that always stole her heart.

"That's easy to say—you've already been in."

"Do you trust me?"

His arms were out, and she knew he wanted her to go into them while he floated on his back like they had innocently as children. It was how she'd learned to swim. Today, at their age, it was a terrible idea. "Yes. I trust you."

His eyes blinked, turning nearly black and he grew serious. "You shouldn't."

"Why not? I've always trusted you."

"Because now that you're eighteen, everything has changed."

"I know it has." She shivered.

"Will you hurry up and wrap your arms around my waist and relax so we float instead of drowning?"

Obliging him, she found herself safely wrapped in his arms, lying on top of his firm body, and she ignored the immediate awakening of hers. She dreamt of moments like these with him and couldn't wait until they truly belonged to each other, so there was nothing improper happening. A sudden sadness washed over her, and she didn't understand why.

"Relax."

"I'm trying," she grumbled.

"Try harder."

After a while, her body relaxed as the sun beat down on them, soothing her all the way to her bones. "Do you really believe our fathers are discussing our marriage contract?"

Before she knew it, she was underwater and glad to be able to touch the bottom of the lake. She stood up, shocked to find the water only at her waist. She spat out the gulp of water she took in as gracefully as she could and without snorting. "What happened?"

His eyes stared into hers, and she felt the intensity all the way to her soul. "Sorry. I lost my concentration." She heard him swallow as his eyes roamed her body. "Christ," he ran his hand through his unruly, wet hair. "You are more beautiful than my dreams led me to believe."

She looked down at herself and was shocked to find her thin chemise transparent and stuck to her breasts and stomach. Her nipples were hard and jutting out. It took everything she had not to cover herself up with her arms. She had nothing to hide from Samuel.

"Clarice," he said, his voice raspy, his hand shaking as he reached out and cupped her breast, running his thumb across the nipple, causing it to harden further. "I've wanted to touch you for so long. I've dreamed of this forever. I forced myself to wait, knowing that when you turned eighteen we would be married."

She sucked her bottom lip inside her mouth as his hand and thumb continued to play with her breast. Other than his hand, they remained apart. Even as her body shivered, heat bloomed between her thighs. There was no denying the explosion inside her heart at knowing they would be married soon. Her father would never turn down a marriage proposal from Samuel. He was the second son of a duke, the son her father never had and always praised. Samuel pulled her into his arms, holding her close so they touched everywhere possible. He murmured into her ear, "Clarice, I have loved you all my life. Will you marry me?"

"Yes." Hearing his proposal was a dream come true for her.

The moment she said yes, he swept her up into his arms and carried her to the edge of the woods, stopping beneath a tree where he laid her down on a soft pile of leaves and moss. "Do you know what I have in mind?" he asked, his voice rough and his eyes heavy-lidded. "If you have any objections, we will wait for our wedding night."

She reached for him. "No. I can't think of a better place or time to finally belong to you—and you to me." She meant what she said. The moment was perfect. Her late-night dreams were about to become real.

Samuel covered her body with his and kissed her deeply. They had kissed before, however, this one was nothing like those kisses. His lips, teeth, and tongue devoured her and stole her breath. He tasted and sipped from her mouth, and she returned the gesture in kind. Never had he kissed her with such intensity that she lost herself in all the sensations coursing through her body. They moaned and groaned freely. The sound was perfect to her ears.

He tore his mouth from hers and kissed his way down her neck and sucked her nipple into his mouth through the wet fabric of her chemise. Her back arched off the ground as she felt the sensation travel down and settle between her thighs. He moved to her other breast and did the same thing, and once again, she felt it all the way to her womanhood.

When Samuel finally pulled up her chemise and touched her down there, she moaned with relief, finally knowing what it felt like to be touched by the one she loved in her most vulnerable and intimate area. Her hips moved against his hand automatically. She had no control over her emotions or her body's response.

Samuel leaned off her and unbuttoned the placket of his breeches, freeing his engorged manhood. She tried not to let it happen, but her eyes widened and her mouth opened. "How is that going to fit inside me?"

Chuckling, he kissed her lips. "Trust me. It will, and I'll be gentle."

He moved on top of her and kissed her while his hand caressed her down there. It didn't take long before she was squirming for more. Samuel moved between her legs and spread them wide. "Don't tighten up. Relax and breathe," he murmured right before she felt his manhood nudge against her opening.

"I'm trying," she giggled, even though there was nothing funny about what was about to happen. She always laughed when she was nervous. His hips moved against hers, pushing and retreating until he broke through her maidenhood. The pain took her by surprise, but as he moved inside her, it eased, and she tingled down there again.

Samuel buried his face in her neck. "I love you so much, and I can't believe we get to spend the rest of our lives together, doing this anytime we want."

"Hmmm, I love you too. But, I'm not convinced about this."

"Trust me, there is so much more, and I promise to make you scream with pleasure the next time we make love."

She frowned. "What about this time?"

"Is that a dare?" He looked at her with his lopsided grin, the one he had perfected at the age of ten that always made her heart melt.

"You bet it is!" she laughed.

"Well then, I'd better do my best and prove myself worthy of worshiping you."

From that instant on, Samuel did as he promised. He worshiped her body until she could endure no more. Nothing, in all she'd read or heard whispered in drawing rooms or ballrooms, had prepared her for the sensitive onslaught and explosive pleasure she experienced with Samuel. Even now, as she lay sleepy, curled up in his arms beneath the large oak tree, her body hummed, her heart sang, and her soul was light and content. Never had she experienced such happiness and fulfillment. And to think she would marry her best friend and the man she loved above all others, hopefully in a short time.

WHEN SAMUEL FIRST saw Clarice approaching the lake, her image took his breath away. He had been half-teasing when he said, "Strip and join me." And when she let him help her undress, he knew without a doubt that she was the woman for him, even though he already knew in his heart she was.

They understood each other, and they always had since they were very young. They were like-minded. He never had to pretend around her, and she probably didn't have to pretend around him either. At least, it didn't seem like she did.

The only thing he regretted was not waiting for her to be his first lover. He'd felt guilty the times he bedded other women, and so very thrilled knowing he would only ever bed Clarice from this day forth.

When he woke up that morning, he never imagined he would be lying beneath a tree, holding Clarice in his arms after making love to her and smiling like a love-sick fool. And this was only the beginning. His heart and soul felt at peace. His mind had also calmed down, which helped him tremendously. Most days, his mind raced with one thing or another. Right now, all it wanted was to hold Clarice and think about what tomorrow might bring. He wondered if he approached the Archbishop of Canterbury, would he grant him a special license so he could marry her within the week? Where would they go on their honeymoon? Where would they live? He chuckled. So his mind wasn't quite as at ease as it seemed.

His arms held her closer to his heart. "Are you awake?" The last thing he wanted was to wake her, but they had been gone for several hours, and he didn't want to risk his father or hers sending a footman or maid to find out where they were.

"Hmmm." She snuggled into his arms, sending his body into turmoil. "Just barely."

He kissed the top of her head. "We should get dressed, make ourselves presentable, and go back to the house."

"It might take me some time."

"I will help you."

Half an hour later, they were dressed and looked acceptable. Clarice's hair might not be perfect, but she could blame the windy weather. Luckily, all their clothes were dry. Hand in hand, they meandered along the path in the woods to the lush green lawn, through the formal gardens, and into the drawing room where both their mothers were dabbing at their eyes with handkerchiefs. A small knot formed in Samuel's stomach. "Is something amiss?"

he asked. Both mothers looked at them and then burst into tears. "Please, tell me what has happened," he demanded, his heart skipping several beats as panic set in. "Has someone died?"

Clarice clutched his hand tightly, and her body stiffened. "Mama, what has you so upset?" she asked with concern.

"My dear Clarice, we must go," her mother mumbled. Her mother hugged Samuel's mother, the Duchess of Stanton. "Goodbye, my dearest friend." She held her hand out to her daughter. "Come, we must not keep your father waiting."

Samuel tried not to let Clarice's hand go, but it was no use. She obeyed her mother and tugged her hand away from his firm grip. As she left the drawing room, her shoulders sagging, she looked back at him, her watery eyes wide and pleading.

"Clarice," he called.

"Let her go, son," his mother said quietly.

Let her go? What did that mean? He couldn't let her go. He was going to marry her.

CHAPTER TWO

CLARICE REMAINED SILENT until their carriage pulled away from Stanton Hall and onto the long road that would take them to one of her father's properties several miles away. When she was born, her father had purchased the property so he and his best friend, the Duke of Stanton, could raise their children together. The duchess had given birth to two sons, Samuel being the second born.

"Why are we leaving? I thought we were staying for dinner." The disgusted look her father gave her chilled her to the bone. What was worse was that her mother still wept into her handkerchief. "Please tell me what is wrong." As she waited for either of her parents to speak, her head began to pound and her stomach ached. Had they found out about what she and Samuel had done down by the lake? But if they had, why would they be upset? She and Samuel were always supposed to marry. And if her parents had somehow found out, wouldn't they be back at Stanton Hall preparing for a wedding?

"I'll . . ." her mother began between sobs, "I'll let your father explain. Since it's his doing."

She had never seen her father give her mother such a hateful look, causing the ache in her stomach to intensify. "Please tell me. I'm going out of my mind with worry."

"I've decided not to negotiate a marriage contract with Lord

Samuel Radcliff." Her father stated it matter-of-factly, as if it meant nothing. When it meant everything to her.

She swallowed the tears clogging her throat, hoping she could speak. "But why? Samuel proposed today, and I said yes. It is what we both want."

"It is no longer what I want for you. Don't talk to me about it again. In fact," he glared at her, making her whole body tremble. "Don't mention the Stanton or Radcliff names ever again. Those people mean nothing to me. Things have changed, and you will marry whomever I choose. Now, be quiet and don't bother me again."

Tears, which she hated to let her father bear witness to, slid down her cheeks as she fought to hold back the sobs that yearned to escape. What had happened behind the duke's closed study doors? How could the duke, her father, or both play with her and Samuel's lives as if their feelings didn't matter? She loved him. Would always love him. The first chance she got, she would write Samuel and suggest they ride like the wind to Gretna Green.

When they reached their modest estate, Clarice said nothing to either of her parents as she hurried up two flights of stairs to her chambers. Fortunately, it was on the opposite end of the corridor from her parents. She couldn't bear to see their faces or hear their voices. In just one day, she had made love with Samuel, and afterward, they'd planned their future together. Then, without warning, her father had shattered her life by taking the man she loved away from her. What truly froze her inside was wondering what her father had in store for her.

Her maid, Mrs. Shelley, an older widow whom she adored, hurried in after her. "I didn't expect you until later, my lady."

"I know. We left early. Could you send up a dinner tray and some fresh hot water for washing? After you do, you may retire for the evening."

She bobbed her head. "Yes, my lady."

While Clarice waited for Mrs. Shelley to return, she stood at a window staring out into the gardens beyond. All the plants and flowers were blurry because of her continuous stream of tears. She had a terrible foreboding that her life was about to take a terrible turn, and there wasn't anything she could do to save herself.

LEAVING HIS MOTHER alone in the drawing room once Clarice and the countess left, Samuel stormed down the hall to his father's study. Seeing the door was shut, he knocked and, without waiting for a response, pushed it open to find his father sitting at his desk, gazing thoughtfully into a glass of amber liquid. "Father, would you please tell me what just happened with Portsmouth?"

His father looked up with sad eyes and murmured, "Pour yourself a drink and have a seat."

Samuel wasn't sure he wanted a drink, but he poured himself one anyway and then sat down in a comfortable wingback chair. "Well?"

"It appears Portsmouth is in serious debt because of a poor investment. He has no dowry for Clarice." His father downed his glass of brandy and clanked the glass on the wooden surface as he set it down. "Her dowry means nothing to me or to you. A marriage contract could have been signed without it."

Taking a big gulp from his drink in the hope of calming his nerves, Samuel asked, "And why didn't you?"

"Because the blackguard wants Lady Clarice's intended to pay him a large sum to marry his daughter, with monthly stipends paid to Portsmouth as long as he, the countess, or the husband-to-be is alive."

Swallowing down his shock and ignoring the pounding of his heart and the sick feeling in the pit of his stomach, Samuel croaked out, "What the bloody hell?"

"Exactly," his father agreed. "Basically, he is selling his daughter to the highest bidder as if she is being auctioned off at Tattersall's. It's immoral, degrading, and downright repulsive."

"I proposed to Clarice today and she said yes." Was it really less than two hours ago that he'd held her in his arms after making love to her and proposing?

"I'm sorry, son. I would have bought Lady Clarice for you, but the amount he asked for, along with the substantial payments expected in the coming years, was more than you could afford. I couldn't, in good conscience, use funds that belong to the dukedom and your brother, Alexander."

"I understand. Is there anything I can do?"

"You could always rescue her and head to Gretna Green."

"My thoughts exactly." Some of the tension inside him eased. It wouldn't be truly gone until she was his wife, and there was nothing her father could do to rectify it.

"But be careful, my son. I don't trust Portsmouth. He's desperate, and desperate men will do anything."

"I will take care. I'll leave right now and take her away."

Samuel took the stairs two at a time to his chambers and packed a bag with two changes of clothes. He rushed out to the stables and saddled his horse, Smokey, and another for Clarice with help from a stablehand. He considered taking the coach, but if Portsmouth pursued, they could move faster on horseback. After stashing his belongings in his saddlebag, he headed out with Clarice's horse tethered to his.

Dawson House was cloaked in darkness when he arrived at the servants' entrance. Although he didn't expect any trouble, he kept a loaded pistol in his overcoat pocket. He turned the doorknob and frowned when it didn't budge. Most servants' doors were unlocked even at night.

"I knew you'd come for her." The unmistakable sound of a pistol cocking sent a chill up his spine.

Samuel didn't need to turn around and look at the person who spoke. He recognized the voice—it belonged to Clarice's father. He pivoted anyway, and not far off, he saw the earl holding a gas lantern in one hand and a pistol in the other. Two footmen flanked him. "You need to leave and never come back."

Despite the pistol aimed at him, he declared his intentions. "I've come for Lady Clarice. She has agreed to marry me, and I plan to make sure it happens with or without your blessing."

"No blessing, and over my dead body."

Samuel reached for his revolver, but before he could grab it, Portsmouth fired, releasing sulfur, gunpowder, and smoke that clogged his nostrils and caused pain to shoot through his upper arm. "What the hell?"

"If you ever try to contact my daughter again, the next bullet goes between your eyes." As he walked away, he spat to his footmen, "See that the earl arrives home safely."

Samuel couldn't believe his father's best friend—until today— and a man he'd known since birth, had just shot him. He used his good arm and took out his handkerchief and pressed it to the wound, hoping to stop the bleeding. One of the footmen approached and examined the wound.

"Yer lucky. The bullet went straight through."

The ride back to Stanton Hall felt like the longest hour of Samuel's life. Not just because of his wound, but because of the gaping hole in his heart. He wondered if that hole would ever heal, or if he would always be missing a piece of his heart, no matter what the future held.

CHAPTER THREE

I T HAD BEEN a fortnight since the best day and worst day of her life. Clarice swore her heart had stopped beating and her emotions had escaped, never to return. She was a walking, living, breathing shell of herself.

She didn't understand why Samuel had never replied to her note or come for her. Was their entire life and the day they spent by the lake together all a lie? Had she allowed her heart and mind to distort what she wanted to see and believe, rather than seeing what truly was? No. She would never believe that Samuel didn't love her. He did. But then why hadn't he come and taken her away from this nightmare her father had created?

They had arrived in London yesterday and were attending a ball at the Viscount and Viscountess Appleton's tonight. According to her father, she was supposed to flirt with any eligible bachelor he deemed worthy. She was not to cause a scandal, but she was to make it clear she was available to the highest bidder.

Highest bidder? He had told her at breakfast that morning that he was in debt and needed money, so he was selling her off, parading her around the wealthy members of Society like one did with horseflesh. The only way to redeem the family name and fill the coffers was for her to do her duty to her family and marry a wealthy man. A man willing to pay her parents for the privilege of marrying her. He laid on the guilt thick, saying her mother would be ruined and it would be her fault. And because she loved her mother and didn't want to see her suffer for her father's deeds, she would go along with her father's plans even though it would break her heart and crush her in the process. But how was she supposed to hold her head high when everyone would know her father was a bloody blackguard selling his only daughter?

She ran to the chamber pot in the corner behind a screen and cast up what little food she'd eaten that day. She didn't even have her mother to comfort her, as her mother had retreated to her rooms and refused to join her father's shocking and abhorrent scheme. That meant her father would be the only parent accompanying her to every event during the fall Season. That is, until someone offered for her.

But why would any gentleman offer? She was nothing special, with her mousy brown hair and brown eyes. Oh, she supposed she had a pleasant face with small features and an acceptable enough figure. Still, what kind of gentleman would buy his bride? One so old and feeble that he needed a wife to nurse him in his final days. One so foolish that no other lady of the *beau monde* would have him, no matter how rich he was. What about the men whispered about in drawing rooms who abused their mistresses? Most fathers kept their daughters away from such men. Her father would push her into their arms regardless of the type of monsters they were, as long as he received the payment he demanded.

"Oh dear," she gasped as she dry heaved into the pot. She needed to shut her mind down. Thinking up all these scenarios wasn't helping her. She crawled beneath her pretty green-and-pink coverlet, curled up on her side, and hoped to sleep. Perhaps when she woke, it would all be a terrible nightmare, and she would have her loving father back. And more importantly, Samuel.

"Time to wake up and prepare for tonight's ball," Mrs. Shelley said as she entered her room some time later.

Clarice sat up and rubbed her eyes. Even though she knew she'd napped, she still felt groggy, tired, and achy all over.

Mrs. Shelley set a tray next to her on the bed. "Eat something, my lady. Midnight is a long way off to wait for supper to be served."

She first picked up the cup of tea and sipped it slowly until she determined whether her stomach could handle any solid food. After finishing the tea, she nibbled on the cold chicken, fruit, cheese, and bread. If she didn't force some of it down, she knew she would feel lightheaded at the ball if she even took one glass of ratafia.

The sound of Mrs. Shelley opening the wardrobe caused Clarice's eyes to follow her hand as she rummaged through her gowns, none of which Clarice had had the chance to wear since she hadn't made her entrance into Society at the start of the Season. As far as Clarice was concerned, this abbreviated Season would be just fine, since nothing mattered to her anymore.

"I think one is perfect." She pulled out a beautiful white gown trimmed with seed pearls and lace. The bodice dipped relatively low, if her memory served. Her father would be pleased. She had the feeling that if he could parade her around naked, he would.

"Let me press it. I'll be back soon."

Finally alone, Clarice stepped off the bed, took care of her needs behind the screen, and slumped into the chair at her dressing table, staring at her reflection in the mirror.

There were dark circles under her eyes, her cheeks were sunken, and her complexion was paler than usual. She felt tingling and discomfort in her breasts. They seemed heavy and sensitive as if her courses were to begin. Just another source of worry caused by the white gown.

"Good, my lady, you are up," Mrs. Shelley said as she swept back into the room, hidden behind layers of white tulle, lace, and silk. "Let's make your first ball special."

Mrs. Shelley worked her magic with her hair, but by the time Clarice entered the hall to find her father waiting for her, all she wanted to do was run back upstairs and hide under her bed like she used to as a child when she was frightened. But now, she was eighteen, and her father was dictating her life. Sighing heavily, she exited the townhouse as the doorman held the door open and then got into the carriage with the help of one of the footmen.

Her father sat opposite her, and his dark eyes swept up and down her person. "You should do nicely tonight," he said in his deep baritone. "All dressed in innocent white."

His words make her tense. Was he trying to make her uncomfortable and nervous for her first ball? Because if he was, he was too late. Her nerves had been torturing her all day. Nothing was spoken for the rest of the drive. When they arrived, her father exited the coach first, then leaned back in with his hand held out. "My daughter." She had no choice but to take his hand, and as they entered the queue for the ball, her father placed her hand on his forearm.

As they moved quietly up the wide, sweeping marble staircase to a large landing where their host and hostess stood greeting their guests, Clarice felt like she was wrapped in a dense fog. Nothing seemed real or normal. She recognized few people because her parents had mostly kept to themselves or were with the Stantons. She had been sheltered. When she reached the Viscount and Viscountess of Appleton, she curtsied and said all the right things, even though she felt disconnected from herself, and the voices echoed as if traveling through a tunnel.

The master of ceremonies announced them, and she found herself being pulled along by her father, her feet barely keeping up, nearly causing her to trip.

"Please slow down, Father. I'm not used to walking in heeled slippers." He did slow his stride but said nothing. "Could you please tie the dance card to my wrist?" Once again, he did as she requested without acknowledging her.

"Let us take a turn around the room," he stated without looking at her, and started walking regardless of whether she was ready or not. "Smile and look pretty. This is when eligible gentlemen scan the young debutantes and decide if they are interested. If you look like you've sucked on a sour lemon or walk like you have a stick up your arse, they may cross you off their list. Smile, make eye contact with the groups of young men gathered around the room." He paused and looked at a group of gentlemen off to the side. "I have it on good authority that the Marquess of Dowding is actively looking for a bride and that his purse is overflowing," he said.

"Which one is he?" The moment she asked, she wished she hadn't. She didn't want her father to think she enjoyed this plan of his.

"He is the red-headed gentleman looking right at you." He chuckled. "You see, my dear daughter, I had my barrister send letters to ten very rich, eligible gentlemen who are seeking brides with information about you and how they may obtain your hand in marriage."

Her feet stopped, the room spun around in circles, and she had to swallow repeatedly. If she didn't, she was going to cast up her accounts. It would serve her father right if she did. All his careful plans would turn to dust. Who would want to marry a girl who lost her stomach at a ball? Now she understood why everyone seemed to be whispering about them. The ladies hid their mouths behind their fans, but their eyes connected with hers. Some looked disgusted, some pitied her, and others glared with hatred. All of this was due to her father's insane plans.

Finally, her father guided them to a corner of the ballroom and took two glasses of wine from a passing footman. As she sipped, several gentlemen approached, asking to sign her dance card. That was how she spent the rest of the night—dancing with strange men, making small talk, or being grilled about her hygiene and daily routines. Some had the nerve to ask to see her teeth. All of it she found invasive. She mumbled answers to the questions she thought appropriate and ignored the ones she didn't. Either way, she didn't give a damn what these men thought of her. If they would stoop so low as to buy her from her father, then she had no respect for them, nor did she want to get to know them.

She found herself in the arms of the Marquess of Dowding, who, she admitted, was handsome with his deep burgundy hair and a smattering of freckles across his cheeks and nose.

"I'm sorry for what your father is doing to you."

It was the first time anyone had mentioned it, and she nearly froze on the spot. Her heart accelerated, and her body quivered from head to toe.

"Forgive me for being so forward and upsetting you. I just want you to understand my feelings on this. I'm dancing with you to please Portsmouth, but I'm not going to buy my bride. I'm neither desperate nor in any hurry to wed."

Things were getting worse for her. She could feel the heat rising up her neck and encompassing her entire face, no doubt turning it bright pink. His green eyes fixed on hers, expecting a reply. "Th-thank you. I'm only allowing this to help my family."

"I'm sorry. I wish I could find it in myself to offer for you and save you from the clutches of a disreputable gentleman, but I'm holding out for the elusive love marriage. I sincerely hope things turn out well for you." He bowed as the dance ended, then escorted her back to her father, who had a hopeful expression on his face.

She could shake her head and alleviate his curiosity, but she refused to make his life easier. Not until he ended his madness.

When they were alone, he asked, "Well, what about the marquess?" When she didn't answer right away, he gripped her upper arm rather tightly, hurting her.

"He is not interested in purchasing a wife. He is also not in a rush to wed." Laughter burst out before she could stop it, and she slapped her gloved hand over her mouth to stifle it. "He is a romantic and holding out for love. I'm going to the ladies' retiring room." Not only did she need to relieve her bladder, but she also needed some time alone without her father. Opening the door to the retiring room, she sighed with relief upon finding it unoccupied. After taking care of her needs, she sat in one of several chairs around the small room. Her feet hurt inside her shoes, and painful blisters had already formed on the backs of her heels. She was about to kick them off when the door opened and two older women, whom Clarice didn't know, entered.

"What a pleasant surprise to find you in here," said one of the ladies, dressed in forest green. "Are you enjoying the ball?"

"Yes, thank you."

"I was disappointed that your mother didn't accompany you this evening," said the same lady as she patted her brown hair streaked with gray. "I've met her several times, and she is a lovely woman."

"She isn't feeling well this evening. Perhaps you'll see her again soon."

"I hope so."

Clarice stood and curtsied. "If you will both excuse me." Before she took a step, the other lady, dressed in navy blue, placed her arm around hers and smiled sadly.

"I'm the Marchioness of Dowding and I saw you dancing with my son, who is now the marquess. Is there anything we can do for you?"

Before she broke down in tears from the marchioness's kindness and her own shame, Clarice hurried out the door. Instead of going into the ballroom, she lingered in the large entryway and sat on a bench between two potted palms. One glance at her dance card showed several names she owed dances to, but there was nothing that would make her step inside that ballroom again tonight.

Her father could drag her kicking and screaming, as far as she was concerned. She would not put herself through any more shame or embarrassment. He would have to find another way to sell her. She refused to be paraded in front of half the *ton*.

It wasn't long before her father sought her out. "Here you are. Why are you out here?" he snapped.

"Because I'm ready to leave. I will not go back in there. I've had enough mortification for one evening." Without waiting to see what he did, she hurried down the stairs, stopped at the door, retrieved her cloak from the butler, and stepped outside. The racing of her heart calmed when she realized he had followed her and was signaling their driver.

The ride home was tense and silent. Her father glared at her, letting her know he was displeased with her. Too bad. It was time she stood up for herself. She would need to if she was to survive what he planned for her.

With Mrs. Shelley's help, she undressed, put on her night clothes, and climbed into bed with a relieved sigh, finally home and back in the privacy of her chambers. What was even more relieving was being without her father's company. After the trying evening, she fell asleep quickly.

Morning arrived quickly as well. Afternoon tea and visitor time came even faster. When Clarice arrived in the drawing room, she froze in the doorway at the sight of four gentlemen standing around talking with her father. Taking a deep breath for courage and strength, Clarice stepped into the room and sat beside her mother on the settee, curling her hand around her mother's, letting her know she appreciated her support even if she looked as though she could collapse at any moment, making her wonder how her father convinced her mother to leave the sanctuary of her chambers.

"You have gentlemen callers, daughter," her father said with a greedy grin plastered on his once handsome face. Oh, he was still handsome for his age, but to her, he now resembled the trolls in fairy tales. "Let me introduce them." He indicated an elderly gentleman with snow-white hair, leaning on a cane. "May I present the Marquess of Chesterfield?" He continued down the line. "The Earl of Banfield, the Viscount Haddington, and Mr. Lewis." His hand swept to Clarice, who stood up. "This is my lovely daughter, Lady Clarice Dawson."

Clarice curtsied. "It is a pleasure to make your acquaintance." She lied so easily.

Each man bowed, even the old marquess, making her believe he was more spry than he let on. As the introductions concluded, she breathed a sigh of relief to be seated again. Her legs felt weak and unsteady.

Her mother poured tea for both of them, while her father served brandy to the gentlemen. They kept talking among themselves as if she and her mother weren't there. One by one, her father took each suitor out of the room, likely to his study to negotiate her marriage. She nearly spat out her tea at how ridiculous it all was. Who would have thought that a month ago, this would be her life?

Pain eviscerated her heart whenever she thought about Samuel, which was almost every minute of each day. Would she ever see him again? And if she did, would he despise her for her father's actions? Oh dear, she needed to think of something else before tears pooled in her eyes and she cried openly.

Somehow, her mother sensed her feelings, squeezed her hand, leaned in close, and whispered, "I'm so sorry, Clarice. I know how much you love Samuel. Perhaps one day . . ."

"Why can't he take out a loan, sell some properties?"

"He has already sold the property near Stanton. Everything else is entailed. He has nothing to offer as collateral for a bank loan. He squandered the money I inherited from my mother. Money I had hoped to put in a trust for you when I die."

"I'm sorry for you too, Mother." Her eyes lifted, and she let them roam over the gentlemen in the room. Mr. Lewis looked to be around forty years old. He was rotund and the ugliest man she had ever seen. His only redeeming quality was that he wore fine-quality riding clothes. When they were introduced, he'd leered at her and smiled, revealing crooked, stained teeth with food particles stuck between them. Dear God, where had her father found these men? And did Mr. Lewis never clean his teeth?

The Viscount Haddington was a tall, thin young man who looked no older than twenty. He had a charming way about him. Why was he here? Was his father or mother pushing him to marry and produce heirs already? The Earl of Banfield was a name she had heard before in passing. He was a widower with four daughters. Perhaps he was hoping to provide his daughters with a stepmother to raise them. Or perhaps he simply wanted male heirs.

The older gentleman, who was with her father at this moment, gave her the chills. When he'd looked at her, his mouth formed a tight grin, his eyes darkened, and she'd swear he'd drooled at one point. But it was his eyes that bothered her most. They showed no sign of compassion for her situation. They were only dark, cold, and calculating. He had the eyes of a sinner, someone who had secrets to hide. Her entire body vibrated, and her skin crawled. Please don't let her father pick him.

If she had the option to choose, she would pick the earl. Could she hope her father would take her preference into account? A niggling inside her mind told her otherwise. Her father would grab the fattest purse strings and couldn't care less who he married her off to as long as his coffers were full once again.

It wasn't long before all four gentlemen bid their farewells, and her father sank into a chair facing the settee, already deep into his cups. "I've made my decision."

All the air whooshed from her lungs, and her heart pounded as she clung tightly to her mother's hand while she awaited her fate. A fate, no doubt, worse than death.

"In a sennight you will marry, by special license, the Marquess of Chesterfield."

Clarice and her mother cried out at the same time, "No!"

"Yes," her father bellowed. "Let me remind you, my dear daughter, that you agreed to do this to save your mother and me from financial ruin. You will marry him and go to Chesterfield House to live. He needs an heir, and you will give him one."

Clarice ran from the room, her hand over her mouth as she hurried up the stairs, tripping twice on her skirts in her rush to reach her chambers. When she arrived, she dove for the chamber pot and cast up her accounts. As she sat back on the floor, she wondered if something was wrong with her. Perhaps she was dying. It would be favorable to marrying the marquess.

A knock on the door startled her; she wrestled with her skirts as she stood up and, on wobbly legs, made her way to the foot of her bed and sat down.

"My lady," Mrs. Shelley called out, "may I enter?"

"Yes."

Mrs. Shelley, tears in her eyes and concern on her face, hurried to her. "I just heard the news." Clarice couldn't hold back her anguish any longer; she dropped her head into her hands and cried. The bed dipped, and comforting arms wrapped around her. "There, there, my lady, let your tears out. I've a good bosom to cry on."

Clarice leaned against Mrs. Shelley's warm body and let the tears flow until she had none left. Gasping several times, she murmured, "Will you attend me after I'm wed?"

"I'm sorry, my lady. According to your father, the Marquess of Chesterfield requests that no one from this household be allowed to travel or serve you. He will appoint your maid from among his loyal servants."

Could things get any worse? Her only hope had been to have Mrs. Shelley with her every day to help her cope with being torn from her family home and forced to marry an old man. "I'd like to be alone."

Clarice asked for a tray to be brought up for dinner and spent most of the night lying in bed, staring at the ceiling. Now that her father had found her soon-to-be husband, he refused to allow her out of her chambers for the week leading up to her wedding. She paced the floor and cried herself to sleep each night wondering where Samuel was. Why hadn't he come for her?

When the morning of her wedding day arrived, she got up, feeling both mentally and physically drained. As she dressed in a pretty, cream-colored gown for her wedding, an invisible veil covered her mind and body, shielding everything inside from the outside world. The only way she could survive the years ahead was if she remained numb, hiding her true self deep inside to protect herself from the outside world and from the man she was about to marry. A man who, two hours later, stood beside her as they recited their vows with icy indifference in his eyes. Why was he marrying her? He didn't look like he was happy about it. And if it weren't for her agreeing to do this to save her parents financially, Clarice would've run out the door and never looked back. But her word was her word.

CHAPTER FOUR

SAMUEL OPENED HIS eyes to find his room in shadowed darkness, lit only by two candles. He noticed several things at once: not only did his arm hurt from being shot, but his entire body ached deep inside to his bones. His stomach felt empty, and when he went to move his arm, he barely had the strength to do so. Also, his mother and father sat beside his bed, looking haggard, tired, and worried. And his valet, Wallace, stood across the room looking as disheveled as his parents.

"Why so glum?" he whispered because that was as loud as he could make his voice go. His throat was so parched it burned.

His mother stood, wiping his hair from his brow, and kissed his forehead. "Because we thought we were going to lose you."

"What do you mean? The physician said I would be fine after he bandaged me up last night."

"My dear boy," his father said as he stood and wrapped an arm around his mother's waist. "You have been in and out of consciousness for a fortnight."

His mouth opened and closed. A fortnight? How was that possible? "That can't be right."

"It is, Samuel," his mother said. "Your arm became infected and the infection spread. Dr. Miller almost amputated it. We insisted that he give you a few more days—thank God we did— and you woke up." She placed her hand on his forehead. "And your fever has broken. Wallace, please ring for broth and tea. We need to get Samuel well and strong again."

After his valet, Wallace, spoke to the maid who came to the door, he helped him sit up in bed, stacking pillows between his back and the headboard. A short time later, a tray arrived. After Samuel drank some of the salty beef broth and tea, his eyelids drooped. He struggled to keep them open. "I think I'd like to rest."

Wallace helped him to lie down. Samuel took a deep breath, his lungs rattling as he sighed with relief at lying down again. Sitting required more energy than he had, and he closed his eyes, picturing Clarice's lovely face, smiling at him as he fell asleep.

The next time he opened his eyes, he struggled to breathe. It felt as if a large dog sat on his chest.

"Try to relax and breathe, Samuel. Your father has summoned Dr. Miller. He should arrive any moment."

"It hurts to breathe," he whispered, which then turned into a wheezing, coughing fit that hurt like bloody hell. Wallace put two more pillows beneath his head, propping him up, which did help with his breathing.

Samuel knew the doctor had come and gone, examining him, but he was too weak to pay attention. All he knew was that he was given vile-tasting medicine, which made the room spin and his body and eyes shut down.

"WHAT HAPPENED?" SAMUEL whispered into his room, not even knowing if anyone was there to hear him. "Why do I feel as though I was run over by both the horse and the carriage?"

His mother's worried, haggard face came into view. It looked as though she had aged years. "Because you have been very sick. The infection in your arm spread to your lungs."

"How long have I been out?"

"A fortnight for the infection in your arm and another for your lungs. A month total." She touched his face and chest, feeling for his heartbeat. "Your lungs finally sound clear. How do you feel?"

"Terrible. Will I ever feel normal again?"

His mother's look was hopeful. "We will hire the best physician to come and stay here until you are back on your feet and back to the healthy man you were."

Samuel heard his mother's words, but knowing how he felt and how much effort and concentration it took to move his arm, never mind his entire body, he wasn't sure if he believed he would ever recover.

But true to her word, his mother immediately hired a young doctor—who used unconventional practices on him—and three months later, Samuel was nearly back to his pre-gunshot wound strength and activities.

He inquired several times about Clarice, but his father and mother would ignore him and immediately change the topic every time. Finally, after an invigorating ride on his horse, Smokey, he had had enough of them tiptoeing around the subject of Clarice, and he burst into his father's study and demanded, "Tell me about Clarice. I'm not leaving this room until you do."

His father sighed, went to the sideboard, and poured two glasses of brandy. After handing Samuel his, his father sat back down behind his desk and downed his drink in one gulp. "Mind you, I haven't heard directly from her father, but I did get a letter from your Uncle David. Portsmouth married Clarice to the Marquess of Chesterfield nearly three months ago."

The pain lancing his chest and the tears clogging his throat made him wish he had never asked. He'd always known she would be married by now, but hearing it made it real. He could no longer pretend they would wed. That it wasn't too late to run off to Gretna Green. If he was suffering so, how much worse must it be for Clarice? He covered his mouth to stifle nervous laughter. His beautiful, sweet, and caring Clarice was married to an old man. An old man rumored to be a vile individual. The marquess wasn't good enough to wipe Clarice's shoes soiled with horse dung. And to think she was married to him? That she had to perform her wifely duties and bed such a beast.

"Bloody hell," Samuel said as he drained his glass. His arm slumped over the armrest, the glass slipped from his fingers, dropping onto the carpet with a thud, while his other hand pulled at his hair. "How could her father marry her to such a man?" he groaned.

"I don't know, son," his father said, staring into his empty glass. "Let's hope he doesn't live long and Clarice becomes a widow very, very soon."

"Yes," Samuel breathed. "Soon."

CHAPTER FIVE

London, 1817

"CAN YOU BELIEVE you are reentering Society?" Clarice said to her friend, another widow her age, Letitia Fernsby, the Marchioness of Rutherford, who lived one street over, as they traveled to the first ball of the Season. They had both been widowed for nearly two years. Clarice had attended several house parties during the last Season, and she had been rumored to be having an affair with one Mr. James Caldwell. However, they had only been friends.

"It's strange to think of it," Letitia said with a smile. "I have no idea what to expect, and I'm shaking with excitement and trepidation. The only time I attended Society functions was on my dear late husband's arm."

Clarice found herself giggling nervously. "Yes. I feel excited and anxious." Letitia and she had many things in common, except that Letitia and her deceased husband had adored one another. Letitia also had a son to keep her busy during long, lonely days and nights. As for Clarice, her marriage had been the kind that nightmares were made of. While her friend had been devastated by her husband's untimely death, Clarice was, and please forgive her for this, thrilled to be free from her husband and tormentor after five long years of marriage.

But Clarice had another reason to be nervous and apprehensive about this Season. What if she happened across her father?

Her mother had sadly passed away the previous year. And from what she understood, her father, at the advanced age of sixty, was looking for a young bride to provide him with an heir. She already felt bad for the poor girl, whoever she turned out to be.

"You turned somber. Are you worried about the Westport Ball?"

Clarice toyed with her pretty, blue reticle that matched her dress. "No and yes. I suppose I'm worried I might see my father. I hear he's looking for a young wife. Please stay as far away from him as possible. He may be handsome and appear charming, but underneath that exterior is a selfish, spiteful, and downright despicable man."

Letitia leaned forward and clasped her hands. "I know, and I'm sorry for what he did to you. If you see him, pretend he doesn't exist. Come to me, and I will help you escape."

"You are a much stronger person than I, Letitia. Thank you for being my friend."

"It is my pleasure, and you are a fighter for what you endured during your marriage to Chesterfield. You are stronger than I am. I would have run away or drowned myself in a lake if I found myself married to someone like Chesterfield."

Clarice gasped. "No, you would not have. And please remind me how strong I am when Chesterfield's great nephew and heir arrives. I don't want to live with him and I'm too young to retire to the dower house. I will essentially be without a home." Her entire being chilled at the thought of it. Just then, their carriage came to a stop. She didn't want to think about her father, or her dead husband, or anyone from her past. She wanted to go to the ball and enjoy herself.

Letitia had insisted on using her carriage, believing it would attract less attention than the one with the Chesterfield emblem on the side. She hoped her friend was right. A footman helped Letitia down the stairs and then assisted her in exiting the coach. When Clarice stood and looked at the line of elegantly dressed members of the *ton* waiting to enter Westport Hall, she almost jumped back into the carriage, telling the driver to take her back home.

The only thing that stopped her was that she wasn't a coward. Not anymore, at least. She had endured a lifetime of misery during her five-year marriage, and she was ready to face whatever the future might be.

Letitia wrapped her arm through Clarice's. "My goodness, all the gowns are gorgeous!"

"They are."

"We were so fortunate to run into the Duchess of Blackstone and the Countess of Langford at Gunter's. Otherwise, we wouldn't have been introduced to Madame Serena."

Clarice had a modiste but had been hoping for an introduction to Madame Serena. No other modiste created such beautiful gowns. "Do you think they will be in attendance tonight?" Clarice asked as they moved quite quickly up in the queue, which surprised her.

"I hope so. I've never met either the duke or the earl, and I'd love to see the duchess and countess again."

"I met the duchess last year before she married the Duke of Blackstone." By now, they had reached the butler, who relieved them of their cloaks. They went up the exquisite marble staircase faster than Clarice could believe, and they found themselves before the elderly Duke and Duchess of Westport.

Clarice curtsied. "Your Graces, thank you for inviting me into your lovely home."

The duke bowed, his eyes lowered to her chest, and Clarice fought not to bristle at his leering. His Grace was certainly no gentleman, and the rumors she heard about him were obviously true. "The pleasure is all ours, my dear."

The duchess smiled at her, saying, "We are thrilled you came. Please enjoy yourself."

Clarice waited until Letitia finished with the receiving line before she moved to the large opening of the ballroom where the master of ceremonies stood introducing the guests. When it was their turn, once again, she wanted to turn around, run down the staircase, and hide inside the carriage until the ball was over. Yet she managed to take a deep, calming breath and stiffen her spine as she handed the master of ceremonies her invitation.

"The Most Honorable, the Marchioness of Chesterfield." When her name was announced, many occupants of the ballroom turned and gawked at her, freezing her in her step, so she waited for Letitia to be announced.

"The Most Honorable, the Marchioness of Rutherford."

Letitia wrapped her arm around hers. "That was quite unnerving, having all these people stare at us. I feel like a lion in a zoo, being seen for the first time."

"Indeed," Clarice murmured, afraid to speak loudly in case people were eavesdropping. "Do you see anyone you know?"

"Let's take a turn around the room. With any luck, we will see people we know and want to see."

They promenaded behind mostly couples. However, several women were taking a turn with either their companion, family member, or friend, as they were.

"Thank goodness," Letitia breathed. "The Duke and Duchess of Blackstone and the Earl and Countess of Langford are over by the open double doors leading to the veranda."

Moving her eyes to that area, she saw the two ladies they had been hoping to find. The duchess had black hair, and the countess had light hair. Both of them were standing, smiling at their handsome husbands. Clarice's insides unclenched. Even though she was only briefly acquainted with them, it was comforting to see familiar faces among the hundreds of guests.

"Let's make our way over," said Clarice.

When the greetings concluded, Clarice found herself intrigued by the four people in front of her. She had briefly met the duke and duchess last Season, had seen the duchess and the countess at Gunter's, but had never met the earl. Even though they knew little about Clarice, they treated her kindly, including her in the conversation.

The Duke of Blackstone kissed his wife's cheek. "Langford and I saw Hollingsworth just arrive with his wife. We'll be back soon."

Once the men left, the Duchess of Blackstone smiled at her. "You two remind me of the countess and me when we first arrived at the Westport Ball two years ago. Except we did have my mother with us, even though she disappeared the moment we were announced. I knew several people, since I'd had a Season when I was seventeen. But much happened in the following ten years." She paused, and a sadness flickered in her eyes for a moment before passing. "Lilly, the countess, knew not a soul but my mother and me, unless you count Langford."

"We must count him," the countess said, smiling brightly, "even if I hated him at first. He did eventually redeem himself," she added, blushing.

"Yes, he did." Her Grace lowered her voice, and everyone leaned closer. "Lilly was married to Langford's uncle, Henry Weston, who was my cousin. When Henry died," she paused, then continued, "Edmund, Lilly's current husband, inherited the earldom from his uncle, Henry. Lilly was already the Countess of Langford. So it was only fitting she marry the next Earl of Langford, even if the start of their relationship was strained."

Clarice listened carefully and believed she had the relationship between the current earl and countess correct. "I think I understand."

"Well then," Lilly began with a smile and a softness in her voice, "it's only fitting if I tell how Blackstone and Emmeline came to be married. During Emmeline's first Season, two gentlemen vied for her favors. Mr. Aiden Fitzpatrick and the Earl of Quincy, who is now the Duke of Blackstone. Quincy bowed out, and she married Aiden. After four years, Aiden died in a horse riding accident. It was six years before Blackstone and Emmeline saw each other again." She twirled her hand around. "Love at first sight again."

The duchess hid her laughter behind her gloved hand. "Not

love at first sight, but we did get there. Anyway, I can't believe it, Lady Clarice. May I call you Lady Clarice?"

"Yes," Clarice replied. "If I recall, I insisted you call me that last year when we met for the first time."

"Lady Clarice it is. As I was saying, I can't believe that you and Letitia are widows. Being young and widowed isn't easy. I'm going to offer some advice. People, mostly gentlemen, treat you differently, and whatever you do, do not dance with the Duke of Westport. Come up with an excuse. He is a horrible creature."

Clarice and Letitia exchanged glances before Letitia said, "I disliked him immediately, but thank you for the warning."

"Yes," Clarice chimed in. "The first thing I thought when he leered down the front of my gown was that he was a vile creature. Much like my dead husband." She slapped her hand against her mouth and mumbled through her fingers. "Did I say that out loud?"

"Yes," the countess said, "but your secrets are safe with us. Even though Emmeline and I are no longer young widows, we consider both of you to be one of us now. I'd say the more, the merrier, but I wouldn't wish widowhood on anyone."

"Except for Clarice," Letitia said with a frown. "She is glad to be widowed."

"Letitia," she groaned, "please don't go around saying such things. People will think I'm a horrible person."

Letitia reached out, took her hand, and squeezed it. "You are a wonderful person. One of the kindest I have ever met, never forget that."

Having never had a female friend until she met Letitia, Clarice fought back a lump in her throat. "Thank you. That is very kind of you." Tears threatened her eyes. "You are all very kind."

"Please call me Emmaline, and the countess Lilly, when it's appropriate to do so. Friends shouldn't have to be so formal and use titles while in private conversation. After all, we did become acquainted last summer at the Waterford house party."

"We did, and I was so very glad when you and Blackstone got married. Not to mention when Caldwell did. Everyone thought he was interested in me, but he never was. We became good friends during those two weeks and nothing more. Although I haven't seen him since." Clarice glanced around the large room, hoping for a glimpse of Caldwell. She had missed him. He was so easy to be around. It was the first time in years she hadn't had to hide her feelings from someone.

"He said he was attending tonight," Lilly remarked as she looked around. "But you know Caldwell, he's always running late."

One moment, she was laughing about Caldwell, and the next, Clarice couldn't find a speck of air to breathe. Her body stilled, and everything in the room faded away, including all occupants, except for the one man standing across the room, staring directly at her.

Samuel Radcliff.

She had always known she would run into him eventually, and she thought she had prepared herself for seeing him, but her mind and body had other ideas. They were frozen and unable to work. After what seemed like hours, which was actually only seconds, she gasped for air, her body quivered from head to toe, and her knees wanted to buckle, threatening to send her tumbling to the floor. Thankfully, that didn't happen. Instead, blindly, she grabbed the nearest arm and held on for dear life.

"Clarice," Emmeline said, her voice sounding far away and muffled. "Are you unwell?"

After taking several gulps of air, she replied, "Yes. No. Maybe. Samuel . . . the Duke of Stanton is staring at me." She bravely looked directly at him, and when their eyes connected, he turned his back on her. "Well, he *was* looking at me."

Emmeline looked concerned, as did Lilly and Letitia. "I know you two have a past. Would you care to go outside and get some fresh air?" Emmeline asked.

Fresh air sounded wonderful. Could she really make it that

far without collapsing? "Yes. Thank you." Knowing she needed support, Emmeline wrapped her arm through Clarice's and the four of them casually strolled out the double doors onto the veranda, which was surprisingly empty, except for one couple just beginning to descend the stairs into the gardens.

Clarice stood with her hands on the railing, and Letitia came to stand beside her. "Just breathe slowly and steadily. That will help your heart slow down and ease your shaking body."

"Thank you," Clarice replied, feeling grateful to have these friends supporting her. As everything started to return to normal, she said softly, "I always knew I would run into Samuel again one day. I believed I would act calm, sophisticated, and worldly. When in actuality, I broke into a million tiny pieces inside." She exhaled shakily. "Do you think anyone noticed?"

Lilly said calmly, "Worrying about what others think about you is pointless. And honestly, I don't believe anyone in the ballroom was paying attention to you, so the answer to your question is no."

"Thank you all for being so kind to me. During my marriage to Chesterfield, I felt very alone. He went out daily and most nights, but we never socialized together as a married couple. He didn't allow me to have visitors or visit anyone. I was essentially a prisoner in his home. I never even saw my mother. It wasn't until after his death that Letitia and I became friends. So thank you."

"We are your friends now," Lilly said with a sad smile. "You went from no friends to one friend to now having three. Please reach out to us at any time."

Clarice fumbled with her reticle's opening, took out her embroidered blue-and-green floral handkerchief, and dabbed her tears away. "Thank you." As she pulled herself together, she knew what she had to do. She needed to speak with Samuel. If she didn't, these panicky, overwhelming feelings would never end. She would be a bundle of nerves at every social event she attended, wondering if she would run into him. Nothing would change, and she wouldn't be able to move on until she faced the past and made peace with it.

THE MOMENT SAMUEL'S eyes landed on Clarice's beautiful face across the room, he locked his knees because they nearly buckled, sending him tumbling to the floor. Last Season, he managed never to run into her. Too bad his luck had run out. It wasn't that he blamed her for anything that happened between them, or for what her father did to him. However, seeing her brought back all his bad memories along with the good ones. Damn his traitorous heart inside his chest. It wanted to reach out and join with hers, even after all the years that had passed. Seven, to be exact. Seven long, lonely years spent with his thoroughbred horses, wiling away the time. His horses meant everything to him. Most people he could take or leave, except for his two friends from Eton, who had stood beside him forever. Without Archibald Fitzroy, the Viscount Greyson, and Mr. Jacob Hunter, he would have given up on life a long time ago. He credited them with saving his life. Credited them for being able to get up in the morning. For him continuing to breathe on a daily basis. No finer friends existed anywhere in the world.

"Don't look," Samuel said, "but Clarice is here talking with the Duchess of Blackstone, the Countess of Langford, and another lady I don't recognize." He nearly smacked Hunter on the back. "I said, don't look."

"You realize that when someone says 'don't look,' the person automatically looks."

"He's right, Stanton," Greyson interjected.

"Yes, well. Anyway, what the bloody hell am I supposed to say to her if the opportunity arises?"

"How about you start with, 'Good evening, Marchioness. How nice to see you again'," Greyson said seriously.

Samuel groaned. "Yes. Greetings are easy. What if she asks

about other things?"

"Don't get ahead of yourself," Hunter added. "No sense worrying about what you'll say until the time comes. And when it does, I have faith in you that you'll say all the right things."

"I'm glad you have faith in me, because mine just ran out the door."

"You can relax now," Greyson said. "She went out on the veranda with the other ladies."

Samuel took a deep breath and exhaled; instantly, his body calmed. However, his mind did not. It played through all the different scenarios of what he could or should say to her. To this day, he honestly didn't know if she knew what had happened to him. And he didn't want to burden her with that guilt by sharing the story if she didn't know. Still, someone was bound to tell her eventually. The *ton* loved to gossip and spill secrets.

"Don't look now," Hunter said, his eyes wide and anger flickering across his features. "The blackguard himself, the Earl of Portsmouth, just entered the ballroom."

Samuel swayed, and his friend Greyson reached out his hand to steady him. "He has some nerve," Greyson droned.

Hunter said angrily, "I heard he's looking to marry again, hoping for a male heir."

"Christ," Samuel raked his hand through his shoulder-length, dark hair. "What father would marry his daughter to a man like him?"

Hunter snorted, "You would be surprised what some will do to procure a title for their daughter."

"I think I'm going to be sick," Samuel mumbled as he swallowed. "I need to be alone for a minute." Without making eye contact with anyone, he exited the ballroom and wandered down a corridor until he found the first empty room, a small salon. He was drawn to a large window overlooking a small garden lit up with lanterns and full of flowing plants and trees. With his arms crossed behind his back, he rocked back on his heels and stared outside, no longer seeing the pretty garden, but recalling Clarice and him when they were young, sitting in Stanton Hall's gardens with their heads together in private conversation.

Soon, he felt a presence behind him, making every nerve ending in his body take notice. "You followed me?" he said without turning.

"So you do acknowledge that you know who I am?"

Her voice, soft yet tense, made him realize how much he missed hearing it. "Did you truly believe I would ever forget you?" The sudden, painful dryness in his throat took him by surprise.

She sighed. "No. As I have never forgotten you. How have you been?"

Her question had him fighting back laughter brought on by nerves and sadness. He cleared his throat and mumbled, "I've been well. And you?"

Soft, nervous laughter trickled into his ears. "I've been good. Are you going to keep staring out the window, or will you turn around and look at me?"

"Forgive me," he said, his body tensing in preparation for facing her. When he did, he almost stumbled. Their eyes met—hers still a warm brown, but guarded and more worldly. No longer the innocent eyes he remembered. He briefly looked her up and down, realizing she had changed very little in seven years. Would she think he looked the same? Perhaps on the outside, but never on the inside. "You look beautiful." Pink shaded her cheeks. He'd always loved making her blush.

"Thank you. You look much the same." Her hands fiddled with her fan, opening and closing it. Her eyes were cast down, and her body shifted from one foot to the other. Eventually, she calmed, lifted her head, and looked deep into his eyes. It was now his turn to squirm under her scrutiny. "After I was widowed, I kept hoping you would visit me."

Oh, how he'd wanted to. During her year of mourning, he didn't dare; over the past year, though, he fought with himself about doing just that. But when she was rumored to be involved with Mr. James Caldwell, he gave up on the illusion that they would ever be together. No sense lying to her. "I thought about it many times. But I didn't want to interfere with your relationship with Caldwell."

He observed her body language and facial expressions, hoping she would reveal some of her secrets. Because he had no doubt she possessed some. Deep, dark secrets. She gave away nothing. "Caldwell and I were friends and nothing more. He is happily married now."

"There were rumors."

"Humph. There are always rumors. Some are true. Some are false. Those rumors were false."

"Did you know your father is here tonight?"

Her mouth opened and closed, her eyes widened, and she groaned as she shook her head from side to side. "No. But truthfully, I knew he would be here. Nobody misses the Westport Ball since it's the official opening of the Season, especially not someone seeking a young bride." She covered her mouth with her hand. "Thinking about my father replacing my mother with some young debutante disgusts me."

"Many older titled men marry young ladies solely for the purpose of producing a male heir. Usually, the bride's family is happy to overlook the age difference if it means marrying into the family of a wealthy, titled lord." Her face flicked to his, and the anguish he glimpsed in her eyes and on her face made his insides tighten at the thought of speaking such callous words. "My apologies," he hurried to say. "That was rude and uncalled for."

"You must hate me!" she exclaimed.

He inhaled and exhaled to steady himself for the conversation that was about to begin. "I could never hate you. It's not in my power to do so."

CHAPTER SIX

WHEN CLARICE MADE the spur-of-the-moment decision to leave her friends out on the veranda and follow Samuel, she hadn't really thought things through, except to get their awkward first meeting together in seven years over with. She hadn't thought about how tough and emotional the conversation between them might be. So far, they had exchanged nothing important, but it was about to change. "I would hate me if I were you." She held her breath as she waited for him to speak.

"Nothing that happened between us was your fault." His voice sounded emotionless. "At least from my recollection, it wasn't, and I have a great memory. The day you rode off with your parents, never to be seen by me again until tonight, is etched in my mind." He winced when he finished. Perhaps he regretted admitting such to her.

"I've never forgotten that day either, or what we shared. Standing with you now makes it feel like yesterday, not seven years ago." She sighed. "What have you been doing for the past seven years?"

He laughed and waved one arm around. "Oh. This and that. Mostly, I spent time with my thoroughbreds. I have two on the racing circuit this year, which takes up most of my life. Not that I'm complaining. I love it. It keeps me busy."

"You always loved your horses and talked about owning

thoroughbreds someday. I'm so happy that you have realized your dream." Perhaps her dream would someday come true. Her dream of marrying and having children.

He laughed again. "Yes, well, it's always good when one of your dreams comes true."

Before she could stop herself, she whispered sadly, "I wouldn't know."

She witnessed his body tense right before her eyes. "Enough about me," he said. "What have you been doing to occupy your time?"

Now it was her body's time to stiffen. There were so many things she wanted to share with Samuel, but tonight wasn't the right time. They needed to get reacquainted first. "I took up watercolors. Chesterfield hired a tutor for me. It helped with the loneliness and isolation during my marriage." Since his death, though, she hadn't picked up a brush. It had been her refuge when he was alive, but painting now only brought back memories she wanted to forget.

"You never had any children?"

Her heart stopped, then ricocheted around inside her chest. Tears threatened to make an appearance. She breathed through the pain of her loss and cleared her throat. "No."

"I'm sorry."

"Thank you. Considering Chesterfield only married me to produce an heir, it made him furious. I'm still waiting for his great-nephew to claim the title. Until then, I'm living at Chesterfield Manor. There's nothing I can do until he arrives from America. He's due sometime this month."

"It must be difficult waiting for the day he arrives." Samuel looked thoughtful. Maybe he was thinking about inheriting his father's title and lands. Something he'd never expected.

"Forgive me," Clarice said. "I never expressed my condolences for the loss of your family. It was five years ago, wasn't it?"

He turned to look at her, his gray eyes filled with sorrow. "Thank you, and yes, five years ago this coming June."

"You must have been devastated. I remember your parents so very well. They were always kind to me, and I loved them. I remember your brother and how he always said we were annoying, but he never meant it. He always had a smile for me and a hard candy treat in his pocket. Is that why you've changed?"

"It took me a long time to come to terms with what happened. I should have been in my chambers and died with them, but I couldn't sleep, so I went to the stables to spend time with the horses." He paused. "The fire spread fast, and by the time I realized what was happening, the flames had taken over and burned too hot. I couldn't get inside to save anyone. Thank God, most of the local servants had the night off and had gone home to their families." His eyes briefly closed, and when they opened again, she saw the pain in his dark-gray eyes. "It was a somber time for the people of Hampshire. What do you mean, I've changed?"

"You appear serious, subdued, and standoffish. The young, carefree gentleman is gone."

He ran his hand through his hair. Something she noticed he did quite often and probably didn't even realize he was doing it. "Well, things happened, and I guess those things changed me."

She decided to let it go. It was clear that he was bothered by the fact that he had changed.

"How are you handling being the duke?" Oh dear, the moment the words escaped, she realized it was another sensitive topic.

He chuckled. "According to Greyson and Hunter, I'm not. I'm spending too much time, money, and energy on my racehorses."

Her eyes widened when she realized he was serious. "Oh. Can't you do both?"

"I'm trying. I might have to give up horseracing next year and my dream of owning a stud farm and focus on the dukedom."

"I'm sorry."

"Don't be. Many would give their right hand to be the Duke

of Stanton."

Uncomfortable silence fell between them, pulsating around like a tangible presence. When she couldn't take it anymore, she said, "I should find the Marchioness of Rutherford; she's probably looking for me." She stepped forward, closing the distance between them, stood on her tiptoes, and kissed his cheek. "You have no idea how glad I am to see you."

His mouth twitched into a grin. "As glad as I am to see you." He extended his arm. "Come, I'll escort you to your friend."

Clarice placed her hand on his forearm. "Thank you." They walked silently out of the room, down the hall, and into the noisy ballroom filled with orchestra music and pulsating voices. "I see her just up ahead."

"You have made some fine friends. I'm not acquainted with the Marchioness of Rutherford, but I know the Duchess of Blackstone and the Countess of Langford quite well, along with their husbands."

"I'm fortunate to be able to call them my friends."

He stopped just short of the ladies and lowered his voice. "Can I be honest with you?"

"Yes."

"When you first arrived at the library, I didn't want to speak to you, but now I'm glad we had the chance to talk." He bowed over her hand. "Until next time."

Clarice stood there, watching his back retreat out of the ballroom, taking some of the vibrancy from the room with him. Was he leaving for good? She had a nagging feeling he was.

"Clarice."

A tight knot formed in her stomach at hearing her name. Samuel mentioned he was here, but Clarice had hoped he was mistaken. Which was silly, because Samuel would never be mistaken about something so momentous. She straightened her spine and tamped down all the emotions suddenly flooding her. She would not give him the satisfaction of thinking he meant anything to her or that she was bothered by seeing him again after so many years apart, years she'd spent hating him. She turned and faced the man who'd sired her but no longer deserved the title of father, even if she referred to him as such. "Father."

His brown eyes assessed her, making it hard to stand still when all she really wanted to do was run outside on the veranda and scream. Or hit him on the side of his head with her reticle. *Where did that violent urge come from?*

"You look well, daughter."

"Thank you. I am well," she said casually.

"I trust your marriage to Chesterfield didn't damage you in any way so that you can marry again and provide your husband with an heir. Something you never did for Chesterfield. Not that I'm surprised. The man was ancient."

Nothing like getting straight to the point and invading the privacy of her marriage. "If you believed he would harm me in any way, why did you marry me to him?" she asked with her most gruff, demanding voice.

"You know why. But seriously," he reached for her arm, but she stepped out of his reach, "did he hurt you?"

Instead of screaming, she now wanted to laugh and laugh and laugh until her stomach hurt. "I hate to disappoint you, Father, but he never laid a hand on me. So no physical damage whatso-ever." Emotional damage was another matter entirely.

"Glad to hear it. Maybe I can help you find your next husband, and you can help me select a new bride. There are so many young ladies to choose from, and it's been decades since I was single, evaluating the young debutantes. I'm out of practice."

He couldn't be serious. "I will find my own husband, on my own time and terms, thank you very much." Her father would never have any control over her again.

"If that's what you wish. However, I hope you will help me. In my advanced years, I seek a wife who can manage my household, bear male heirs, and fulfill my needs. I'm not looking for a companion or friendship. Just a wife who does what's asked of her. Who, in your opinion, fits that description?"

"Really, Father." Trying not to laugh, she glanced around the room, observing all the young ladies. "I'm familiar with three ladies here tonight. Two are married, and one is widowed."

He huffed. "That won't do. I suppose I'll have to ask several young ladies to dance, and if they pass my test, I'll pay morning calls on them tomorrow. I suppose I'll have to send flowers and sit through endless cups of tea in my quest to find a bride. No thanks to you, my daughter."

"I wish you luck, Father," she said in a strained voice. It felt wrong and disrespectful to her mother's memory to be discussing her replacement. "If you'll excuse me, I have someone I must speak to." She curtsied out of habit and hurried away as quickly as she could, giving her father no chance to say anything else. She needed to find Letitia and persuade her to leave.

After frantically scanning the ballroom, her eyes landed on Letitia, standing off to the side alone, opening and closing her fan out of boredom. She made her way over to her. "I'm sorry I disappeared. I followed Stanton and then ran into my father."

"Oh, dear, how did both those conversations go?"

"The conversation with Stanton went better than I expected. The one with my father, not as well. Do you mind if we go home?"

Letitia's eyes moved around the room, and she sighed. "No, I don't mind."

"Who are you looking for?"

"There is this gentleman who caught my eye. He is most handsome, and he smiled at me. We kept locking eyes from across the room. Even when I wasn't looking his way, I felt the heat from his stare. Unfortunately, he has two lovely young ladies following him around like puppies."

"Did you get an introduction?"

Letitia sighed. "Sadly, no."

"Do you see him now?" Clarice asked as she looked around the room for a handsome gentleman with two puppies . . . young ladies in tow.

"No."

She linked her arm through Letitia's and gently nudged her toward the exit. "Perhaps next time you can manage an introduction, and you can find out if he's serious about either of the two puppies."

Giggles escaped Letitia's lips. "Thank you for making me feel better. I never realized how difficult it would be to enter Society. In my dreams, I thought I'd meet a man and we'd fall instantly in love." She huffed. "What a silly notion."

"It's not silly," Clarice said. "I have the same dream. Although mine involves seeing Stanton again, and we fall in love on the spot. Sadly, that didn't happen tonight."

Letitia squeezed her arm. "Don't despair. You two have a past, and pasts tend to come back around." Letitia's steps slowed, and she whispered, "Oh my. There he is, gathering his greatcoat and helping the two ladies with their cloaks. They seem to be leaving with him." The disappointment in her voice surprised Clarice.

"Relax," Clarice said. "That's one of Stanton's oldest friends. I met him years ago. He is Archibald Fitzroy, Viscount Greyson. And if memory serves me, he has twin sisters. Don't you see the resemblance?"

"Now that you mention it, all three of them have warm brown hair with light highlights. Are you right? Are they his twin sisters?"

"It would be quite a coincidence if he were escorting some other twins. So, yes, I'm positive they are his sisters." Clarice tugged Letitia along. "Let's hurry, and I'll introduce you."

Letitia's feet halted.

"What's the matter?"

"Nothing. An introduction would be helpful so that the next time I see him, I won't have to stare from across the room, wondering who he is and if he'll speak to me."

As they approached the butler to request their cloaks, Clarice cleared her throat to get Greyson's attention. "Excuse me,

Viscount Greyson."

He pivoted around and smiled warmly at Clarice, and when his eyes landed on Letitia, the entryway's temperature seemed to rise.

"I was hoping to introduce you to my friend."

"Please." His eyes never left Letitia's face.

"Marchioness, may I present Archibald Fitzroy, Viscount Greyson. Greyson, this is Letitia Fernsby, Marchioness of Rutherford."

Clarice did not need to say or do anything else. Greyson stepped forward, took Letitia's hand in his, bowed most gallantly, and kissed her hand. When he straightened, he said, "A pleasure to meet you, Lady Rutherford."

Letitia curtsied. "It's an honor to make your acquaintance, Viscount."

"Forgive my lack of manners," he said, indicating his sisters. "Lady Chesterfield. Lady Rutherford, these are my two sisters, Miss Aurora and Miss Anastasia Fitzroy."

His sisters curtsied, and Miss Aurora said with a warm smile, "It is nice to meet you both."

"Yes," Miss Anastasia chimed in. "Very nice to meet you both. The Duke of Stanton was shocked—in a good way—when he saw you this evening, Lady Chesterfield."

Greyson groaned. "Anastasia, you shouldn't say such things."

"Well, it is true."

Clarice's stomach fluttered. "May I be honest with you? I was shocked—in a good way—myself as well. He appears much the same as I remember."

Greyson snorted. "Excuse me, ladies, but I must escort my sisters home." He leaned toward Letitia and lowered his voice. "May I call on you tomorrow?"

Her friend visibly melted, and her cheeks pinkened. "Yes. I would like that very much."

He took her hand in his and brought it to his mouth, brushing his lips over her knuckles. "I look forward to it then."

Letitia didn't move; she stood in the doorway, staring at Greyson's back. She sighed, and her eyes became dreamy, which Clarice envied. "I'm never going to sleep tonight thinking about that man and his deep-green eyes and that smile. And his voice, I felt the vibrations deep inside me."

Clarice linked her arm through Letitia's, feeling joyful for her friend, and led her down the outside stairs to their waiting carriage. Once inside, she said, "That meeting was intense. I've never witnessed anything like it. You two connected on a deep level."

Leticia exhaled as she leaned against the squabs. "I felt something. I know we just met, but I felt as though I could see into his soul and he into mine. It was disconcerting, peculiar, and welcoming all at the same time." She looked at her, her eyes questioning. "Do you believe he will call upon me?"

"Greyson appears to be a man of his word, although I can't say for sure. What I do know is that he's a good brother to be his sisters' chaperone."

"Are his parents still alive?"

Clarice tried to remember what she knew about Greyson, but she couldn't think of anything. "I don't know about his mother. Except if his father had passed, he would no longer be Viscount Greyson, but the Earl of Danbury."

Leticia closed her eyes. "It doesn't matter. When he pays me a call, I'm sure he'll tell me all about his family." Without opening her eyes, she asked, "Do you think Stanton will call on you?"

That was a good question, and one she couldn't answer. But deep down, where she once knew everything about Samuel, she knew he would come. They had unfinished things to discuss. Her insides tightened. She wouldn't be getting any sleep tonight either.

And true to what she thought during the carriage ride home, she lay on the chaise longue in her chambers with a light blanket over her, dressed in her night rail, wide awake. Well, her mind was alert, but her body was exhausted. She wasn't used to such late hours. As she lay restless, visions of Samuel haunted her. Visions of when they were young. And when her memories arrived on the day they last saw each other, tears trickled down her cheeks.

It was the most wonderful day of her life, until it wasn't.

The day he proposed.

The day they believed their fathers were negotiating a marriage contract.

The day they made love under a tree and held each other as they rested in the shade.

The day they both believed would be the start of a happy life together, only to have everything they thought and believed ripped away from them. Their united hearts were torn apart and shredded because of her selfish father. How Samuel must hate her father—and her. Except he said tonight that he didn't hate her. Perhaps he didn't anymore, but he must have then.

Not that she deserved his hatred, pity more like. She often wondered—well, more than often, more like daily—what Samuel thought about her being married to Chesterfield. An old man. A mean, nasty, resentful old man. He had hated most everyone except for a handful of friends and the world because his first wife, whom he had loved more than life itself, died in childbirth. Their premature and unthriving infant son had died five days later. His second wife, whom he said he'd cared for, had died from a fever. And then came Clarice. He despised her. He loathed everything she represented. Youth, vitality, and fertility, yet not when it came to his seed.

Someday, she would need to have a serious conversation with Samuel.

Her eyes fluttered shut, and her breathing slowed as she drifted into a sleep filled with memories of the past.

She trembled as his loud footsteps stomped closer and closer to her chambers. It was her wedding night to the Marquess of Chesterfield, and she dreaded what was to come. With the help of her new, stern-faced, middle-aged maid, Mrs. Johnson, she was bathed, perfumed from head to toe, and dressed in a see-through, light-blue night rail and matching robe. She had to force her arms to stay by her sides instead of crossing them over her chest.

"My lady, sit on the end of the bed and await his lordship."

The maid left, and Clarice, on wobbly legs, eased onto the mattress. The time had come to face her husband. Would he know she wasn't a virgin? More importantly, what would he do if he found out? Just as nerves made her skin crawl, he burst into her chambers from the corridor, shut the door, and leaned against it. His eyes made contact with hers, and she shivered from his icy stare. Her husband, though seventy years old, stood tall and large, with a shockingly enormous amount of snow-white hair. He was opposing and frightening.

"Before we get down to business, I have one question to ask you, and if you lie, I will know. So, for your own good, I suggest you be honest. I don't take kindly to liars, and you'll find out soon enough what I mean if you lie. Did Lord Samuel Radcliff take your maidenhead?"

Her entire body shook upon hearing his question. She wanted to lie. But she could tell by the look in his eyes and the words he spoke that she would be wise to speak the truth. Best to face his wrath after admitting to the truth than to face it later. She looked him right in the eye and said one word, "Yes." And she was shocked that the hatred she witnessed in his eyes could intensify.

"How long ago?" he demanded as he gripped her upper arm painfully.

"Th-three weeks," she stuttered.

"Have you bled?" he bellowed.

"N-n-no."

"I will not bed you until you bleed. No bastard of Lord Radcliff's will inherit my title and lands. When you bleed, Mrs. Johnson will inform me. If you don't bleed, God help you."

"Wait!" Clarice cried out as she sat up, gasping for air and her heart pounding inside her chest. When she realized where she was, she flopped back onto the chaise longue and tried to calm her out-of-control emotions. She'd dreamed about this memory before, but tonight it felt like it was happening all over again. As if tonight were her wedding night to Chesterfield. Sometimes she felt he haunted her from his grave, even if she didn't believe in such nonsense. Although, this was his house. She was an intruder, so maybe he *was* haunting her.

The new Marquess of Chesterfield couldn't get there fast enough.

Maybe she'd dreamed of her wedding night because of the guilt plaguing her after seeing Samuel. She had kept a terrible secret from him. If he didn't hate her now, he certainly would when he found out. Not that she'd had any control over what had happened. Chesterfield had ensured she was punished in the worst way possible, and he had enjoyed watching her go almost insane with grief. She might marry again, but she would never give that kind of control over to another man ever again.

CHAPTER SEVEN

AFTER SAMUEL ESCORTED Clarice back to the ballroom and begged off, he left without so much as a by-your-leave to Greyson or Hunter. He hailed a hackney and headed to Brooks's for a nightcap or two or three. What did it matter how many he had? He'd tried drinking Clarice out of his mind for years, and he never succeeded. Perhaps he would visit Tattersall's in the morning to see the display of fine horses for sale. Sundays were always a good day to see the new horseflesh available for sale come Monday. Not that he was in the market for a new thoroughbred. He'd had as many as six at one time, but he only had two now, and both of them were descendants of the Darley Arabian. His horses, Zeus and Clover, were racing in the upcoming season. He had more than he could juggle between that and his commitment to his title and lands.

Since this was his first season on the racing circuit, he wouldn't miss a race or neglect caring for his horses. But after the season ended, he had several difficult decisions to make. Did he hire someone to oversee his two thoroughbreds while he focused on the dukedom? Did he speak to Greyson and Hunter and ask them to invest in the stud farm? If they refused, would he be able to drum up another one or two investors? Of course, most of these decisions revolved around how well Zeus and Clover did in the upcoming races.

Meanwhile, in a sennight, he would travel to Newmarket. He was a new member of The Jockey Club, and he needed to prepare for the first race at Newmarket.

Was a week enough time to smooth things over with Clarice? He needed to make his intentions known quickly before he lost her again to some other gentleman. He needed to explain what had happened to him and why he had never come for her. She must have believed he didn't love her enough to rescue her. Which was the farthest thing from the truth.

He wished he could go back to that night and do things differently. Could he have reached her another way? What if he had contacted her maid for help sneaking her out? He had gone over these different scenarios for years, but the reality was, you couldn't change the past. It was what it was. Only the future could be shaped, molded, and controlled into what you wanted it to be. Well . . . to a certain extent, it could. Nothing was etched in stone until it happened. He knew for certain now that his love for Clarice had never died, only been dormant. When they were in the private salon, his heart had decided to come out of hibernation and overflow with his long-suppressed love.

It had taken all his strength and willpower not to pull her into his arms. If he had, he never would have been able to let go. But before he declared himself to her, or kissed her, or showed her any physical affection at all, they needed to have a serious conversation about the past.

He finally signaled the waiter for a drink. "A glass of brandy and leave the bottle."

"Yes, Your Grace."

No matter how much it would hurt her to hear about her father, she needed to know. She needed the knowledge now that she had entered Society more fully, so her father could never manipulate her again. She was a grown woman and a widow, free to do as she chose. Her father truly had no control over her. Yet somehow, Samuel didn't think that would stop the man from using his daughter to get what he wanted.

"So this is where you ran off to," said Hunter with a knowing smirk as he sat in the chair beside him and signaled the waiter. "A glass, please." When the empty crystal tumbler arrived, he poured from Samuel's bottle of brandy without so much as another word.

"I'll have you know, I didn't run. I walked, hired a hack, and sat my sorry arse down for some peace and quiet. That is, until you showed up."

"Well, hold your horses, because Greyson's heading this way."

"I'm so glad we are creatures of habit," said Greyson as he walked over. "I almost went to White's, but I knew better." He signaled the waiter, "A glass." Once again, Samuel watched as a friend poured from his bottle of brandy, which was slowly disappearing. Greyson took a deep swallow and exhaled. "Nice and smooth going down. How did it go with Lady Chesterfield?"

So much for peace and quiet. Downing his glass, he refilled it and held it in his hands, staring into the amber liquid, hoping to find answers about his future. But, alas, he wasn't a fortune teller. Not that he believed in such things. Still, wouldn't it be nice to see something of his future? Something to give him hope that Clarice and he would marry and have a family, as they should have years ago.

"The conversation was polite and strained until the end, when we discussed hating each other. Which neither of us does. Hate the other, that is."

"Did you explain what happened that night and that you didn't abandon her?" Greyson asked, his eyes wide.

"Yes," Hunter added, "did you?"

Samuel couldn't help himself; he burst out laughing more from the relief of tension coiled tight inside him than from anything humorous. "You should see your faces; you'd think you each had something to lose."

"Well, now that you mention it," Greyson said as he raised his ankle to rest on the opposite knee. "Lady Chesterfield introduced me to her friend, the Marchioness of Rutherford. She is the woman I kept staring at across the ballroom. She is also a widow. I'm going to visit her tomorrow, and it would be good for me if you and the marchioness were on friendly terms again."

He snorted as he took a sip of his drink. "I want that. However, it's not going to happen unless we talk about the past and make peace with it."

"I know. Believe me," Greyson added. "I want nothing more than for you two to reunite and enjoy a long, prosperous life together."

"Me too," Samuel muttered as his stomach turned. Not so much from thinking about Clarice, but because he had eaten very little today and was starting to feel the effects of the brandy. Still, he couldn't get up and leave.

Hunter asked, "Are you going to Tattersall's Repository in the morning?"

"What a stupid question to ask," Greyson said with a smirk. "Whenever Stanton is in London, he visits nearly every day, regardless of whether there is any action happening. He has become quite friendly with the owner, Richard, who shares the same last name as the establishment."

"We are not chums or friends. He likes that I visit and we have some fine horseflesh conversations. And he knows that when I'm in the market for new horses, I will always purchase from him. He sold me Zeus and Clover before he showed them to anyone else, and for that I'm grateful."

"Are you excited and ready for the racing circuit?" Hunter asked.

"If being excited means you want to lose your dinner when you think about it, then yes. Once I arrive at Newmarket, I hope my nerves will settle down. As for Zeus, he's in his prime and ready. He was bred for racing, and I have faith in him. And Clover gives her all every time she hits the track. I just hope Mr. Tobias Burns, my jockey, is ready."

Hunter and Greyson shared a look, and Samuel prepared

himself for what was coming.

"I don't mean to pry," Greyson began.

"Yes, you do."

"Well, you're right. I'm just worried. When you inherited the dukedom, it wasn't that solvent. Which makes me wonder how you're managing all the costs of owning and racing two thoroughbreds."

"I'm managing fine. No need to be concerned." He wasn't ready to get into a conversation with Greyson and Hunter about money, his thoroughbreds, or anything racing related until the time was right.

Hunter said, "Come. Let us drop you home."

Standing up and swaying, Samuel grabbed the chair to steady himself and mumbled, "I believe I've overindulged."

The three friends left Brooks's and headed home in Greyson's carriage.

CHAPTER EIGHT

TWO DAYS HAD passed by since Clarice had seen Samuel, and she was disappointed he hadn't called on her. Perhaps he wasn't interested in pursuing what they once shared, she mused as her maid, Mrs. Shelley, styled her hair. She no longer had the dour-faced maid loyal to Chesterfield. Mrs. Shelley had been her maid before Clarice had married and had come to her once Chesterfield died. She remembered how shocked the butler, housekeeper, cook, and her maid—who had all treated her poorly—were when she let them go and hired ones loyal to her. The new hires had already promised to relocate with her when the new marquess arrived and she found suitable housing. Her father had done one thing right by her when drawing up her marriage contract to Chesterfield: He had ensured that she received two thousand pounds annually as his widow until her death or until she remarried.

"My lady, could you please stay still? I don't want my hand to slip and burn you with the curling rod."

"I'll be as still as a statue." It was hard, but she forced herself to settle down. Worrying about why Samuel did or did not call on her and where she would live would not be solved as Mrs. Shelley styled her hair.

The Earl and Countess of Langford were hosting a small dinner party this evening, and she wanted to look perfect because

Lilly had sent her a note informing her that Stanton would also be attending. Thinking about seeing him again sent her heart skipping. She wanted to look so beautiful that he would trip over his own feet when he saw her.

If he wouldn't take the reins, so to speak, to move their relationship forward, she would. Yes, she was still hurt that he hadn't rescued her from Chesterfield, but perhaps he had a good reason. Indeed, nothing could change the past. The future . . . could be theirs. She admired her hair in the mirror. Mrs. Shelley had curled every strand, pinned half of it up loosely, and left the other half down to caress her neck, shoulders, and back. "You did a splendid job with my hair, as always, Mrs. Shelley." When she stood, she spun from side to side, causing the silk skirt of her gown to swirl around her legs. She sighed as she admired the lovely new gown Madame Serena had delivered just that afternoon. It was beautifully designed, featuring a beaded bodice and a flowing silk skirt with subtle touches of beading here and there, all done in shades of smoky topaz and cream. The colors complemented her hair with just the right amount of contrast to make it interesting. Her slippers and reticle were the same shade of topaz as her dress, but her cloak was cream, trimmed with topaz ribbon and beading. She had never possessed a more elegant gown. It suited her mood and purpose tonight perfectly.

With any luck, Samuel would take one look at her at the dinner party, collapse to the ground on his knees, and declare his undying love. She exhaled and fought back the nerves prickling her skin. She had nothing to be nervous about. If Samuel didn't want her, then at least she could move on with her life instead of pining for a long-lost lover.

Thank goodness, Letitia was also on the guest list. She made her way down two flights of stairs and into the drawing room. No sooner had she walked to the windows facing the street than she saw the Rutherfords' black, well-appointed carriage pull up.

"My lady," Williamson, her butler, announced from the open doorway, "the carriage is here."

"Thank you, Williamson. That will be all."

Once she entered the coach with the help of one of the Rutherford footmen, she took a deep, calming breath. "I have pins and needles on my skin. If we weren't attending the Earl and Countess of Langford's dinner party, I may have begged off, I'm so nervous."

Letitia giggled, looking stunning in a deep sapphire-blue gown and cloak that contrasted with her light hair and made her blue eyes shine. "I feel the same, knowing Greyson will be there. I tried on three gowns before I chose this one."

"It's perfect. The contrast between dark and light will hopefully mesmerize Greyson."

"Yours as well. That color makes you glow."

Now Clarice giggled. "I think that's a compliment, and I don't actually glow like a lantern."

"Sorry, no. I should have said your complexion looks radiant—soft, creamy, and glowing in a good way."

The carriage ride was brief, and since it was a small gathering, the long queue of carriages normally found at large gatherings was nonexistent. Moments later, they found themselves inside Langford House, where the butler helped them with their cloaks. A footman guided them up the stairs and into a large salon, nicely decorated in hunter green and cream. She had heard somewhere that the previous Earl of Langford had possessed a flair for decorating, and it showed.

What Clarice noticed next was the sound of voices from the twenty or so male and female guests blended together in a musical rhythm. It was surprising how beautiful all the voices sounded without being overwhelming. She never admitted to anyone, but sometimes loud, crowded rooms made her feel lonely, uncomfortable, and invisible. It was silly that she could feel lonely surrounded by so many people. She had no explanation for why it happened. It had happened for the first time last Season when she'd attended two house parties. After that, she turned down most invitations, preferring to stay home . . . alone.

Which, to be sure, made no sense whatsoever.

Lord and Lady Langford, looking elegant, were both dressed in blue. The earl in navy and tan and Lilly in a soft blue, stood off to the side, greeting their guests. Clarice and Letitia meandered toward them. Clarice curtsied. "Lord and Lady Langford, it is an honor to be included among your guests this evening."

Langford bowed. "Lady Chesterfield, it is good to see you again."

Lilly took her hands in hers. "I'm so glad you could make it. Please mingle and enjoy yourself, and we will speak later." After Letitia made her greetings, they moved deeper inside the salon.

Letitia grabbed her hand and held it tightly. "Greyson is near the open double doors, talking with Stanton and another gentleman. The same one they were with at the Westport Ball."

"I see." It was hard to ignore the excited flutter in her chest when she saw Samuel, handsomely dressed in a cream linen shirt and a cravat tied perfectly into an intricate knot, a brown-and-cream patterned waistcoat, and a tan cutaway coat perfectly paired with dark brown breeches, hose, and shoes. He stole the very air from her lungs. He would always be the most handsome and desirable man to her. "That is Mr. Jacob Hunter. Those three have been thicker than thieves since their first days at Eton." Clarice squeezed Letitia's hand. "They have spotted us and are coming this way," Clarice breathed out, hoping she didn't faint from the bees swarming inside her stomach most uncomfortably.

"Oh my," Letitia said, turning pale. "I don't know if I'm ready for this."

"Me either, to be honest." Being with Samuel was what she wanted and desired most in the world, but it also terrified her. Her feelings and the depth of those feelings, still to this day, frightened her. They wound around the very fabric of her heart and soul so deeply and tightly that she would never be free from them, whatever might happen between them.

Being in a loveless marriage was simple. She had known from the very first night what her life would be like married to

Chesterfield. Although it hadn't been easy, she'd had no expectations or delusions of love and happiness. She had made peace with her bleak future with Chesterfield—until he died and she saw Samuel again. But seeing him unlocked the door to her feelings, pouring out her hopes and dreams of love, happiness, and a family. Of being in love and being loved in return. She knew she would never be able to lock it all back behind a door, even if things soured between her and Samuel.

"Ladies." Greyson bowed. "What a pleasant surprise seeing both of you here." When he spoke, his eager eyes fixed on Letitia, causing her to blush. Clarice was happy for her friend and hoped all went well between them. "I don't believe you have met my friends. Lady Rutherford, may I present the Duke of Stanton and Mr. Jacob Hunter?"

After the formalities concluded, Greyson and Letitia went for a stroll through the gardens since it was a lovely, warm, and dry evening.

"It's very nice to see you again, Lady Chesterfield," said Hunter, taking her hand and bowing over it. "You are as lovely as ever." He stood without letting go of her hand, his eyes shifting from Samuel to her. And Samuel practically growled at his friend.

"Please, call me Lady Clarice. And it is a pleasure seeing you again after all these years, Mr. Hunter."

"Lady Clarice it is," he replied as he brought her hand to his lips, making a show of kissing her hand.

"Mr. Hunter, that is enough," Samuel interjected.

Hunter chuckled. "Why don't I give you both some privacy? I know when I'm not wanted."

"Is he upset?" she asked as she watched him walk away.

"No. It takes more than just feeling unwanted to rile Hunter up. He is the easiest-going man I know."

"I only met him a few times and don't remember much about him."

"He hasn't changed much. Neither Greyson nor Hunter has. They're still enjoying their bachelor lifestyle."

"Greyson appears interested in Lady Rutherford."

A frown appeared on his face. "He does, and I sincerely hope he doesn't break Lady Rutherford's heart. Greyson tends to break hearts all over London."

"Letitia is a grown woman and can look after herself." Clarice hoped her words proved true. Maybe Greyson was just looking for a dalliance with the young widow. She would keep a close watch on him. She did not want to pick up the pieces of Letitia's broken heart. On the other hand, perhaps her friend only wanted a liaison and nothing more serious. However, she didn't believe that.

"It's good to see that you, Greyson, and Hunter are still good friends," Clarice said.

"Yes. I can sometimes get lost, and they always find me." He appeared uncomfortable after divulging that little tidbit. Which made her wonder what he meant by getting lost.

She smiled sadly and clasped her hands together to resist reaching out and touching him. "You aren't lost now."

He snorted, "No, I'm not."

The bell rang for dinner, and Clarice was grateful because of the sudden awkwardness that had developed between them.

Small dinner affairs often disregarded the proper rules of etiquette by lining guests up according to title; tonight was no exception. Samuel extended his arm. "May I escort you into the dining room?"

"Yes." She placed her hand on his forearm, and they filed behind other couples as they entered the large dining room with a table set for twenty. Clarice wasn't shocked when the fancy gold place card with her name on it was on the place setting beside Samuel's. Lilly was doing her best to help her in her quest to win back Samuel's heart. And she truly believed she needed all the help she could get. Across the table from them sat Letitia, Greyson, and Hunter. Lilly had placed Hunter next to one of Greyson's twin sisters, Anastasia, she believed, whom Clarice hadn't realized was in attendance until just now. The other sister was seated several chairs down from her, next to a young gentleman she didn't recognize.

The Duke and Duchess of Blackstone, who had arrived just moments ago, sat farther down the long table on the same side as Letitia. Emmeline nodded and smiled at her in greeting. Clarice nodded and smiled back. What a strange and wonderful feeling it was to have friends.

She had spent the five years of her marriage mostly eating alone in the large dining room at Chesterfield Manor or in her chambers. Chesterfield preferred to dine at his clubs. He rarely spent time in her company, except for several nights a week when he performed his husbandly duties. During those nights, Clarice closed her eyes and prayed for it to end. His breath was always foul and reeked of strong spirits. He wasn't gentle when he did bother to touch her. Thankfully, he didn't bother most nights and got right down to his business. He would spill his seed trying to produce an heir and then leave quickly afterward, for which she was very grateful.

His tongue was sharp, but he never laid a hand on her in anger. He used his words to hurt her. She wouldn't lie and say his words never stung. Yet she reasoned with herself that he didn't matter to her, nor did his words. And that's how she survived those years. That, and her watercolors. It was the only concession in their marriage that he ever gave her.

"You're awfully quiet." Samuel's deep voice pulled her out of her unhappy thoughts.

"Forgive me for my woolgathering and being a terrible diner companion." Picking up her glass of wine, she took a large sip.

"You are no such thing. Being beside you, whether we talk or not, is a pleasure I never thought to have again. Ah, the first course has arrived."

It puzzled her why her thoughts had drifted to Chesterfield, why her tongue was tied and her hands were trembling. Sitting next to Samuel was all she'd ever wanted, and somehow she needed to relax and enjoy his company. She picked up her spoon and ate her turtle soup like everyone else at the long table. Most conversations had stopped, aside from a few words here and there.

The soup was taken away, and a footman refilled all the wine glasses. She was surprised to realize she had finished her entire glass. It never took much wine to make her tipsy. She would have to limit herself to just one or two more; otherwise, Letitia would be carrying her home.

The courses came and went. Clarice nibbled on everything on her plate, but she couldn't possibly finish everything she was served. The conversation between her and Samuel was still stilted and awkward. When dinner ended, instead of the men staying behind for port and cigars as usual, everyone went back to the salon. Clarice promised herself she would relax, not think about her marriage to Chesterfield again, and enjoy the evening spent with friends.

Most importantly, she wanted to enjoy the evening spent with Samuel.

CHAPTER NINE

"WOULD YOU CARE to stroll through the gardens?" Samuel asked once they entered the salon, and the uncertainty in his voice astounded her. The Samuel she once knew was never unsure of himself when it came to her. Perhaps her unusual behavior at the dinner table caused it.

"I would love that." She smiled, feeling lighter and happier but still guarded. "The gardens and fresh air sound perfect."

"Shall we?" He extended his arm, and instead of placing her hand on his forearm, she looped her arm around his elbow.

"We shall." How wonderful it felt to be close to him. If only they both weren't holding something back. There was an invisible wall of unease, uncertainty, and a past to navigate through before they could be at ease with each other as they once were. She hoped it wouldn't take long.

They strolled leisurely out of the double glass doors onto the veranda, down a few stairs, and into gardens lit by glass lanterns hanging from tall poles. "How long have you known the Earl and Countess of Langford?" she asked as their feet crunched on the gravel path and they walked farther away from the veranda.

"I met Langford last year at Tattersall's. He was buying a mare for the countess and a matching four for his carriage. I offered him my help."

"That was very thoughtful of you."

He shrugged his shoulders. "I was also very much in awe of him, Blackstone, and Mr. Caldwell for building their import and export empire. I had never met them personally, although we would have had overlapping years at Eton; however, I had heard a great deal about them. So I took the opportunity to introduce myself and offer any assistance I could. When he realized my vast knowledge regarding horseflesh, he took my recommendations. Since then, I've become acquainted with Blackstone and Caldwell as well. They could never replace my friendship with Greyson and Hunter, but they are friends of mine as well. Greyson and Hunter have also become friends with them. They have another friend, the Marquess of Hollingsworth, whom I've met and become friendly with. He and his wife are away at the moment and couldn't attend this evening."

"I'm glad for you." She genuinely was. They were both making new friends, which would help make life less lonely.

"What about you? How did you meet the Earl and Countess of Langford?"

"Letitia's mother and the Duchess of Blackstone's mother have been close friends for a long time. Letitia has known Emmeline her entire life and met Lilly when her first husband died and she came to live with Emmeline in London." She paused and inhaled. "I only met them recently, but we have become friends thanks to Letitia."

"I'm also glad for you. I can't imagine that being married to an older man gave you many chances to meet other young women like yourself."

They arrived at a black wrought-iron bench and sat so close that their shoulders, hips, and thighs brushed against each other. Neither moved to create space between them. The warmth of his body felt nice against hers. "To be truthful, Chesterfield didn't allow me out of the house. Well, that's not entirely true. I was allowed on the grounds. We never attended social functions together. He went out, but I was stuck at home. Honestly, I was glad not to be around him, and he certainly didn't want to be anywhere near me."

He turned and took her hands into his, sadness shining in his eyes. "I don't understand. If he didn't want to be with you, why did he marry you?"

Her cheeks reddened, and she looked down. "He wanted an heir, and that was all. He couldn't be bothered with me . . . except . . . for . . ." She didn't believe her face could get hotter, but it did. She was utterly mortified that she was sharing these intimate details about her marriage with him.

He gently squeezed her hands. "I'm sorry."

"What happened and what was done is over. I never gave him an heir, and he went to his grave despising me for it. Cursed me to a barren life." Tears pooled in her eyes, and she blinked them away.

"I'm sure you'll have children someday. Chesterfield was old. He was undoubtedly the one who was barren."

What Samuel said was true. But now was not the time for that conversation. Nor did Clarice know if the right time would ever come. If he went away and she never saw him again, he should never know. Why should he suffer as she had if she could spare him from the pain? She'd suffered enough over the years for both of them, cried enough to create a river full of her tears and carried a constant pain in her chest from the loss, enough to break a weaker woman. She suddenly had to blink back tears.

"Can I ask a question?" His voice was quiet and unsure.

"Yes."

"Did you ever think about me?"

She pulled her hands away from his in shock as anguish and pain pierced her heart. How could he ever think she hadn't? She gasped, "How can you ask such a question?"

Before she continued, he took her hands in his again, gently brushing his thumbs over the back of her hands. "Forgive me. That was rather insensitive of me. What I should have said was I thought of you often."

"I thought of you as well. I realize we have a lot to talk about, but could you hold me and let us enjoy this lovely evening without dredging up the past or my unhappy marriage?"

"This I can do." He let go of her hands, wrapped one arm around her shoulders, and pulled her close so their bodies touched everywhere. Clarice rested her head on his shoulder and inhaled his familiar scent. A scent that hadn't changed. Samuel always smelled of a mix of hay, horses, and the outdoors. Some might think it was a bad smell. To her, he smelled like coming home and heaven all in one.

"I missed this," he murmured as he rested his head on hers.

"Me too." He took her free hand in his, and their hands rested on her lap. His thumb gently stroked the underside of her wrist where the glove met her skin, and she wished she hadn't put her gloves back on after eating. The circles he drew with his thumb made her skin tingle in a very good way. The sensation traveled up her arm, down her stomach until it settled between her thighs. She moved her bottom on the bench, trying to heighten the sensation. Desire wasn't something she'd felt in forever, and she wanted to enjoy it.

Samuel chuckled. "Are there ants in your gown? Because you seem squirmy all of a sudden."

Mortified because she hadn't realized it was so obvious, she giggled nervously. "No ants. My body's enjoying being close to yours." She gasped, tugged her hand from his, and slapped it across her mouth. "I can't believe I said that."

Samuel chuckled, but she knew he wasn't laughing at her, but with her. "I'm not going to lie—I could stand to adjust my breeches." Before she could understand the meaning of his words, he used his strong arms to pull her onto his lap. Her legs dangled on the bench, her arms wrapped around his neck, and they stared at each other. She didn't breathe, nor did she think Samuel did, but she could feel the rapid beat of his heart against her side. She felt the intimate gaze of his dark, mesmerizing eyes penetrate straight into her soul.

"You are beautiful." His voice deepened, and his eyes shifted from hers to her mouth and back multiple times. "May I kiss you?" he breathed out.

Her lips curled into a smile, and she exhaled, "Yes."

She turned toward him as his lips pressed against hers. How could it be that he tasted the same as she remembered? His soft lips, larger than hers, even settled against hers in the same way. They both moaned as the kiss deepened. Her tongue swirled around and around with his. They reacquainted each other with their tongues. The fingers of one of his hands skimmed up and down her back, then drew circles around and around, fueling the heat between her legs. His other hand moved to the side of her neck, and his thumb moved lazily across her neck, collarbone, and the sensitive spot behind her ear, making her rub her bottom against the hardness growing in Samuel's breeches, and he groaned out.

Lips left hers and travelled down her neck and throat until he licked the swell of her breasts exposed by the low-cut neckline she'd worn specifically to entice him. "Christ, Clarice, you are driving me mad with lust. You, only you, have ever made me feel this way. Like I could lose myself in you and die in your arms, a happy, contented man."

She wiggled her bottom again as she took his hand and placed it at the bottom of her skirt. "Touch me, Samuel."

He didn't hesitate to comply. He moved his hand beneath her skirts. Clarice bit her bottom lip to keep from crying out as her core vibrated with anticipation. When his fingers finally found their way up the inside of her thighs and tunneled through her curls, she buried her face in the crook of his shoulder as her entire body trembled. His fingers parted her folds, stroking her as his thumb circled around and around her nub. She kept her face buried because of the sounds escaping her that she couldn't hold in even if she tried. To have Samuel's hands on her again was almost more than she could endure.

Her hips jumped when he inserted a long finger inside her channel, and while he moved it in and out, he continued to tease her nub. It was only moments before her legs shook, her stomach coiled up tight, and her body exploded. Thankfully, his clothing muffled her cries as her pleasure continued on and on, and he continued to stroke her more gently and more lightly as time went on, until he removed his hand, tugged down her skirts, and inserted his index finger into his mouth and moaned.

"Samuel." Having left euphoria, she smacked his arm.

"Did you really think I would waste your juices after waiting seven years to taste you again?"

Embarrassed, she buried her face again, and he wrapped his arms around her waist, making her feel cherished.

"IT'S ME. WE have never been embarrassed by anything we've done together." He kissed the top of her head and rubbed his cheek against it. "Please don't be now. Time has passed, but we remain the same. Everything I felt for you before is still inside me."

Samuel's skin had tingled alive when he pulled Clarice into his arms, acutely aware of her breathing, the steady beat of her heart, and the softness of her curves. The lavender scent of her hair drove him wild with desire, but at this moment, it was all about her. He wanted to give her pleasure. When she said "touch me," he nearly lost control. When his fingers first ran through her curls and felt her wetness, her heat, he sighed as his body stilled and hers awakened. When she came on his fingers, he knew he had to taste her. He hoped he hadn't shocked her too much, especially since her face was still buried. As time passed and she said nothing, his stomach tightened. "Is something wrong? Did I do anything wrong?"

When she said, "Nothing is wrong," in a muffled voice, he understood her perfectly.

"Will you look at me?"

A groan escaped her lips as she slowly raised her head and looked into his eyes. Tears streamed down her cheeks, making his heart race and his voice falter, "What is it? Why are you crying? Did I hurt you?"

Her head shook from side to side until she finally answered him. "I'm fine. Better than fine." She hiccupped. "I got a little overwhelmed with emotions and sensations, making me cry."

Leaning his head back against the bench, his chest rose and fell with deep inhalations full of relief. He had been so afraid that he had done something to upset her. Looking up into the night sky, his eyes took in its vastness and all the stars. He always wondered what it would be like to travel up into the sky and explore what was there. What the planets and stars were really like. But right now, he had everything he ever wanted or needed right down here and cradled in his arms.

"Do you remember what I used to tell you?" It wasn't really a question, so Samuel kept going. "That we never have to pretend with each other. That we are the other half of each other's hearts, minds, and souls. Nothing we could ever do or say would shock the other. That we could confess our deepest, darkest secrets and nothing would change. We would love, respect, and cherish each other until death."

"I remember. Please let me up." Regrettably, he released his grip on her and helped her stand, where she began smoothing down her skirts and patting her hair. "How do I look?"

He joined her in standing. "Perfect."

Her eyes drifted down to her skirts, and she giggled. "You'd say that even if I wore a sack. But, oh well, there's nothing I can do about the wrinkles. Shall we head back to the house?"

He held out his hand, and bloody hell if he didn't grin like a love-sick fool. "Yes."

They neared the double doors leading into the salon as Lady Rutherford and Greyson stepped onto the veranda. Samuel lowered his head and asked quietly, "I know you arrived with Lady Rutherford, but was it your carriage or hers?"

"Hers."

"Would you allow me to see you home?"

Instead of replying to him, she said, "Letitia, Stanton has offered to take me home. You don't mind, do you?"

Lady Rutherford smiled at Clarice. "Not at all. Are we still going shopping on Bond Street tomorrow, late morning?"

"Why, yes, of course."

"Greyson, Lady Rutherford," Samuel said, "enjoy your stroll through the gardens."

Before they could respond, he led Clarice into the salon, where they approached Lord and Lady Langford to say goodbye.

They exited the townhouse hand in hand. Once beside his coach, the liveried footman opened the door, lowered the steps, and Samuel helped Clarice inside. He spoke to his driver, then entered the carriage, sat down, and tapped the roof, sending the carriage on its journey. Samuel reached for Clarice's hand and held it throughout the ride to Chesterfield Manor.

CHAPTER TEN

CLARICE'S HEART RACED inside her chest as she settled into the carriage, which bore the Stanton ducal crest. She faced a dilemma. Should she invite Samuel in for a nightcap or send him on his way with a polite thank you? Part of her was excited and afraid of what might happen if she invited him in. Another part worried that if she let him go, she might never have another chance to see him again. Which was silly, of course, but ever since she had first seen him tonight, her insides and her mind had been all jumbled up.

"We have arrived," Samuel said.

Before she lost her nerve, she asked, "Would you care to come in for a nightcap?"

He exhaled loudly and replied, "I would like that." He knocked on the door, and the footman opened it, lowering the steps. Samuel exited first, leaned back in, and held his hand out to her. She took it and never let go as she led him up the stairs and through the door her butler opened.

"Welcome home, my lady," the butler said with a bow.

"Thank you, Williamson." She handed him her gloves and cloak, and Samuel took off his greatcoat and handed it over as well. "You may retire for the night."

"Thank you, my lady," he said as he handed her a candelabra to light their way.

Clarice led the way up the stairs to the drawing room where she received visitors. She sat on the settee, placing the candle on the oval table in front of the settee. "Do you mind pouring us brandy from the sideboard?"

"Not at all." Her eyes never left Samuel as he strolled across the room, poured two drinks, turned around, and joined her on the settee.

"Do I have something on my face?" he asked, as he handed her a glass half-filled with amber liquid.

"You pour a healthy drink, and no, there's nothing on your face. I just couldn't stop myself from looking at you. I'm worried that if I look away, you'll vanish, and tonight will have been just my imagination."

He took a deep sip of his brandy. "I'm real, but I understand how you feel. It's occurred to me that I might be dreaming."

They both laughed, and she allowed herself to relax against the back of the settee instead of sitting on the edge with perfect posture. She didn't need to impress Samuel with her manners or posture.

"I believe I mentioned that I have a horse on the racing circuit this year."

"You did."

"I leave for Newmarket soon." He removed her glass from her hand and placed both their glasses on the table. He turned toward her, so she pivoted toward him, causing their knees to touch. He reached out and took both her hands in his. "I'm hoping you will allow me to spend as much time as possible with you before I leave."

"Nothing would please me more." She could hardly contain her excitement. And when his thumbs stroked the underside of her wrist, she gazed into his mesmerizing gray eyes full of desire and need, causing her entire body to tremble. Pulling her hands away, she stood and held one out. "Come with me."

One of his brows arched in silent question, but he stood, took her hand in one of his and picked up the candle with the other, and followed her up another flight of stairs and down the corridor to the large chambers she moved into the day Chesterfield died. Thank goodness she told Mrs. Shelley not to wait up for her. Once the door was closed, she turned the lock.

Once again, Samuel looked at her with one brow raised. The difference was that this time he didn't stay silent. "Clarice. Is this really what you want?" he asked as he placed the candle on the bedside table.

Maybe she should have thought this through. But no. If she had, she would have found many reasons why this was a bad idea. And all she wanted was to be with Samuel. To feel his skin against hers. To feel his strong arms around her. To feel the quick beat of his heart as he made love to her. She wanted it all. Suddenly nervous, she walked to a window, pulled aside the curtain, and stared out into the darkness.

Samuel stepped up behind her, and his large arms wrapped around her waist, pulling her back against his chest. He dipped his head and whispered into her ear, "You didn't answer my question."

One of her arms raised, and she placed her palm on his razor stubbled cheek. "My answer is yes. I've had seven years to dream about this. To want this. I thought you'd be married by now, and we would never have another chance to be together. Since we're both unmarried and free, I can't think of anyone I'd rather be with than you."

Samuel groaned as he spun her around, cupped both her cheeks, and crashed his mouth to hers. The kiss was raw in its intensity. Their teeth clashed, and their tongues tangled. She grabbed his shoulders, not trusting her legs to support her. Just as her head began to spin from lack of air, he broke the kiss, his lips traveling down her neck. "I will never tire of kissing you. Turn around so I can unbutton your gown."

She obliged. He fumbled with the buttons until he released enough to tug her dress down and over her hips, and it pooled at her feet. He tugged off her petticoat and untied her corset strings, freeing her to inhale deeply for the first time since her maid tied them. "How do you breathe with this thing on?"

She giggled. "You get used to it." Once her corset was off, he stepped in front of her and unlaced the front of her chemise, his eyes, almost black with desire, never wavered from hers.

"These ties are easy," he said with a wink. He slipped the chemise off first one shoulder, then the next, tugging it down further until one breast peeked out and then the other, and still he gazed into her eyes. She had trouble breathing even though her corset was gone. When her chemise hit the floor, his head and eyes lowered and she heard him inhale. "You are beautiful." Without warning, he scooped her up into his arms, carried her to the bed, tossed the covers aside without dropping her, and gently laid her on the top of the snow-white sheets, dressed in absolutely nothing.

It was her turn to watch him as he undressed down to nothing but toned muscle. The bed dipped as he joined her and murmured, "Have you any idea how beautiful you are? I could spend the rest of my life just looking at you."

As his eyes roamed over her body, heat caressed her skin. She wanted to tell him he was beautiful, but she was too shy to say it. "Samuel." One of his knees slipped between her legs, and he leaned down and kissed her. This time, the kiss was soft. He sipped from her mouth, his tongue gentle. It was sensual and indulgent. He adored her mouth with his. Kissing had never felt so amazing and exciting; she never wanted it to end.

Just as she thought that, he moved his mouth. His sinful lips lightly kissed down her neck and chest. He took one nipple into his mouth and sucked it deep inside, causing her hips to rise off the bed. His mouth moved to her other breast and did the same to that pebbled nipple, causing her hips to rise again. He buried his head between her breasts and chuckled. "You like that, don't you?"

"Mmmm," was all that she was capable of saying because his lips were trailing down her stomach. His tongue swirled around her belly button, causing sensitivity overload. But he wasn't done. He nudged her thighs open and kissed her there, and she was thrown back in time to when she'd experienced this once before. The time she lost her innocence to Samuel. "Samuel," she moaned as his fingers opened her folds, followed right behind by his tongue. He gently nudged her thighs wider, sucking her nub into his mouth, and she thought she would float right off the bed. When he added a finger, the trembling in her legs started. He stopped, lifted his head, met her eyes with a confident grin, placed her legs over his shoulders, and bent back down. A loud moan escaped her as his mouth and fingers took her over the edge into a world vibrantly alive and pulsating with pleasure.

He crawled up her body, placing butterfly kisses here and there, keeping her skin tingling. "You taste so good. I could do that for hours," he said in a deep, guttural tone. And then he was kissing her in that raw and desperate way he had earlier. She felt the push of his manhood at the entrance to her channel, and she let her knees fall open. One deep push and he was completely inside her, her body stretching to accommodate his length and size.

His hips began to move, and she joined him in perfect rhythm. A rhythm as old as time. The closer they came to falling over the edge, the faster their bodies worked. Clarice put her hands on his hips, pulling him as deep as she could into her body and holding him there as her entire being trembled, and she felt her inner muscles clamping around Samuel's member. A loud animalistic groan came from him, his body tensed, he groaned again louder than before, then collapsed down on her, nuzzling her neck. Her arms and legs were splayed out on the bed, trembling, yet somehow lifeless.

Samuel rolled onto his side, taking her with him. "I'm sorry, I must've been heavy," he murmured into her ear as his arms wrapped around her.

"A little. But it felt good," she sighed as she wiggled back against the front of his body. His chest hairs tickled her back.

Being held against the hard, strong, and broad expanse of his chest made her feel safe and cherished.

She almost thought *loved*, but it was too soon to bring love into the equation. Indeed, she knew without a doubt that she still was in love with Samuel. Always had been, always would. However, she didn't want to put that pressure on him. It had been years, and perhaps he had feelings for another. She was the one who had asked him to stay. Led him to her bedchamber. Mentioned they were free and unmarried. She was anyway. But maybe he was courting someone. Or had a lady friend.

No. No. That couldn't be right. Hadn't he said he wanted to spend all his time with her before he left for Newmarket? Could his lady friend live in Newmarket? Oh dear, tears leaked from her eyes, and the last thing she wanted was for Samuel to notice.

"You're being quiet? Are you regretting . . ."

"No. Never," she interrupted. Even if it turned out he had a special someone, she would never regret what had happened between them. Sharing herself with Samuel before her marriage and dreaming about doing so again was what had kept her sane during her unpleasant marriage. Chesterfield was no kind old man. He was the type who snatched treats from babies, stole donations from the church, and looked down his nose at almost everyone.

"I apologize, but I must go." His lips brushed the back of her neck. He climbed off the bed and pulled up the covers. She immediately missed his warm body against hers. With heavy-lidded eyes, she watched him dress. The bed dipped when he sat down and tugged on his boots.

"Must you leave?"

"We don't want to make it easy on the gossip rags. With my carriage parked outside your townhouse all night, it would give them proof that we are having an affair. Even if I send it home, some busybody who prides herself on spreading the latest gossip—like Lady Hornsby, who lives across the street—would put the pieces together." Once he finished pulling on his boots, he stood, leaned down, and brushed his lips across hers. "It's probably too late for rumors, but I don't want my late-night visit causing you any embarrassment."

"Lady Hornsby does love to gossip, but believe it or not, since Chesterfield passed, she has been kind to me. I hope she will continue to be my friend and keep my private affairs to herself. She always did before."

"I apologize for offending Lady Hornsby. Maybe I am mistaken about her."

Clarice laughed. "Oh, she loves to gossip, just not about me or Letitia."

He leaned in and kissed her again, this time lingering, sweeping his tongue in and tasting her, which sent heat rushing through her. "Good night. Sleep well, my love."

He exited and quietly shut the door. She wasn't worried about her servants seeing Samuel leave late in the evening or perhaps early in the morning, depending on the case. She had removed anyone who wasn't loyal to her. Williamson, Mrs. Shelley, and the housekeeper, Mrs. Jones, managed them well. With a contented sigh, Clarice snuggled beneath the coverlet and fell asleep with a smile and a full heart.

"Good morning, my lady," Mrs. Shelley said cheerfully as she entered her chambers as the next morning came all too soon. She placed her breakfast tray on the table next to her comfortable chaise longue and continued to open the curtains on the mullioned glass windows. "It is a lovely day. The sun is actually shining."

Clarice blinked several times, adjusting to the light streaming through the windows. She pushed the covers off her, swung her legs off the bed, and stood with her arms up, stretching to ease the pleasant soreness in her muscles from last night. Her lips curled upward into a smile, and her cheeks warmed as the pleasant memories resurfaced. She slipped into her robe, which matched the night rail she had donned during the night, and made her way to the chaise longue, laughing as she relaxed on it.

"You're in a good mood today, my lady. I take it the dinner party last evening was worth attending?"

"Hmmm, yes, Mrs. Shelley, it was. I ran into an old friend whom I haven't seen since before I married Chesterfield."

"I'm happy for you. You need more friends. If you'll excuse me, my lady, I'll leave you to your breakfast and come back in half an hour to get you ready for your Bond Street adventure with Lady Rutherford."

"Thank you."

No matter how hard she tried, Clarice could not stop staring at nothing and smiling. When she realized Mrs. Shelley would be back any moment, she drank her now lukewarm tea, ate her cold toast with jam, and her poached eggs. It wouldn't do to have her stomach grumbling while shopping with Letitia. The two of them had only recently started going out shopping on Thursday mornings. Shopping while in mourning was not enjoyable. The two of them had been stared at and whispered about, so they'd stopped until both their mourning periods were over.

While Clarice waited for her maid, she opened the wardrobe and rummaged through her walking dresses, pulling out her favorite green one with a matching spencer. She laid the dress and spencer on the bed, then entered her dressing room where her hat boxes were stacked. Somewhere in the pile was a green bonnet to match her dress. Sighing, she decided to wait for Mrs. Shelley. No doubt, she knew exactly which hat box it was in.

"I see you picked your favorite green dress. It always highlights your brown eyes and the green hidden within. I'll get the matching bonnet." It took Mrs. Shelly two tries, and she found the correct box. "Ah, here it is. The flowers on the band just need a little fluffing."

Clarice stood as Mrs. Shelley removed her robe and night rail, replacing them with a linen chemise, corset, and petticoat. Finally, her dress was slipped over her head and pulled down into place. The dress featured a scooped neckline and short, puffed sleeves trimmed with the same lace as at the hem. The high waistline was encircled with green ribbon, which Mrs. Shelley tied in the back with a perfect bow. She sat on the dressing table chair as Mrs. Shelley slid her stockings up to her mid-thigh and tied them with ribbon to keep them secure.

"Let's do your hair," Mrs. Shelly said as she picked up a brush and began to run it through her long tresses. "I swear your hair has grown and gotten thicker since yesterday."

"I know. It's too much," she said with a frustrated exhale. She always wanted to have straight blonde hair.

"Most young ladies admire your hair. The color isn't your typical plain brown. It has stunning auburn and blonde highlights. It shines in the sunlight and under lantern light. It also falls in soft, natural curls. I rarely need a curling rod, which is good because they can damage hair."

Mrs. Shelley twisted Clarice's hair into a nice, neat chignon, and secured it with multiple pins. To complete her outfit, she placed Clarice's bonnet on her head and secured it with several pearl hat pins and a ribbon sash tied to the side beneath her chin.

"See, you look perfect." Mrs. Shelley helped her stand and patted her arm. "You are a vision. Perhaps you will see your gentleman friend during your shopping outing."

Her mouth dropped open, then she quickly closed it. "I never said my friend was a man. Perhaps she is a lady friend I haven't seen in forever."

"Not by the twinkle in your eye and the smile on your face this morning. Your friend is most definitely a man. And good for you, my lady."

Clarice's stomach fluttered at the thought that she might see Samuel today. He did know she was shopping on Bond Street. So perhaps. "Thank you, Mrs. Shelley, for everything. I don't know what I would do without you."

She dabbed at her teary eyes. "Oh, pish-posh, my dear lady. You would do just fine without little ole' me taking care of you."

She did something she'd always wanted to do but never had. Clarice hugged her—quickly, not wanting to ruin everything Mrs.

Shelley had worked so hard on. Before tears welled up in her own eyes, she headed toward the door, paused, and then turned around. "Mrs. Shelley, we forgot my walking boots."

"Oh my, we can't have you leaving the house in your stockings. What will the neighbors say? Sit down. Let me get them." She hurried into the dressing room and returned carrying a green drawstring pouch and two brown walking boots that tied at the mid-calf. "Now you are ready."

"I am."

When Clarice reached the front door, Williamson bowed and said, "Lady Rutherford's carriage has just arrived." He opened the door.

She exited and, with the help of Letitia's footman, Clarice entered the carriage and sat beside her friend. "Thank you for picking me up. What a lovely day for shopping."

"Yes. It is," Letitia replied with a smile. "Perhaps we should go to Gunter's for ices or confections after shopping."

"Yes, that's perfect. Where should we go first?"

"I was thinking about Marietta's Milliner Shop. I could use a new cream bonnet. I left mine on my bed, and the new puppy tore it apart. Little Freckles is quite the naughty puppy, but I love him, and Percy smiles and giggles whenever he sees him. It warms my heart. They are nearly inseparable. Just last night, I caught Freckles sneaking into his room and curling up on the foot of his bed."

"How sweet," Clarice said, thinking of Letitia's precious little boy. A heaviness and sadness tugged at her heart. She shook her head—no sense torturing herself with the past when what was done was done. "I could use several pairs of white kid gloves for all our upcoming social events. Some of mine have yellowed from overuse and cleaning. I know Mrs. Shelley frets over getting them back to pure white, but it's time to admit they are old and worn. And some colorful pairs will be fun for the daytime."

"You must," Letitia commented.

"I know. You should too. Tell me, how was your time with

Greyson last night?"

Letitia sighed and relaxed against the squabs. "He is so handsome and kind and witty. It's strange, but I feel as though I've known him for longer than I have. How is that possible?"

"It happens, or so I've been told. Two souls meet and connect."

The carriage came to a gentle, rolling stop. A footman opened the door, lowered the stairs, and helped them out of the carriage one by one.

"Thank you, Herbert," said Letitia. "We will be shopping for a while."

Arm in arm, they entered the fray of fashionably dressed shoppers strolling down Bond Street. Some window shopped, while others went into the shops to make purchases. Clarice and Letitia nodded to acquaintances as they navigated the crowds. Clarice should have known that on a pleasant day, weather-wise, Bond Street would bring out the shoppers en masse.

"Marietta's is just ahead," Letitia said.

When they reached the door, it opened, and several ladies exited the shop. One of them spoke, "Good luck, my ladies. It's a veritable crush inside."

"Thank you for the warning," Clarice said as they went in anyway. "Maybe there's a sale. I've never seen so many buying bonnets."

"Oh, look," Letitia said as she approached a display filled with bonnets in every color imaginable. She picked up an ivory one with a wide brim across the front, but not in the back. It was trimmed with white and ivory ribbon and flowers, and tied beneath the chin with wide ivory ribbon.

"It's lovely," Clarice said. "Try it on."

Letitia removed her hat, put it on, and turned to her, smiling. "It fits perfectly. How does it look?"

"It's like it was made for you. The contrast against your dark hair is striking, and your blue-and-cream dress looks lovely. I would wear it today."

"I shall."

After she made her purchase, leaving her old bonnet in the new hat box with the proprietor to be delivered to Rutherford House later, they exited the shop and entered the bustling crowds, only to come face to face with Samuel and Mr. Jacob Hunter. They both bowed and said, "Ladies," at the same time, making Clarice smile. When she looked at Samuel, who was looking at her, she knew by his look that he was remembering last night, as she was, and her cheeks burned.

"We were just thinking of going to Gunter's for ices," Samuel said. "Would you ladies care to join us? My carriage should be pulling up momentarily."

Letitia and Clarice looked at each other and smiled. "As a matter of fact," Clarice said, "we were planning on going there as well. We would love to accompany you."

"Perfect," Samuel said as his easily recognizable carriage pulled up. "Good thing I didn't bring my phaeton; there wouldn't have been room for four."

The footman opened the door and lowered the stairs. Samuel helped Letitia and then her into the coach, and she found herself sitting beside Samuel, their knees brushing. Remaining quiet during the ride, Clarice listened to the men discuss the upcoming racing tour. All the while, her body burned with desire for the man beside her. Could he feel the heat radiating off her? She didn't know how he could miss it.

They arrived shortly after at Berkeley Square and found a nice table for four against the wall. They all ordered lemon ices charged to Samuel's account.

When they were finished, Mr. Hunter asked, "Would you ladies care for a walk in the park before going back to Bond Street?"

"That would be nice," Letitia replied. Then she asked, "Where is Greyson today?" Hunter winced, and she blushed before immediately saying, "Sorry. I didn't mean to imply your company is not enough."

He chuckled. "I understand. No harm done. He's escorting his sisters to a luncheon at their aunt's house on the Thames." He winked at Letitia. "I'm quite positive he would rather be here with you."

She blushed a deeper shade of red.

CHAPTER ELEVEN

SAMUEL LED THEM out onto the pavement as the four of them left Gunter's. Clarice's arm was wrapped through Samuel's, and Letitia's through Mr. Hunter's. Once a clear path across the street appeared, they crossed the road and entered the park. Samuel distanced them from Hunter and Letitia. "Sorry if I made you walk fast to keep up with me, but I wanted a word alone with you."

"I managed fine."

He led her to a bench under a large elm tree, and they sat down. He turned to her and took her hands in his. "How are you today?"

Pink tinted her cheeks. It was a telltale sign she understood he was referring to last night. "I am good. Better than good."

He raised an eyebrow and tilted his head. "No regrets, I hope?"

"None." She glanced at their joined hands and smiled. "In fact, I look forward to doing it again soon."

He moaned, slightly surprised by her assertiveness. Surprised, yet completely elated.

"That is, if you are agreeable to it," she added.

"I am most agreeable. In fact, are you free this evening?"

"Why, yes. My social calendar is wide open."

Raising her hands to his mouth, he kissed the sensitive underside of one wrist, then the other, and he could see her body tremble visibly.

"You are a rakehell, Samuel Radcliff, duke or no duke."

He burst out laughing.

"I love your laugh. I was worried I'd never hear it again," she said.

"Since it makes you happy, I will laugh often."

"We should go. Letitia and I have one more shop to visit. Come for dinner. I have an excellent cook."

"Dinner it is."

He stood and held out his hand, and she placed her hand in his and rose to her feet. They strolled, hand in hand, over to where Letitia and Hunter sat on a nearby bench. Hunter was talking nonstop, and Letitia was laughing at what he was saying.

"I believe Hunter is spilling secrets about Greyson," Samuel said, chuckling. "When he finds out, they will come to fisticuffs."

"Truly?" Her eyes widened as she looked concerned.

"No. I'm teasing. Let's get you ladies back to your shopping."

"Here is the glove shop," Clarice said, hurrying to the door and stepping inside, only to find herself face to face with her neighbor across the street, Lady Hornsby.

"Lady Clarice, my dear, what a lovely surprise to run into you," Lady Hornsby said with a worried expression. Then her eyes scanned the room where several old biddies were whispering and glancing their way. Lady Hornsby frowned, leaned in close, and whispered, "I should warn you that rumors are going around that the Duke of Stanton spent the night with you." She touched her arm. "I dispelled the gossip, saying I witnessed him drop you off in his carriage just after midnight, and he left immediately after escorting you to your front door."

Clarice suddenly felt a queasy sensation in her stomach. Many widows took lovers and had affairs, and it was perfectly acceptable, so the gossip shouldn't bother her. To some members of the *beau monde*, it would ruin her reputation in their eyes, but to others, not at all. Not that she was terribly worried about her reputation. It was nobody's business but hers and Samuel's. Except it was something of a sport for the *ton* to spread rumors and gossip. She didn't want to cause undue discomfort for Samuel. Not with his upcoming races. No doubt he had enough worry to deal with.

"Thank you, Lady Hornsby. I appreciate you dispelling the rumor. As you know, His Grace did not spend the night, but he did visit for a spell."

Lady Hornsby smiled sadly. "My dear, after being married to that horrible Lord Chesterfield, you deserve to live your life as you please." Her eyes twinkled. "And good for you for snagging Stanton. He is a fine and worthy duke." Lady Hornsby paused, looking thoughtful. "I'm just shocked that after what your father did to him and the months of recovery it cost him that he would want to have anything to do with you while your father still lives."

The patrons' voices in the shop grew louder, and the walls seemed to close in around Clarice.

Her whole body trembled, making her heart beat irregularly.

Her lungs refused to work, causing her to gasp for air—air that no longer seemed to exist.

Her eyes no longer focused; all she could see were grey streaks that turned to black and then vanished.

"Clarice, can you hear me?" She heard Letitia's voice, clear and concise, yet sounding distant. And what an odd question to ask. Of course, she could hear her. But why was she lying on a hard floor, with a cold cloth over her eyes and many soft voices chatting around her? Taking her time to answer her friend, Clarice took several deep breaths, hoping to slow her pounding heart.

"I can hear you," she said as she reached up and took the

cloth off her face. She opened her eyes, blinking several times to clear the fuzziness. When she did, both Letitia and Lady Hornsby were kneeling beside her with worried expressions. "What happened?"

"You fainted, my dear," Mrs. Hornsby said as she took her hand. "How are you feeling?"

"Fainted? I've never fainted in my life." She looked around at all the wide-eyed ladies whispering to each other, and dread settled deep in her stomach. Clarice could imagine what they were whispering. How Stanton spent the night in her bed, and she was already enceinte. There could be no other reason a lady would faint dead away. Except there were many reasons, but these ladies would not entertain any of them. Oh, dear. What would Samuel think when he heard about this? "Help me up, please."

Before Letitia and Mrs. Hornsby could help her, they needed help getting off their knees. Two kind sisters, Lady Grace and Lady Faith, helped them to their feet. With Letitia's and Lady Grace's help, Clarice was pulled upright. She wobbled a bit, then steadied herself. Glancing around the shop at everyone present, Clarice's face heated.

Looking at Lady Grace and Lady Faith, she murmured, "Thank you for your kindness." Turning to Letitia and Mrs. Hornsby, she said, "I'd like to go home now."

With Letitia's arm through one of hers and Mrs. Hornsby's through the other, they made their way out the shop door. It was amusing, really, how the ladies parted to let them pass. She didn't have the pox, but you'd think she did.

"Lady Hornsby, will you wait here with Lady Clarice while I signal my driver?" Letitia asked.

"Yes, dear, go ahead. I won't leave her side."

"Thank you, Lady Hornsby," Clarice murmured. She was surprised how much energy it took to speak.

"I believe it's time we used first names, my dear Clarice. Please call me Ellie, short for Eleanor."

"Ellie, I like that."

"Here's the carriage."

A footman approached and helped Clarice into the carriage, where she sat beside Letitia. Then Ellie entered and sat across from them. The door closed, Letitia tapped the roof, and they slowly moved into the line of coaches along Bond Street. It would be a slow ride home.

"I hope you don't mind my intruding, Lady Letitia. I just wanted to see Clarice home safe and sound."

"Not at all," Letitia said. "What happened to you in the shop, Clarice?"

She leaned against the squabs and sighed. Honestly, she had no idea why she'd fainted, except that it was probably related to what Ellie said about her father doing something to Samuel. How could all these years have gone by without her ever hearing about any incident between the two—something Samuel would have had to recover from? She wouldn't ask Ellie to explain. This was a conversation she needed to have with Samuel.

"Maybe the lemon ice I had at Gunter's didn't agree with me. All I knew was that everything around me started closing in and turning black. Then I realized I was awake and lying on the floor. How humiliating."

"Nonsense, my dear," Ellie said. "Most ladies faint dead away at some point in their lives. Just last week, the young Mrs. Woodbine fainted during a stroll in Hyde Park."

"Yes," Letitia said, "isn't she increasing?"

Ellie blushed and said, "Yes. Perhaps that was a poor comparison."

Clarice closed her eyes and tried to relax, but failed. Increasing? She would pay close attention to her courses from now on if she was going to keep sleeping with Samuel.

The carriage finally came to a stop, and Ellie and Clarice stepped out with the help of a footman. "Thank you, Lady Letitia, for the ride." She looked at Clarice. "Get some rest, my dear, and you will feel better." Clarice watched as Ellie crossed the street and entered her townhouse.

"My thanks, Letitia, for your help," Clarice said into the carriage. "Shall we have tea tomorrow?"

"Yes, please," Letitia replied. "If you need me for anything, just send word."

"Thank you."

Clarice's hands gripped the railing as she climbed the stairs slowly, her legs still a bit unsteady. Williamson opened the door and hurried down several steps to assist her. "My lady. Are you ill? Should I send for the physician?"

"I'm fine. Just tired from shopping."

"Lord Portsmouth is here in the drawing room. He insisted on waiting. Shall I tell him you're indisposed?"

All she wanted to do was climb into bed and take a nap. Instead, she would have to deal with her father. After their conversation at the Westport Ball, she couldn't understand why he was calling on her. "No. I will see him. Please send in refreshments, but please tell the entire household that if the Earl of Portsmouth comes here again, he's to be sent away. I'll not have him in this house again."

Right before she entered the drawing room, she took a deep breath, exhaled, and straightened her back. This was the last person in the world she wanted to see, but she would be strong and forthright. Under no circumstances would she cave or show weakness to the man who had sired her but was no father to her. He'd proven that when he'd sold her to Chesterfield.

"Good afternoon, Father," she said as she swept into the room, acting as if she hadn't a care in the world and hadn't just fainted dead away in a shop less than an hour ago. He stood looking out the window. "Would you care to sit? I've requested refreshments."

"Don't mind if I do," he said as he turned around, walked to a chair facing the settee, and waited for her to sit.

As she settled into the settee and adjusted her skirts, her father sank into the chair and looked at her thoughtfully, with an unhappy expression on his face. "I heard gossip that Stanton spent the night in your bed after a small gathering at the Earl and Countess of Langford's."

It took all of Clarice's willpower not to blanch and give her father any satisfaction regarding his rude comment. Nor confirm the gossip. "You know the good members of the *ton* love to make up rumors and spread gossip. Some of the older ladies live for it as they have nothing better to do."

"*Is. It. True?*" he practically growled at her, his dark eyes narrow and full of hatred.

What had she ever done to deserve such contempt from him? She swallowed the hard lump forming in her throat, told her heart to slow its erratic beating, and ignored his question. "I also heard some disturbing news today. What did you do to Samuel?"

He glared daggers at her. "That is between him and me, and I will not discuss it. Regardless of whether he spent the night in your bed." He paused as a footman entered the room and placed a tray with tea and biscuits on the oval table in front of the settee. Once the footman retreated, he continued. "I forbid you to ever see that rakehell again. He has bad blood running through his veins—the blood of his lying, cheating father." He paused and inhaled. "Of course, you have the blood of your lying, unfaithful mother in you. Perhaps you two deserve each other." He jumped up and began to pace. "They had an affair." He swung in her direction, his features twisted in anger. "Did you know that? The blackguard—my best friend—and your mother had an affair that lasted *years*. How dare he touch what was mine?"

The only thing she could think to say was, "When?"

"When!" he bellowed. "Does it matter when? What matters is that the man put his cock and spilled his seed inside my wife. All I can say is thankfully it happened years after you were born, otherwise . . ."

His crude words shocked her, but the upset in her stomach eased somewhat at the realization that she'd already been born. She couldn't even imagine the alternative. Then something clicked into place. "Did you find out the day Samuel proposed to me?"

Her father combed his fingers through his hair and groaned. "Yes. My wife's cuckolding me with Stanton broke me. Two people I loved betrayed me. I suspected for some time your mother was having an affair, but not until that day was it confirmed, and with whom."

Now everything made more sense. And when the previous Stanton and her father had sat down to discuss the marriage contract, the truth must have come out, and he'd used his lack of funds as a convenient excuse and made the most of it. No wonder her father acted so cross and irrational that day and in the days, months, and years afterward. Although she never actually saw her father during her marriage to Chesterfield, she'd heard things about him. Not that she was forgiving him for how he'd treated her or her mother from that day onward, but it did shed light on her father's state of heart and mind.

Honestly, though, nobody becomes an unreasonable monster overnight unless those traits have been hiding inside all along.

"So I will say again, I *forbid* you from seeing Stanton." Once more, he glared at her with hatred and anger twisting his once handsome face.

"I'm sorry for what you endured, through no fault of your own. However, I am a widow and a grown woman. You have no say over what I do or over me. I will see Samuel if I choose to." She swallowed the rest of what she wanted to say. She hoped to marry him and have his children, but part of her still feared her father and what he might do to either her or Samuel.

"Where is Chesterfield's heir? It's been two years. I'm shocked that Prinny hasn't taken everything back and gifted the title and lands to one of his favorites. Or someone who has served him and the Crown well."

"He should arrive soon." Her father had voiced something she had often wondered about herself.

"Good. When he arrives, I will speak with him. Since he is

now your guardian, I will have him forbid you from seeing Stanton, and I will help him choose your next husband."

Her heart stopped at her father's words and his delusions. She stood up, suddenly emotionally drained, not that she would let her father see. Instead, she let her simmering anger come to the surface. "I would like you to leave now. And please refrain from ever coming here or approaching me ever again. You ceased to be my father when you sold me."

With her head held high, she left the drawing room and spoke to two footmen standing outside the doors. "Please escort this man from the premises."

Before she broke down, she lifted her skirts, hurried up two flights of stairs and down the corridor, and entered her chambers. She closed the door behind her and sank to the floor, pressing her back against the hard door, her knees drawn up as she wrapped her arms around them. She let her tears fall. Now she understood what had truly happened that day to cause a rift between their families at Stanton Hall. She had been wrong to think her mother had retreated to her rooms and refused to see anyone because Clarice was being sold to the highest bidder. A part of her wanted to believe her mother had loved her enough for that to be the reason. Deep down, Clarice knew now that the real reason was that her father had found out about her affair. Had her mother loved the duke? How long had it been going on before her father discovered it? Wait, hadn't her father said it lasted for years? Had Samuel's mother known? Did Samuel know?

A little niggling feeling inside her wondered if her father told the truth. Was there any way of discovering what had happened with both her mother and Samuel's father dead? Perhaps some of the servants knew. It was something to consider looking into.

The change in her father back then now made complete sense. He was already a broken man and in debt, at risk of losing any properties and possessions not entailed. Then he discovered his best friend for most of his life was having an affair with his wife—or at least believed it to be so. Clarice rested her cheek on her knees. Did the truth about Stanton and his traitorous behavior hurt her father more, or was it that his wife had cheated? Clarice would bet anything that Stanton's betrayal had hurt her father more. Her father always spoke of loving her mother. But did he really? She didn't think he was capable of loving anyone but himself.

Tears kept flowing as she remembered the day of her wedding when she last saw her mother. She had been a shell of her once vibrant, beautiful self. Was that what happened when someone loses a loved one, even by removal rather than death? When Clarice lost Samuel seven years ago, she was young and strong. Chesterfield was strong, but old, and it had only been a matter of time before he died—that knowledge had kept her going. But her mother seemed to have given up, seemed not to want to live anymore. Clarice unwrapped and rewrapped her arms around her legs, shivering. Her mother had died alone in her chambers without love. How tragically sad. "I'm sorry, Mama," she murmured. "I wish I could have consoled you somehow."

After a spell, with her skirts in disarray and twisted around her legs, she struggled to stand and rang for Mrs. Shelley.

"My lady," she gasped upon seeing her appearance. "Are you unwell? Can I get you something? I heard your father visited. Did he cause this?"

Fighting back the sudden urge to laugh, she replied, "Thank you for your concern, Mrs. Shelly, but I am well. I needed a good cry after my father's visit. But don't worry, I told Williamson never to let him step foot in this house again." She cleared her throat. "Meanwhile, can you tell the cook that I'm having a visitor for dinner? She need not make anything fancy. The Duke of Stanton, if I recall, will eat practically anything."

Mrs. Shelley's eyes widened, and her mouth opened when she said the Duke of Stanton, but she didn't comment.

"Before you leave, can you help me out of this dress? I want to rest a bit."

Once undressed down to her chemise, Clarice climbed beneath the coverlet and quickly fell asleep dreaming of Samuel.

CHAPTER TWELVE

AFTER SAMUEL AND Hunter dropped the ladies off on Bond Street, they visited their tailor, Mr. Brooks, then headed to White's for an afternoon drink. They greeted several acquaintances upon entering and made their way to the back, where a popular grouping of chairs was surprisingly vacant. Once seated, Samuel signaled a waiter, who poured each of them a brandy. After nearly half an hour of relaxing, Samuel was feeling good and sipping on his second drink.

"You seem relaxed," Hunter said. "You clearly did not see the Earl of Portsmouth enter just now."

The sip of brandy he had just taken threatened to come back up as a lump formed in his throat and his heart accelerated. "Bloody hell. I knew running into Clarice today and being invited to dinner was too good not to be spoiled by something." He ran a hand through his overly long, wavy hair. "I briefly saw him at the Westport Ball, but we didn't come face to face. For some reason, I don't think I'll be so lucky today. Shit," he swore, "here he comes with a murderous expression on his aged face."

"I hope he's unarmed," Hunter remarked, his brows drawn in concern.

"Good afternoon, gentlemen," Portsmouth said with a tight smile. "May I join you?"

He didn't bother waiting for an answer; he simply took a

vacant chair facing Samuel and waved to a servant, who poured him a brandy. He downed the liquid in one gulp and set the empty glass on the side table next to his chair. "If you would excuse us, Hunter, I would like a word with Stanton."

Hunter looked from him to Portsmouth and back again, clearly reluctant to leave.

"Do me a favor and see what all the fuss is about with the betting books?" said Samuel.

As if Samuel needed confirmation. No doubt they were betting on whether Portsmouth would kill him or not. Or, if they came to blows, who would win. Samuel would have the edge in bets over fisticuffs because of his age and strength. But if Portsmouth had a pistol, the outcome might change. Still, Samuel didn't think he would aim to kill, if it came to that. Killing a duke would require severe punishment, regardless of Portsmouth's title. The man wouldn't want to rot in Newgate until death or hang in disgrace. Hunter, not looking pleased, left the two of them to talk.

"What is it you wish to speak to me about?" he asked once Hunter was out of earshot.

Portsmouth leaned forward in his chair and stared at him with his hard, dark, hateful eyes. "I've just come from seeing my daughter. After hearing gossip about you spending the night with her, which has spread throughout London faster than a fire, I wanted to know the truth." He leaned back in the chair, pretending to be relaxed. Samuel wasn't fooled. The man's veins were prominent in his temples and neck. He stretched his legs out and crossed them at the ankles. Samuel was still not fooled. "Do you know why your father and I had a falling out?"

Samuel started a bit—internally at least—at the swift change of subject, but he had often wondered what had really happened that day. It had begun with longtime friends enjoying each other's company and ended with their fathers as enemies, leaving Clarice and him utterly devastated. And then Portsmouth had shot him, nearly killing him and forcing him to endure months of painful recovery. It gnawed at his insides to admit he didn't know why it all had happened. "My father refused to tell me."

Portsmouth burst out laughing. "I knew it. I knew he didn't tell you or your poor mother—whom I regret never bedding when I had the chance before she wed your father. Ah, I can see your mind at work. You did not know your mother was sweet on me before she decided on your father." He flung his arm out and leaned forward, lowering his voice. "Doesn't matter. What matters is your father fucked my wife."

Before Samuel could stop himself, he gasped.

"Yes. Your so-called honorable, perfect father, whom you looked up to, was involved in a long-term affair with my wife. I caught them together that day, sneaking a kiss in his study. They didn't see me, but that's why I dismissed you from the marriage negotiations. I confronted your father. He didn't deny it and admitted it had been going on for nearly five years."

Samuel's mind wandered back to that day, reliving everything he could recall, yet it still seemed unlikely. "I don't believe you."

"Oh, come now, Stanton. You're no fool. What else could end a friendship that had lasted more than thirty years except a woman?"

"Perhaps it was money. You admitted to being broke."

"Yes. But the money I owed wasn't to your father. So no, it was their affair. The two most important people in my life made a fool of me. However, I found satisfaction in refusing to allow the marriage between you and Clarice to take place. And locking my wife in her chambers ended their affair. They never saw each other again, and my poor departed wife died a broken woman with a shattered heart."

Listening to Clarice's father speak with such hatred and disregard for her mother saddened him. Yes, an affair was wrong, but how sad. Had he noticed a difference in his father after that day? Honestly, he'd been battling to recover from the bullet wound and then the lung infection, and he hadn't noticed. Except in the year leading up to his death, he had appeared quiet. Samuel had always attributed it to his lost friendship with Portsmouth. But perhaps it was that he missed Lady Portsmouth. His stomach twisted painfully. Had his mother known? She had also seemed sad, but she had lost her best friend, Clarice's mother. Unfortunately, he would never know. His entire family was gone. There was no one left to tell the story.

Of course, there was the possibility that Portsmouth was making all this up. Except looking back, he had occasionally found his father and Lady Portsmouth in a room together, but he'd thought nothing of it at the time. But now, if his memory served him correctly, there was an intimacy in those moments between them that bespoke of lovers in retrospect.

"I can see by your expression that you're coming to terms with what I've said." He signaled the waiter. "Would you like another?"

"No." He didn't trust anything else going into his stomach.

"Now we get down to the real matter at hand. You will leave London and go back to your racehorses. You will never speak to my daughter again, or I will reveal the secrets of your father. And I'm not talking about his affair with my wife. No one cares about infidelity. Everyone's doing it. I'm talking about other things from his past—mistakes he made when he first inherited his title. Of course, I have no proof of what I'm saying, just my word. Unless I can find the other parties involved. Even so, we know how the *ton* loves to gossip. Whether or not what I say is true, it will spread, and his legacy will be tarnished regardless. And you know how the sins of the father trickle down to the son." He paused and grinned. "Some might even think he set the fire at his estate to kill himself and take his family with him. Weren't you staying there at the time? From what I understand, it was pure luck you weren't in the house." He finished his drink and set the glass down on the table beside his chair with an audible click. "Even more believable would be that you burned the place down, killing everyone to inherit the title. Your life will be ruined."

Samuel jumped up, ran into the water closet, and lost the

contents of his stomach into a chamber pot. When he exited, Hunter was standing outside the door, looking worried. "What the hell did he say?"

"Not here. Let's take a ride," Samuel said as he walked, slightly unsteady, out of White's, avoiding eye contact with anyone. He didn't need to see to hear all the whispers and bets being made about him and Portsmouth.

As he reached his carriage, he said to his driver, "Drive through Mayfair. Don't drop Mr. Hunter off for half an hour." Once inside, he collapsed against the cushions, legs stretched out, and inhaled deeply, causing his lungs to rattle. Hunter sat opposite him, and Samuel tapped the roof, signaling the driver to go.

Now that they were moving, Samuel shared everything with Hunter, including the embarrassing and threatening parts.

"What a blackguard. You can't be serious about listening to his threats," Hunter said with wide eyes and a frown.

And wasn't that his dilemma? Did he ignore Portsmouth, hoping he wouldn't have to face his threats? Did members of the nobility respect Portsmouth enough to believe his slanderous words about his father? About him killing his family? Even thinking it sickened him. After last night and pouring his heart out to Clarice, could he survive without her? Was any of this fair to her? "I haven't made up my mind. I'm having dinner with Clarice tonight. Perhaps I'll discuss it with her, or not. I don't want to burden her with my problems."

"If I were you, I would speak to her. The threats are coming from her father."

"I know this!" he bellowed, then flinched. "Sorry."

"What if you retire to your estate with Clarice? You don't need London Society; you never did. You prefer your thoroughbreds. You could start that stud farm of yours. And if Portsmouth leaks the secrets he claims to have, you need not care. You will have the love of your life with you."

"In theory, it sounds promising. But there are several problems. Who will buy a thoroughbred from me if my reputation is tarnished? What about any children Clarice and I have? Who will marry them? I'm not concerned with something my father did years ago being gossiped about. I am worried that Portsmouth will go for my jugular. That he will spread rumors that I started the fire that killed my parents, my brother, and three of the servants. People believing that will ruin everything I've worked for and destroy any hope of a life with Clarice. If she'll even have me."

Hunter sighed. "Ask her tonight and you will know. Tell her everything. Tell her about what her father did to you. She is bound to find out at some point. Better to come from you."

"I want to talk to Greyson."

"He will tell you exactly what I did."

Samuel was relieved Hunter didn't take offense. "I know. I'm still trying to wrap my head around everything he said, try to figure out what is truth and what is lies. How did such a promising day turn into a nightmare?"

"Because Portsmouth is toxic."

The coach arrived at the bachelor lodgings where Hunter rented rooms, then continued on to Stanton House. Samuel walked the halls and paced his rooms as he tried to speed up the clock. Finally, when it was close to seven, with Wallace's help, he dressed for dinner and left to travel several blocks to Chesterfield Manor in his carriage.

CHAPTER THIRTEEN

CLARICE, DRESSED IN a lovely pink taffeta evening gown, waited in the parlor for Samuel's arrival. Feeling nervous, she stood by the window, looking out at the street. When Samuel's carriage pulled up, her uneasiness grew. It should have subsided once he arrived, but thanks to her no-good father, it didn't. She had no idea how she would bring up the affair with Samuel.

While she awaited his entrance, she poured sherry into two crystal-stemmed glasses and set them on the table in front of the settee. She needed the fortified wine to calm the storm churning inside her.

"The Duke of Stanton," a footman announced.

"Please have a seat. I took the liberty of pouring us a drink. I hope sherry is acceptable."

Samuel's eyes followed her every move, and once she sank down onto the dark green velvet settee, he joined her. He picked up one of the wine glasses and handed it to her. "I believe you could use this. I heard about your father's visit." She took the glass from his hand and took a sip, her eyes widening at his knowledge of her afternoon visitor. He picked up his glass and drained half of it. "That is good. Thank you."

They both turned toward each other at the same time. Clarice giggled nervously, and Samuel chuckled. "Perhaps we should get the discussion about my father's visit over with so we can relax and enjoy the evening," Clarice said as she took another sip, then set the glass down on the table.

"What did he say to you?" Samuel asked, setting his now-empty glass down and taking both her hands. "And keep in mind that he cornered me at White's and shared several shocking tales with me."

Clarice opened her mouth, then closed it. She cleared her throat and said, "I see. So he told you about the affair. Do you believe him?"

"I want to believe he's lying."

"Except," she prodded.

He sighed. "When your father told me, my first reaction was that it was a lie. My father and your mother would never participate in an affair and hurt the people they loved most. Then I remembered several times when I came upon the two of them alone. At the time I had no reason to suspect anything between them. Thinking back now and picturing the circumstances of them in a room alone with the door closed and the two of them on a settee together looking flushed, I think I believe your father. But I had no notion of it until today. I had no idea my father was having an affair with your mother."

"Perhaps you could talk to your servants who were in residence then. Maybe one of them saw something and could corroborate my father's accusations."

"It's not necessary." He swiped his hand through his hair. "The more I remember little details here and there, the more I'm convinced it's true."

"Now I understand why my father acted so irrationally and why my mother retreated to her rooms. I thought it was because of me."

"My father was not the same after that day. But I don't believe my mother ever knew. She worried about my father's health. I'm not certain she would have been so concerned if she had known. She did appear lost without your mother's friendship." Samuel released her hands, pulled a starched white handkerchief from his jacket pocket, and handed it to her. "It's so sad, really. I think my father and your mother must have loved each other deeply."

"Thank you." Clarice took the handkerchief and dabbed at her tears. "There's more. What happened between you and my father? There's something else, isn't there?"

Samuel stood and moved to look out the same window she had when she saw his carriage pull up. "I often wondered if you knew what happened after."

"I don't."

"I realize that, now. But still, I can't believe you never caught wind of it. Chesterfield really did keep you isolated."

"He did."

Turning around, Samuel leaned against the window, his sad eyes looking right into hers. "You remember the day I proposed and we made love by the pond? The day we thought our fathers were negotiating your marriage contract? The day your father took you away from me? I didn't take the news well when my father told me, and I went to your house that night to take you away to Gretna Green."

Hearing his words, more tears dribbled down her cheeks, but she didn't bother to wipe them away.

"Your father and several footmen were lying in wait for me at the servants' entrance. Your father had a gun and threatened that if I ever came back or tried to see you, he'd put a bullet between my eyes. And to prove he was serious, he shot me in the upper arm."

"What?" Clarice yelled as she stood and went to him, fighting the need to run her hands all over him to convince herself he was unharmed. Silly, since all that happened seven years ago. "How did I not notice the scar last night?"

"Maybe because you were distracted. Anyway, I also got a lung infection and almost died. It took months before I was strong enough to leave the house. By then, you had married Chesterfield."

She wrapped her arms around his waist, resting her head on his chest. The steady beat of his heart sounded in her ears. "I am so sorry for what my father did. Clearly, he lost his mind."

"He seemed sane to me. He took his vengeance against my father out on me." His arms went around her, and he kissed the top of her head. "He threatened me today with some seriously damaging stuff. Did he threaten you as well?"

Hearing his words chilled her to the bone. "He told me that if I continue seeing you, when Chesterfield's heir arrives, he would contact him. Between the two of them, they would marry me off to someone of my father's choosing." She scoffed. "I'm of age and have my own money, so they have no control over who I court or marry." She swallowed. "At least I believe so. I'm not willing to take unnecessary risks in that quarter, though. My father would find a way, even go so far as to kidnap me, I'm sure."

"What will you do?" The desolation in his voice pierced her heart.

"I don't know. Tell me what he warned you about?" Clarice stepped back from Samuel so she could see his handsome face. One marred now by sadness, frustration, and anger.

He went on to explain the uncomfortable conversation he had with her father. "Whether people believe any of that nonsense or accusations, my reputation will be damaged or even ruined."

"He is a monster," Clarice breathed out. "What will you do?"

Samuel inhaled and exhaled with a groan. "The racing circuit is starting. I'll be gone for a while. It'll give us time to think and plan how to move forward with our future . . . together." He paused. "That is, if you'll have me?"

She threw herself into her arms. "Yes. I'll have you."

"I should go. No doubt your father has someone watching your house." His strong arms wrapped around her, and she buried her head in his chest, holding on tight. Afraid she wouldn't feel the safety and comfort of his arms again for a long time, if ever.

"Look at me," he murmured.

Tilting her head up, her eyes met his somber, dark-gray ones, and she couldn't breathe. When she gasped for air, he moved in and kissed her deeply. Her fingers curled into his lapels, and she held on tight. Groaning, he tore his lips away and stepped back. "I would take you to Gretna Green now if I thought your father wouldn't interfere. But I think we both know he would, and it would cause a disaster for us. We need to plan and think. Once my horses have completed their races, we will be in a better position to face your father and secure our future. Meanwhile, if you need me for anything, I will be staying with Baron and Baroness Ramsbury in Newmarket. Don't hesitate to send word." He leaned forward and brushed his lips across hers. "I love you, before, now, and forever. Remember my words when you believe all hope is lost. Trust me, we will prevail and come out the victor."

He left without saying another word, giving her an additional kiss, or looking longingly at her. Clarice left the room and addressed the first footman she saw. "My guest has left. Please have a tray sent up to my rooms." Once inside her chambers, she sank onto the chaise longue, wrapped her arms around her aching stomach, and let the tears come again.

Never in her wildest imagination, when she found out something had transpired between her father and Samuel, had she expected to learn that her father shot him. Samuel had always been like a son to her father. How could someone go from being a decent, caring father and friend to appearing as a monster so easily? During private moments alone with her mother, had her father been mean and careless with her? Had his kind, caring self only been a façade while in public? Had Samuel's father ever witnessed her father's bad temper and behavior? Would he have stayed friends with him if he had?

Clarice wanted to understand how the affair had started. Were there any signs of their love and affection for each other out in the open? She didn't believe they had ever treated each other with anything more than friendship and respect. Had her father been so cold and cruel that her mother had sought comfort from the duke, and it had turned into physical desire and then love?

"Oh dear," she sighed. She could go in circles forever trying to find the answers. But the truth of the matter was that she would never know. The truth was buried with Samuel's father and her lovely mother, Countess Portsmouth.

"Enter," Clarice said as a knock sounded on her door.

"My lady," Mrs. Shelley said as she entered. "I've brought your dinner tray."

"Thank you. Please put it on the dressing table." Clarice wasn't sure anymore if she could stomach eating. "That will be all for tonight, Mrs. Shelley."

"Yes, my lady," she said as she curtsied and left, quietly shutting the door behind her.

Clarice curled up on the chaise longue, reached down by her feet for the lightweight throw, and covered herself with it, closing her tired, burning eyes. If only she could go back to when her mother was alive and talk to her, discover all her secrets, so she could understand her past. She wanted to help her mother overcome her heartbreak and melancholy. However, back then she'd been dealing with her own heartbreak and was petrified about her future with a husband chosen by her father.

The Marquess of Chesterfield was a complicated man. Due to his advanced age, he expected everyone except dukes and duchesses to obey his commands. From what she gathered from several of their rare conversations, he was a powerful force in Parliament and had fought against other Parliament members over any reform that could benefit the lower classes. He was truly an abomination.

Memories flooded her mind of her years being married to him. Even though she was the daughter of an earl, he believed she was far beneath him. When he found out she wasn't pure on their wedding night, he threw a fit. Later, when he discovered she was with child, Samuel's child, he forced her to drink vile potions in the hope that she would miscarry. Those poisonous potions didn't work. The son she carried wanted to be born, and born he was.

During those many months, while she was increasing, Chesterfield kept her locked inside her chambers. The only people she saw were the housekeeper and her maid. Both women were mean right down to their souls. Fortunately for her, the delivery had been an easy one. Chesterfield refused to risk a scandal, so no midwife or physician was called to the townhouse. The housekeeper and maid attended to her themselves. Secretly, she knew Chesterfield hoped the baby would die in childbirth. Possibly herself as well.

Tears rolled down her cheeks and soaked the small pillow she rested her head on. The moment the baby was born and the umbilical cord was cut, the housekeeper had whisked him away from the room. Clarice had gotten a quick glimpse at the baby to confirm it was a boy before the housekeeper swaddled him in a blanket and took him away. She swallowed the sobs trying to escape. It never mattered how much she had cried, prayed, and wished for her son; no one would tell her what happened to him. For all she knew, Chesterfield had killed him and he was buried in the garden.

Her lungs rattled as a loud, heart-wrenching groan tore from the depths of her soul. If he were alive, how old would he be? A little older than six. And if he lived, where was he?

Maybe he had been sent to a monastery. Perhaps he lived with a loving couple who adored him.

Right before she drifted into a sorrowful sleep, she wondered how she would tell Samuel. And would he blame her for the baby's fate?

CHAPTER FOURTEEN

S TUCK IN HIS carriage for two days during his travels to Newmarket in Suffolk, Samuel replayed the shocking information he had learned from Portsmouth. Had Samuel been so selfishly wrapped up in his own life that he never noticed any signs of his father's indiscretion? Although "indiscretion" wasn't quite the right word or description. A love affair was more apt. Because evidently, they cared for each other deeply. Well, if Portsmouth was to be believed.

And wasn't that the biggest dilemma facing him? Did he believe the earl? Portsmouth might be fabricating the affair to push his own agenda, using Clarice's sympathy to get back into her life. But she had no sympathy for her father. And Clarice was too clever to let him manipulate her. Had he not nearly ruined her life by marrying her off to Chesterfield in the first place?

Had he lied about Samuel's father's past? Was everything he said a lie to get what he wanted? And what Portsmouth wanted was to separate him from Clarice. Regardless of truths or lies, Samuel should have known her father would interfere with their future the moment he caught wind of them courting, even if the courtship had barely started. The evil earl hadn't wasted any time showing his true colors by using threats to tear them apart because of the affair between his wife and Samuel's father.

An affair that had nothing to do with them. This caused a

sharp stabbing pain in his temples as his thoughts circled endlessly—truths, lies, smoke, and mirrors. He groaned. How was he supposed to know what was real and what was the figment of a deranged earl's imagination? He couldn't, and wasn't. That, perhaps, was the crux of the problem.

Samuel's heart was splitting down the middle in a jagged line. The pain was even worse this time than the first time he lost Clarice. Luckily, he would be busy with Clover and Zeus and could lose himself in the day-to-day tasks of training, caring for them, and preparing for the first race of the season, the 2000 Guineas Stakes at Newmarket Racecourse held the first week in May. Seven days away.

Before the manure in the form of the Earl of Portsmouth stunk up their lives, Samuel had been planning to surprise Clarice by asking her to join him as a guest of the Baron and Baroness, acquaintances of his through their shared love of thoroughbreds. They owned a stud farm and bred some of the best racehorses around. Samuel rented a small stable from them to house Zeus and Clover until he could set up his own stud farm and stables.

His carriage stopped in front of Ramsbury Ridge Farms. When Samuel got out, he saw Bartholomew Hamilton, Baron Ramsbury hurrying down the front steps to greet him. "Stanton, welcome," Ramsbury said with a curious look. "We didn't expect you for several more days. Is Lady Chesterfield with you?"

Samuel winced and shook his head. "I hope you don't mind me arriving early. And sadly, Lady Chesterfield did not accompany me." He didn't offer a reason, nor would he.

"I see." Ramsbury indicated the stairs. "No matter whether you're early or not, your room is always ready." He motioned for Samuel to go ahead of him up the front stairs. "Anna will be thrilled to see you. She is taking tea in the drawing room. Come, let's join her."

The only things Samuel wanted to do were to freshen up and visit his horses. However, first he needed to pay his respects to his host and hostess and join them for tea. Just then, his stomach growled, letting him know he was famished. When he and Ramsbury joined Anna, she poured tea and settled several biscuits on a plate for each of them. While Samuel sipped his tea and ate the biscuits, his mind strayed.

The first race was coming up fast, and he needed to spend every minute of every day with his jockey, Tobias, his trainer, Albert, and of course, Clover and Zeus. Zeus would race in the 2000 Guineas, the Derby, and St. Leger Stakes. Clover would race in the 1000 Guineas Stakes and the Oaks. Samuel was still undecided about the Royal Ascot Heath.

As the owner of two thoroughbreds racing for the first time, there were nightly parties that he was expected to attend. Unfortunately, he wouldn't have Clarice on his arm as he hoped. His stomach clenched tightly.

Fortunately for him, Baron Ramsbury sponsored his membership to The Jockey Club, an essential institution for any thoroughbred owner and stud farm hopeful. The Tea Room was where everything related to the horseracing industry was discussed. Fortunes were made and lost there, as well as reputations. He would have to show his face there daily.

"Stanton," Anna's soft voice drew him out of his musings, "you look tired. Go to your room and get settled."

He stood and bowed. "Forgive me, I have much on my mind."

"Go," Ramsbury said as he ate another biscuit. "We will see you at dinner."

Samuel made his way up to the room he used whenever he was in town and found to his surprise his valet had already unpacked everything. He eyed the bed and wanted nothing more than to fall face first onto it and sleep. Instead, he put on his riding clothes and headed to see his horses.

"CLARICE," LETITIA SAID as she swept into her chambers, with Mrs. Shelley on her heels, to find her curled up on her chaise longue with a book of poetry. For the past two days, she hadn't left her rooms. It took too much effort to smile and act natural and normal while she sorted out the things her father had told her.

"Letitia," Clarice sat up, swiping her long hair from her face and tucking it behind her ears. Standing, she turned and faced her worried friend. "You may leave us, Mrs. Shelley."

"Yes, my lady."

As the door closed behind her maid, Letitia stepped forward, her concerned eyes scanning her from head to toe. "You look dreadful. I suppose I'll have to forgive you for canceling tea."

"I do not look dreadful, and I'm sorry for canceling," she huffed. Clarice went to her dressing table and glanced at herself in the mirror, made a face, and laughed nervously. "Oh dear, I do look dreadful."

"Sit down. Let me brush your hair."

With a heavy sigh, Clarice sat on the small chair, picked up her hairbrush, and handed it to Letitia. "You know, Mrs. Shelley can do this."

Her friend met her reflection in the mirror. "I know, but I would like to brush it in the hope that you will indulge me and explain what has happened that has you hiding in your chambers."

Her stomach twisted. She'd been so lost in her head about what transpired between her, her father, and Samuel that she hadn't considered how her actions might have affected Letitia when she canceled on Letitia without an explanation. "I'm sorry." She went on to explain everything that had happened, leaving nothing out, knowing she could trust Letitia with her secrets.

Letitia's hand paused as she brushed her hair, and sadness and shock appeared on her face. "I'm sorry." She continued the downward stroke of the brush. "I don't even know where to begin to be sorry. Your father is . . . there are no words." Her hand faltered. "He called on me yesterday, sent flowers, and invited me to the theater. Naturally, I declined. He was very gracious about my rejection."

"He's up to something."

"He is." Letitia agreed. "He's trying to ruin your life. Can you imagine me courting your father?"

Clarice shivered. "No."

"Me either." Pink stained her cheeks. "Greyson called on me right after your father left. Phew! That was a close call. After what you just told me about the earl, I'd rather he not find out about Greyson and his intentions."

Clarice locked eyes with Letitia in the mirror and tilted her head in silent questioning. "And what, exactly, are Greyson's intentions?"

Removing the brush from her hair, she swung it around. "Damned if I know."

"Letitia," Clarice exclaimed. "I've never heard you swear before. You really care for Greyson, don't you?"

Letitia's pink cheeks and dreamy eyes revealed it all. "Yes," she huffed. "Unfortunately, it's a bad time for us. His social calendar is booked solid all the way through spring and summer, with one house party after another as he escorts his sisters because his mother isn't up to participating or won't leave his sick father's bedside. Not that I blame her for staying with her husband, except that the responsibility of chaperoning his twin sisters falls on him. And I'm being selfish and silly wanting him all to myself."

"It is uncommon, but not unheard of, for a brother to escort and chaperone his sisters. Perhaps you are attending some of the same house parties?"

"Not really. I declined most invitations because I wasn't sure how I would feel rejoining Society."

Clarice turned around in the chair. "I know. Let us go to Newmarket for the races. Surely he would not miss an opportunity to watch Samuel's horses race." It would also give her an opportunity to watch Samuel from afar. She would have to be very careful when out in the open so as not to draw attention to herself. She would not want any news of her being seen with him to reach her father. She would prefer her father never know where she'd gone off to. It would be better for all involved if he believed she was holed up inside her townhouse.

A frown marred her face. How would she sneak away? Her butler had confirmed her and Samuel's suspicions: Her father had men watching her house and each exit at all hours of the day and night.

"My father has men watching me. We need a plan if I am to leave the house and travel to Newmarket undetected. Samuel is a guest at Baron and Baroness Ramsburys'. I don't dare send him a message until we arrive. I can't risk it getting into my father's hands."

"Hmmm," Letitia said as she returned the brush to its rightful place on top of the dressing table just as her stomach growled.

Clarice jumped up and exclaimed, "Where are my manners? Let's go to the drawing room for tea and refreshments." She didn't bother trying to smooth the wrinkles out of her sage-green linen day dress. It was well-creased from lounging on her chaise longue for most of the morning and into the early afternoon. On the way to the drawing room, Clarice spoke with a footman and sent him to the kitchens to ask the cook to send in a tea tray.

Sitting together on the settee, the tea tray newly arrived, Clarice poured the tea and handed the fine china cup and saucer to Letitia, then picked up her own.

"I've been thinking, do you think it's worth the risk traveling to Newmarket, knowing Stanton is there, too?" Letitia sipped her tea. "You definitely don't want your father making good on his threats, even if you stay away from the duke."

"Wonderful question." One she would have said no to the day Samuel left for Newmarket. But after wallowing in self-pity and heartbreak for two days, she was willing to risk anything to see him again. Even if she didn't have the chance to feel the warmth and safety of his arms around her. To witness the amusement in his dark eyes when he was carefree and the desire that could come on instantly—her body tingled. It would be hard to keep her distance from him, but she believed Samuel when he said he would find a way for them to be together in marriage.

"I refuse to let my father ruin the rest of my life. He took years away from me, years when I was married to Chesterfield, and I won't let him take any more. What we need is a plan. Will you come to Newmarket with me? And will you help me escape my father's men?" She knew it was a lot to ask her friend. But she was hopeful. She also knew he wouldn't be fooled for long and would eventually find out where she was. But if she had a week or so of freedom, she would be happy.

Letitia reached out and took her hand. "Of course. What are friends for? We'll need some help from your servants, though."

"They will help me."

"Good. Let's plan."

TWO MORNINGS LATER, during a windswept rainstorm, Clarice paced her drawing room, waiting for Letitia and one of her young housemaids, who was close in height and weight to her, to arrive.

Last night was the longest night of her life, filled with worry about today and what might happen. She wondered if they could fool her father's men with her escape. She panicked about where they would stay when they reached Newmarket. The Red Lion Inn would be their first hope, but with the racing season beginning, she imagined they were already booked solid. But she couldn't stay here and do nothing. She'd been biting her nails until they bled ever since Samuel left, and the end wasn't in sight. Not until she came face-to-face with him.

She and Letitia had a plan, but knowing how things could go wrong, they needed to be flexible.

"Marchioness Rutherford has arrived, my lady," a footman said as he entered the drawing room with Letitia on his heels.

"Thank goodness," Clarice said as she hurried forward to greet her. "I'm going crazy with worry and nerves."

"I know," Letitia replied, "So am I. And before I forget, tell you, thank you for indulging me with this excursion in the hope of running into Greyson."

"You're most welcome, even if I'm only going to feast my eyes on Stanton."

"We are both doing favors for the other," Letitia said. "It is ghastly outside, which should work in our favor. The man guarding your front door looks miserable, trying to stay dry, hunched in his greatcoat. He barely gave us a passing glance when we arrived. Today is a good day to slip away."

"I thought the same thing when I woke up and saw the rain. Come, sit down and have some tea. We must make it look like you spent a respectable amount of time visiting with me before we leave." Clarice picked up the teapot from the tray, which had arrived shortly before Letitia's arrival, and poured the hot tea into two cups, doctored them with cream and sugar, and handed one to her friend. They sat side by side on the settee.

"Is everything arranged?" Letitia asked as she sipped her tea.

"Yes. Williamson, Mrs. Shelley, Mrs. Jones, and one trusted housemaid know what we have planned. I had the housemaid, Penny, pack her old trunk with my belongings and travel to the Black Pigeon Coaching Station, take two rooms, and wait for us to arrive."

Letitia set her now-empty teacup down. "I was wondering how you planned to get your things out of the house. What an ingenious idea."

"I can't take credit for it. Mrs. Shelley suggested it, and it's perfect. We'll stay at the Black Pigeon tonight and be in New-market tomorrow. With any luck, we'll find rooms to rent." She set her cup down and picked up a sweet roll. "I don't ever recall my father being interested in horseracing, and let's hope it stays that way. I would hate to do all this and have him show up out of the blue. It's one thing if he arrives after he finds out I've left London, which, honestly, I expect, given all the newspaper reporters writing about the races and who's attending from the *beau monde*. But for him to be in Newmarket purely by coincidence would make my blood boil."

"We should probably go," Letitia said.

Hands wrapped around her stomach, Clarice groaned. "I shouldn't have drunk or eaten anything. Please excuse me while I go to my chambers. I'll be right back." She stood and left the drawing room, hurried up the two flights of stairs, and down the hall to her rooms. Once inside, she ducked behind the privacy screen and took care of her personal needs.

When she moved around the screen, she saw Mrs. Shelley entering the room with an unfamiliar cloak. "This belongs to Lady Rutherford's maid. Let's get you ready for your adventure."

Indeed, she was going on an adventure, but would it have a fairytale ending?

Mrs. Shelley extended the cloak, and Clarice slipped into it. The dampness from the rain immediately chilled her. "Perhaps I could wear one of my cloaks underneath."

"Oh my dear," Mrs. Shelly exclaimed. "What am I thinking? You'll catch your death wearing this damp thing."

"Will you give Lady Rutherford's maid one of my cloaks in exchange for hers?"

"Don't you worry, I will take good care of that girl. After all, she is doing us a big favor by helping you today."

"Thank you, Mrs. Shelley," Clarice said. "What would I ever do without you?"

"You would manage just fine. Now let's get you on your way."

Clarice met Letitia in the front entry, standing with Williamson, who bowed when she approached and said, "In front of Rutherford House, you will find an unmarked black coach with Kirkland in the driver's seat. He will see you safely to Newmarket."

"Thank you, Williamson."

Mrs. Shelley approached her from behind. "Now, off you go."

Pulling up her hood to hide her face and block the rain, Clarice followed Letitia to her carriage, pretending to be her maid. Once inside the coach, she sighed with relief and pushed off the hood. "I didn't notice my father's man. Did you?" she asked Letitia.

She shook her head as she removed her hood and wiped rain droplets from her face with her gloved hands. "I was too busy trying to hide from the downpour to notice. If he was there, which I'm sure he was, he wouldn't be able to recognize you. And nothing seemed out of the ordinary. So I would say we are safe."

Clarice reached out, taking Letitia's hands in hers. "I can't thank you enough for doing this. I know it was a lot to ask with you having to leave your son behind."

"I have to admit, when you first asked, I was a little nervous that it might not work, and I didn't want to face your father's anger. Especially after I turned down his theater invitation. Then I thought, why not? You and Stanton deserve to be together and happy."

"I can't believe my father called on you. Well, actually, I can. You already have a son, so he knows you can have children. You are wealthy, which is very important to him. I just can't imagine you and him . . ." She groaned. "No, I will not think about it."

Letitia was startled and snorted in a most unladylike way. "Please don't."

They both laughed, and Clarice knew it was out of relief rather than genuine humor.

The carriage came to a stop. "We're here," Letitia said. "My trunk should already be loaded onto our new conveyance."

A footman opened the door, lowered the steps, and escorted first Letitia, then Clarice out of one carriage and into the other with Kirkland in the driver's seat. Once they were inside the well-appointed carriage, sitting side by side, the other bench covered with two blankets and a basket of food, she removed her wet cloak and settled in for the long drive to the Black Pigeon Coaching Station. Letitia did the same.

Feeling drained all of a sudden, Clarice reached for both blankets, handed one to Letitia and wrapped the other around herself. She leaned back against the cushions and closed her eyes. "If you don't mind, I'm going to close my eyes. I didn't sleep a wink last night."

"Rest," Letitia said as she snuggled into the blanket Clarice gave her. "I'm going to as well. I couldn't sleep last night either, and we might as well sleep since we will be on the road for hours."

The sway of the carriage and the warmth from the blanket soon lulled Clarice to sleep.

CHAPTER FIFTEEN

WHY WAS HER bed rocking? Was she on a ship in the middle of the ocean? It took Clarice a moment to pull herself out of the deep sleep she had fallen into. She needed time to clear her mind and distinguish fact from fiction while her eyes fluttered open. She looked beside her at a still-resting Letitia, leaned forward, moved the curtain aside, and was surprised to see the Black Pigeon coming into focus. "Letitia," she said as she gently shook her arm. "We have arrived at the coaching station."

"Hmmm," Letitia moaned. "We are what?" She opened her eyes and rubbed them. "I can't believe we've arrived. I must have slept the entire time. So much for being good company for you."

"Don't feel bad. I slept the whole time, too," Clarice said. "We obviously needed our sleep."

Kirkland opened the door, flipped down the stairs, and reached inside to help Clarice out. "Thankfully, the rain stopped a while back, and we made good time. I'll have everything ready for departure after breakfast tomorrow. Mrs. Shelley wanted me to remind you to take your meals inside your room and keep the door locked. I'll be in the stables with the horses, watching who comes and goes. Send word if you need anything or see anything suspicious."

"Thank you, Kirkland," she said as she stood on the ground next to the carriage while he helped Letitia out.

Once they were both standing outside the carriage, Kirkland reached under the seat and took out two portmanteaus. "I'll escort you inside and see you to your room. Mrs. Shelley also thought it was best if you stayed in one room to keep each other safe."

Letitia huffed. "I believe I need to find myself a Mrs. Shelley. She certainly does think of everything."

Clarice laughed. "She does." They entered the Black Pigeon, and Clarice blinked to adjust her eyes to the dimness inside. The gloomy day and the sparse lighting from the candles didn't help illuminate the room. The taproom was full of guests enjoying a meal or an ale to quench their thirst. The smell of food made Clarice's stomach clench as she realized she hadn't eaten anything from the basket on the ride because she'd been asleep the entire time.

The three of them headed to the bar, and an older gentleman who looked like the proprietor said, "Welcome to the Black Pigeon. I'm Mr. Dunphy, the owner. How may I help you?"

"Good evening and thank you," Clarice said. "I'm looking for Miss Jones. I believe she's here and has a room reserved for us for the night."

"Ah, Miss Jones," he said with a friendly grin. "She's waiting for you. Come this way." He took a key from a peg, stepped around the bar, and climbed the narrow but sturdy stairs up one flight and down a long corridor, stopping at room number four. "This is your room. Miss Jones is next door in room six." He unlocked the door and pushed it open.

"Thank you."

"Mrs. Dunphy will bring your dinner at seven."

"Thank you, again," Clarice said as she entered the room, followed by Letitia and Kirkland.

He placed the bags on the floor and bowed. "If there's nothing else, I'll go see to the horses, my ladies."

"Could you knock on Miss Jones's door and tell her we've arrived and don't need her services until the morning?"

"Yes, my lady."

Kirkland left, closing the door behind him, and she immediately locked it and looked around, taking in the room. It was decorated in deep blue and beige. The large bed occupied much of the space. There was also a small table with two chairs, a bedside table, and a tall chest of drawers. A privacy screen was in one corner, and, of course, an unlit fireplace. Perfect for the two of them for one night.

"What side of the bed do you sleep on?" Letitia asked as she walked around the room, taking everything in.

"Right."

"Good. I sleep on the left." Letitia moved to the window and pushed the curtain aside. "You do realize we never gave the proprietor our names? I feel like a spy on assignment for the Crown."

Her comment caused the tension in her body to ease somewhat. "Now that you mention it, it does. Except we aren't doing anything remotely dangerous or honorable like spying for England."

Letitia turned and looked at her with complete seriousness. "Dangerous is a possibility, since we know your father shot Stanton when he tried to run off with you to Gretna Green."

Her tension flared up again. "You are right. My father is a dangerous man. One who is determined to get what he wants." She huffed and sank onto the side of the bed, causing it to dip and squeak from her weight. "I thought I was done with him when I married Chesterfield. Never, in my wildest imagination, did I think he'd come back into my life demanding I marry for a second time a man of his choosing. I will do everything in my power to see that he fails. My wants and needs will prevail if it's the last thing I accomplish in my life."

It wasn't long before Mrs. Dunphy arrived with their dinner, a tasty rabbit stew with carrots and potatoes, rolls, tea, and blueberry pie for dessert. After they finished eating, Clarice was full and sleepy again. "I'm going to bed. I can't keep my eyes open."

"Go ahead. I feel the same way. Besides, the sooner we go to sleep, the sooner tomorrow comes, and we arrive in Newmarket to find your Stanton."

"My Stanton. I love the sound of that." Knowing she would be on the road today, Clarice dressed in a traveling dress that buttoned in the front, making it easy to remove, along with her corset and petticoat. Wearing only her chemise, she climbed beneath the covers. She knew Mrs. Shelley had packed a night rail for her to wear, but she was too tired to put it on. Her soft, linen chemise would do just fine. Curling up on her side, she said, "Good night, Letitia. Thank you for coming on this journey with me, and let us hope we find your Greyson in Newmarket as well."

Without opening her eyes, she could tell Letitia was undressing. The bed dipped on the opposite side as she climbed in. "Good night, and you are most welcome," Letitia murmured. "I believe I shall sleep well dreaming about Greyson."

Moments earlier, Clarice could barely keep her eyes open; now she was wide awake, listening to Letitia's soft, even breaths as she slept, along with noises and voices from the taproom below. Eventually, the sounds lulled her. Her eyelids fluttered closed, and her heart beat slow and steady as she drifted into dreamland. She dreamed of Samuel and his thoroughbred horses and how happy and content he was with them.

Birds chirping outside the window and the early morning light had Clarice sitting up and stretching in bed. Her eyes drifted to Letitia, already dressed, and Mrs. Dunphy entering with their morning meal. She set it on the table and quickly left without a word. "I can't believe I slept so late."

"You've been going through a lot recently. You clearly needed it. I woke up at sunrise and couldn't fall back asleep."

Clarice got out of bed, went behind the screen, and took care of her morning necessities. Then she searched her bag for a clean chemise. She quickly swapped the chemise for yesterday's and put on her traveling clothes from the day before. There would be plenty of time to wash up and change into clean clothes once they arrived at the Red Lion Inn and her trunks were unloaded.

Joining Letitia at the table, she was pleasantly surprised to find fried eggs, sausages, and toast with jam, along with strong black tea for breakfast. One glance at the clock sitting on the fireplace mantel, and she was shocked to see it was already half past seven. "We should try to be on the road soon so we can reach Newmarket before afternoon tea."

"That sounds perfect."

"It seems like the rain has let up, and if Kirkland had noticed anything suspicious, he would have sent word. So everything must be fine with sneaking away."

"Yes. Let's hope the good luck keeps going."

An hour later, they were back inside the carriage with the housemaid Penny and her trunk filled with Clarice's belongings. While visiting Newmarket, Penny would serve as a maid to both Letitia and Clarice.

The ride was slow going at first because of the ruts in the road, which were overflowing with rainwater leftover from yesterday. But as they got farther and farther away from the Black Pigeon Coaching Station, the road conditions improved.

When they were nearing Newmarket and about an hour from the Red Lion Inn, the road became congested with other travelers heading to the horseracing town. The first race, according to what Clarice remembered from Samuel, was less than a sennight out, and all the festivities leading up to the first race would be in full swing, social parties that most racing enthusiasts didn't miss.

"I'm nervous," Clarice admitted. "We planned this on a whim, with no guaranteed place to stay and no formal invitations to any social events. The only person we know in Newmarket is Samuel. What were we thinking?"

Letitia giggled, then covered her mouth. When she took her hand away, she said, "I thought I was the only one nervous. And I agree with you, what possessed us to do this?"

"Gentlemen."

"Oh, dear, you are correct," Letitia agreed. "You want to see Stanton, and I hope to see Greyson. But really, what if the inn is full? What will we do then?"

"We will think of something. I can always send word to Staton letting him know we're in town and have nowhere to stay. Perhaps he has friends we can stay with." She tried not to notice how worried Penny looked upon hearing they didn't have a definite plan for their visit to Newmarket. "If the worst happens, we turn around and go home. It's better than having stayed home, wondering what could have been." And it was. Better to have tried and failed than never to have tried at all.

Letitia sat up and looked out the carriage window. "You're right. We're coming into town."

Clarice leaned forward, peering out the window on her side of the carriage, her eyes widening with surprise. "So we are. Look at all the people and carriages. I wonder where the Red Lion Inn is located. Do you suppose it's in the heart of town?"

Neither of them knew the answer to that question, but they found out shortly when they turned off High Street onto Rous Road. It seemed the inn was made up of several buildings that stretched across Rous Road. Many people were coming and going, giving the impression that it was quite a popular place to stay. Kirkland opened the door and helped them exit. Two waiting stable boys and two footmen were ready to assist with the carriage and their trunks.

"My ladies," Penny said with a curtsy, "I will go and inquire about available rooms."

"Thank you, Penny. Two nearby rooms would be ideal," Clarice replied.

"Yes, my lady."

While they waited for Penny to return, the footman removed the trunks from the top of the coach and carried them into the hotel. "Oh, dear. I hope they have rooms for us," Letitia said as she watched them go inside.

"As do I," Clarice said as Kirkland removed their small portmanteaus from inside the coach and Penny's bag, placing them on the ground beside their feet. Then he spoke to the two stable boys, who led the horses and carriage away to what Clarice assumed was a very large stable.

Penny came back with a smile, and the tension inside Clarice immediately slackened.

"My ladies, they had a last-minute cancellation. I was able to secure two rooms side by side with a connecting door."

"Thank God," Letitia said with a deep exhale. "I didn't look forward to being homeless or traveling the two days back to London."

"Me either," Clarice agreed. "Shall we?"

The footmen picked up their bags and followed both Clarice and Letitia into the largest of the hotel buildings, with Penny walking at the back. They were greeted by a uniformed hotel worker who directed them to their rooms on the first floor. It was down one corridor to another when they reached their rooms, twelve and fourteen. As soon as the door was unlocked to each room, the footmen arrived with their bags and trunks. Penny indicated where each trunk belonged.

Clarice entered the room and was pleasantly surprised by how well-furnished and bright it was. She immediately approached a wooden door with a slide lock and knocked. "Letitia, are you there?"

"Yes."

Clarice heard her unlock her side of the door, and she did the same. Then she swung into Letitia's room and found her smiling at her. "This will be convenient."

"Indeed."

They had afternoon tea in their rooms and then visited the inn's spacious yet cozy dining room for dinner. After eating more than her fill, Clarice and Letitia went to bed early so they could wake up refreshed and ready to explore the town. Clarice had written a letter to Samuel and given it to the hotel concierge, who promised to deliver it first thing the next morning. What would he think when he read it? Would he be upset that she'd risked her father's anger by coming to Newmarket? She hoped Samuel would be as excited to see her as she was to lay eyes on him.

Clarice lay in bed, listening to Penny make soft snoring noises as she slept on a pallet by the door. Her mind refused to rest as she imagined all sorts of scenarios involving her and Samuel sneaking private moments together. She wanted that more than anything, but she had to be careful of her father finding out. It wasn't just her future she needed to worry about; Samuel's future was at risk if her father caught wind of them together.

What frightened her most was that her father had shot Samuel once. Would he be so bold as to ignore the law and hurt a high-ranking member of the aristocracy again? Deep down, where her woman's intuition resided, she believed her father would.

Rolling onto her back, she sighed deeply and stared up at the ceiling. If only she could see into the future, see that Samuel would be safe from harm, and she wouldn't somehow be forced to marry another old man who was as mean as a troll. Curling onto her side, she closed her eyes and eventually gave in to the pull of sleep.

CHAPTER SIXTEEN

SAMUEL HAD SPENT the past few days preparing Zeus for the 2000 Guineas Stakes. But he couldn't neglect Clover since the Sunday after that race, the 1000 Guineas Stakes would be held.

In the small stable he rented from Ramsbury, he was checking on Zeus after his morning exercises and practice runs on Ramsbury's half-mile track he had recently built. Zeus had run the half-mile track twice for a good time. He knew Zeus was not a favorite for the 2000 Guineas, but Samuel believed he would surprise those running the betting books at The Jockey Club. Maybe he wouldn't win, but Samuel thought he'd place second or third.

Every day since he'd arrived in Newmarket, Samuel's mind had wandered to Clarice and how she was doing. Had her father tried to see her again? It was a constant ache in his chest whenever he thought of her and her father's devious plans for her.

Tonight, Baron and Baroness Ramsbury were hosting a pre-race ball. He would have begged off, except he needed to be involved with the racing enthusiasts and other members of The Jockey Club as much as possible. But it didn't mean he had to enjoy himself when every lady he saw would remind him of Clarice.

He had left the main house at Ramsbury Ridge Farms before sunrise and returned now with tired, aching legs and a growling, hungry stomach. The butler immediately handed him a note. Before he looked at it, he said, "Jerome, could you please have a tray sent to my room? Anything the cook has left from breakfast will be fine."

Jerome bowed, "Yes, Your Grace."

The moment Samuel entered his room, he sighed with relief upon seeing Wallace straightening up.

"Your Grace, I didn't hear you come in." He examined him critically and shook his head, clearly displeased with the dirty and disheveled appearance he presented. Wallace never minced words and often said he didn't think a duke should be getting his hands dirty with racehorses. It was one thing to own thoroughbreds, but another to care for them and get one's hands dirty during training. His man was quite the gentleman's valet and Samuel knew he shocked him from time to time. "I'll ready your bath," he said as he exited the room, presumably to order a tub and hot water.

What was the point of owning thoroughbreds, though, if you didn't spend time working with them? He knew many owners did nothing but oversee their care and cover the costs of feeding, housing, training, and managing them. But Samuel had always felt a connection to horses and didn't care what others thought about him being involved in their day-to-day needs.

It was then that he realized he was still holding a letter, now quite crumpled. He raised it up, noticing the handwriting, and began to tremble. He quickly unfolded the piece of paper, scanned the contents, and couldn't decide whether to laugh or cry. Clarice was in Newmarket and staying at the Red Lion Inn. How on earth had she managed to get a room there on such short notice? Everyone involved in the racing business had booked rooms months or even a year in advance. He himself hadn't been able to secure a room. He had hoped not to impose on Ramsbury, but was thankful he always had a guest room available. Not to mention it was quite convenient having his horses on site with him.

Dear Stanton,

Lady Rutherford and I have arrived at the Red Lion Inn. It was probably unwise to come to Newmarket, but I couldn't stay in London with my father's men watching my every move without losing my mind. Please forgive me if this causes any trouble with your upcoming races. You don't need to make time for me. Seeing you from afar is enough to soothe my worried mind.

Yours truly,
Clarice

He folded the letter and placed it on the table beside the bed, then smiled like a fool. She was here. Bloody hell, she had risked much to come to Newmarket. His heart raced, and his vision blurred with the overwhelming urge to see her. He wanted to jump on his horse, Smokey, and ride like the wind to the Red Lion Inn. Pull her into his arms and kiss her. Drag her into her hotel room and make love to her.

Slow down and avoid doing anything rash that might draw attention.

It was a good thing Wallace returned at that very moment with a footman as they wheeled in a bathtub, followed by several other footmen carrying buckets of hot water—much-needed hot water to loosen his tired and sore muscles. And when he was done bathing and presentable, he would seek out the baroness and ask her to invite Clarice and Lady Rutherford to tonight's ball. He knew it wasn't the wisest thing to do, having Clarice and him at the same function, but he needed to lay eyes on her. Even if he couldn't speak with her or dance with her, seeing her safe and well would be enough.

Or so he told himself. He knew himself well enough to suspect he wouldn't be satisfied with just that when the time came.

While he bathed, a tray of food arrived, and Samuel hurried to scrub off the dirt and smell of the stables. With Wallace's help, he dressed and got a shave. Being in desperate need of a trim, Wallace snipped an inch off his hair and brushed it into some semblance of control. "Thank you, Wallace. Where did you put my paper? I need to send a letter."

"Everything you need is in the middle drawer of the writing desk."

"That will be all for now."

"Yes, Your Grace." Wallace bowed and exited the room. Samuel knew that once he went downstairs, Wallace would be back to take the tub out and tidy up once again. Wallace was extremely fastidious.

Finally, he lifted the cup of coffee from the tray and drank it, lukewarm and all. He grabbed a piece of toast and went to the desk against the far wall, sat in the chair, and just as Wallace said, paper and writing implements were in the middle drawer. He wrote a short note to Clarice, telling her he had received her message and to expect an invitation to tonight's ball. He folded it, sealed it with wax, and used his Stanton ring, with the letter "S", to seal it.

Exiting his chambers, he made his way down the stairs, stopping to speak with Jerome. "Could you please have this letter delivered? But wait for another from the baroness."

"Yes, Your Grace. And please forgive me but I mistakenly gave this letter for you to Lord Ramsbury." He handed Samuel the letter, the seal still intact.

"Thank you," Samuel said as he tucked it inside his coat pocket. "I would like a word with the baroness. Where can I find her?"

"She is in the ballroom, Your Grace."

He continued on his way to the large ballroom, where the baroness, a petite, beautiful woman with two young children, was overseeing the placement of flower arrangements with the housekeeper. "Excuse me, Baroness, may I have a word?"

She turned around and placed her hand on her chest. "Stanton, my goodness, you surprised me. Yes. How may I help you?"

Samuel approached, "I just received a note from Lady Chesterfield, and she's in town staying at the Red Lion Inn. I was hoping you could invite both her and Lady Rutherford to tonight's ball."

She raised her eyebrows and smiled. "So I will get to meet Lady Chesterfield after all. Of course, I will have an invitation sent right away. Won't Greyson be pleased to see Lady Rutherford?"

"How do you mean?"

"Greyson's sisters and I attended the same luncheon yesterday, and they mentioned a mysterious Lady Rutherford who had caught their brother's eye."

Samuel couldn't help but laugh. "Poor Greyson. He can't have any secrets without his sisters sharing them."

Anna, the baroness, giggled. "Ladies do like to share juicy tidbits. My brothers were very happy when Ramsbury and I got married, and I was no longer living with them. They could finally keep secrets from me."

"How are your brothers? I haven't seen them in ages."

"They should be arriving today. I told them they must attend the ball tonight. They are hellions and testing my papa's patience, especially Thomas. As the heir, Papa wants him to settle down, but Thomas, at twenty-eight, believes he's too young. Stephen, at twenty-five, falls in love every other day."

Samuel couldn't help it; his face fell in sadness. Anna stepped forward and touched his arm. "I'm sorry, Stanton. I shouldn't have gone on and on. You must miss your brother and father terribly."

"I do, and you did nothing wrong. I asked about those two devils. I look forward to spending time with them."

"I'm sure they look forward to seeing you, but I admit they will be disappointed to lose another friend to love."

Samuel shook his head. "I predict that when they find the right lady, they will fall hard and fast."

She laughed. "I agree, and I can't wait."

"Thank you, Anna, for everything."

"You are most welcome, Your Grace."

Samuel exited the ballroom through the double glass doors onto the terrace, then down the steps onto the garden path of crushed stone, and strolled aimlessly until he found a bench to sit on. He leaned against the wooden back, his legs stretched out and crossed at the ankles, and smiled, thinking about Clarice. She was here. In Newmarket. To see him. He glanced around the gardens, hoping there weren't any gardeners watching him smile like a love-sick fool. Which, of course, he was. In love with Clarice, that is. A love that never died when she married Chesterfield. A love that not even getting shot by her father could eradicate.

He removed the letter from his coat pocket and noticed something he hadn't when Jerome handed it to him. It had the royal seal. He eagerly broke the seal, unfolded the paper and read the several lines of fine handwriting. Those few lines and words had his heart lighter and the muscles in his chest easing now that he had Prinny on his side.

After about an hour of relaxing on the bench, Samuel left the gardens and went to his room to think more about Clarice and how he couldn't wait until that night to see her again.

CLARICE AND LETITIA sat in the outdoor dining area at a small round table with two chairs, having luncheon, when an inn worker bowed and handed her two notes. "These are for you, Lady Chesterfield."

"Thank you," Clarice said as her heart pounded, knowing one or both came from Samuel. She opened the one addressed to her in his smooth, looping handwriting.

My Dearest Clarice,

I don't know whether to be worried or thrilled that you have arrived in Newmarket. I look forward to seeing you, but I'm also concerned. We must be very careful not to draw attention to ourselves.

You and Lady Rutherford can expect an invitation to a ball tonight, hosted by the Baron and Baroness Ramsbury, where I currently reside. I can't wait to see you.

Always and Forever Yours,
Samuel

"Well," Letita said as she stared at her excitedly, "is it from Stanton?"

"Yes. He says we should expect an invitation to a ball being held this evening." Clarice broke the seal on the heavy cardstock of the second note and unfolded what appeared to be the invitation. "It's an invitation from Baron and Baroness Ramsbury. The 'Off to the Races' ball starts at seven. I have the feeling it's a dress for the races theme."

"It sounds like it," Letitia replied. "I'm sure Penny can take care of everything."

"I'll inform Kirkland that we need the carriage tonight."

"Oh my," Letitia whispered, "Greyson and his sisters are coming this way. I had hoped . . . but didn't really think . . ."

"Take a deep breath and relax. You don't want to seem nervous or overly excited."

"I know, but it's difficult. The man is so handsome and makes my heart flutter in song."

"Song?" Clarice asked. "He makes your heart flutter in song?"

"You know what I mean. Oh my, he's stopping."

"Lady Rutherford, Lady Chesterfield, what a lovely surprise to find you here," Greyson said as he nodded. "You remember my sisters, Lady Aurora and Lady Anastasia."

"Yes," Clarice and Letitia said in unison.

"Lady Chesterfield, does His Grace know you're in town?" Greyson asked, looking concerned.

"Yes. We exchanged correspondence today."

"Glad to hear it. Will we see you lovely ladies tonight at the Ramsbury Ball?"

"Yes," Letitia replied, blushing.

"Well, then," he dipped his head and grinned, "until this evening."

Both Clarice and Letitia watched them walk away and sit at a table nearby.

Letitia leaned forward in her seat and murmured, "I can't believe Greyson's really here. I had dreamed of running into him, but now I'm so nervous. It felt as though I had a cloth tucked inside my mouth; it was so dry and hard to speak. I don't remember ever feeling that way before." She patted her hair nervously. "Indeed, when I met Rutherford, I was young and naïve and overwhelmed with his kindness and generosity. I loved him deeply, and he made my stomach constrict and my heart pound. But Greyson, I cannot explain what he does to me, except to say it's so much more than what I felt with my husband, and I hardly even know him. It makes no sense at all."

When Clarice spoke, she did so as softly as Letitia, so neither Greyson nor anyone else could overhear their conversation. You never knew when a busybody might be straining their ears, hoping to overhear gossip. "I've never heard of anyone falling in love at first sight, but I believe that is what you did."

"I never thought it happened in real life, only in novels," Letitia exhaled. "Perhaps it is something else altogether. Perhaps I'm just attracted to him, and it is simply desire and nothing more that I feel for him. It makes sense since it has been . . . well, you know what I mean. Rutherford and I enjoyed the marriage bed." She touched her cheeks. "I'm blushing. How embarrassing. However, if I can't talk to you about it, who can I? Anyway, as I said, perhaps it is a physical attraction and nothing more."

Perhaps what Letitia felt was only a physical attraction to Greyson, since they hardly knew each other. But Clarice believed it could, and would, if given the chance, develop into something much more. And she wished for both their sakes that it would.

They left their table and entered the hotel through glass doors leading into a spacious salon where guests could enjoy tea or simply relax and chat with friends. On a long, narrow wooden table, the hotel had tea and biscuits ready at all hours, and Clarice and Letitia helped themselves to tea and sat on a settee.

"This inn is very accommodating," Clarice said as she sipped her tea. "Not that I've ever stayed in an inn before, except for last night. And somehow, the Black Pigeon is nothing compared to here. Have you stayed in a large hotel or inn?"

Letitia giggled. "As far as large inns go, this is a first for me as well. Rutherford and I once spent time in Bath, but we stayed with friends and at a small coaching inns along the way."

"I can see the appeal of a big inn if they are all as nice as this one."

For a short while, they watched guests of the Red Lion Inn come and go. Clarice recognized several people, but mostly they were strangers. It was sad, really, that she never got to know many of the members of the *ton* close to her age. Even sadder that she hadn't become close to Letitia or Lady Hornsby until she was widowed. And she'd only recently met Emmeline, Lilly, and their husbands. She was thankful to have them among her friends. Adding Mr. Hunter, Greyson, and his sisters, Clarice felt truly fortunate.

During her marriage to Chesterfield, she never thought she would ever be free of him or have friends of her own. He never let her leave the house or entertain guests, which kept her from making friends. So many years lost, trapped in her own home—a home that belonged to the new Marquess of Chesterfield. Part of her was afraid of his arrival. Another part couldn't wait, so she could move into a townhouse of her own and be free. What troubled her was that he should have arrived by now, and she was worried for his safety.

She forced those maudlin thoughts of the next Marquess of Chesterfield away. "Shall we retire to our rooms and rest before tonight's ball?"

"That's a splendid idea," Letitia agreed. "Sitting here has made me sleepy. I'm having trouble keeping my eyes open."

"Oh dear," Clarice chided. "We can't have you causing a

scandal by falling asleep in your teacup and then spilling it down the front of your pretty yellow day dress."

Both of them stood and giggled. "No, we can't," Letitia replied.

Once inside her room, Penny helped her undress down to her chemise, then went into Letitia's room to do the same. Climbing beneath the soft coverlet, Clarice turned onto her side and exhaled. It wasn't until she mentioned to Letitia about resting that she realized how tired she was—both mentally and physically. All the worry about sneaking off without her father's knowledge and the two days of travel had caught up with her in the salon. The door between her room and Letitia's opened and closed, and she knew Penny had returned. Before long, she felt herself drifting off and enjoyed the sensation of falling asleep.

It seemed only a moment had passed since she fell asleep, but she knew by the sun's rays entering the room at a different angle that hours had gone by. She sat up and called out, "Penny?"

Penny ducked her head through the doorway from Letitia's room. "Yes, my lady?"

"How long was I asleep?"

"About two hours. I'm helping Lady Rutherford dress and do her hair for the ball. If it's acceptable to you, I will finish and then be right in. While you napped, I took the liberty of pressing your green gown with the cream trim."

"The green gown is a perfect choice. Thank you, and take your time finishing up with Lady Rutherford." It would give her time to clear her foggy mind and fully awaken. She climbed out of the bed and found fresh water in a pitcher, a bar of floral-scented soap, and clean linens. While she waited for Penny, she slipped off her chemise and washed her entire body, except for her back, which she couldn't reach. Feeling refreshed and wide awake, she went to the wardrobe, pulled out a clean chemise, and put it on. She then sat down at the small dressing table, which doubled as a desk, and stared at her reflection in the fine-quality glass mirror.

Brown hair and brown eyes framed by nicely arched brows. Nothing particularly unusual. Her skin was porcelain white with high cheekbones, a round chin, and a small, straight nose with a slight upturn and tiny earlobes. Still, nothing extraordinary. No one called her a "diamond of the first water." It didn't bother her. Samuel called her beautiful, and that was all that mattered.

As she examined her reflection in the mirror, trying to see herself as he did, she finally recognized her beauty. Her eyes weren't just brown, but had gold flecks in them. Her hair wasn't plain brown either, as red and blonde highlights shimmered depending on the light. How had she never noticed she was anything but plain?

Maybe because she listened to Chesterfield call her plain. His plain wife, with hair and eyes the color of mud. Well, he was gone now, and it was time for her to start regaining her confidence and believing in her beauty, both inside and out. Samuel saw it. Others might as well. But Samuel was the only one who truly mattered. Oh, dear. Her hand flew to her stomach as it seemed to tumble down to her toes.

"My lady," Penny said as she hurried into the room. "I'm so sorry to keep you waiting. Shall we do your hair first?"

"Yes, that would be nice." As Penny worked her thick, wavy hair into an elaborate arrangement, Clarice was stunned by her talent. "If you're so good with hair, why are you a housemaid?"

Penny blushed. "My husband, Mr. Peter Welch, works as an underbutler in your household. We wanted to stay together, and you didn't need an abigail. I told Mrs. Jones I didn't mind being a housemaid."

"I apologize for taking you away from your husband for this trip. I had no idea you were married. Perhaps when we return, you can assist Mrs. Shelley. Besides being my maid, she takes on too much."

"Thank you, my lady."

Penny dressed Clarice in the gorgeous green silk gown with a high waistline and scooped neckline, complemented with a cream shawl. The only jewelry she'd thought to pack was a simple gold locket given to her by her mother and engraved with two entwined hearts. She had always planned to put likenesses of Samuel and herself inside and pass it down to their daughter someday. Perhaps her plan would come to fruition. They were still young enough to marry and have children.

"You are ready, my lady. You look beautiful," Penny said. "Kirkland should be waiting outside the inn with the carriage to take you and Lady Rutherford to the Ramsbury Ball."

"Thank you." As Clarice was about to leave the room, Letitia entered, looking beautiful in a medium-blue gown with a matching shawl. "That dress looks stunning on you. Your blue eyes are practically glowing."

"Thank you. Green looks gorgeous on you." Letitia paused. "We are missing something to complete our outfits. We are supposed to be dressing as though we are attending the races, are we not? Penny, do you have the things I asked you to purchase?"

"Yes, Lady Rutherford, coming right up." Penny disappeared into Letita's room and returned with two hat boxes, which she placed on the bed. She then left and came back with two parasols—one blue, one green.

"Thank you, Penny. Your style is impeccable," Letita said as she opened the hat boxes, pulled out the green and cream wide-brimmed bonnet trimmed with flowers and feathers, and held it out to Clarice.

"This is gorgeous. Thank you, Letitia." Clarice put on the hat and tied the wide green ribbon to the side by her chin. "It fits perfectly." The hat was cut out in the back to allow for a lady's chignon.

Letitia's hat was similar in design, but it was blue and white. Each parasol matched the hats in color and trim.

They exited the room and headed to the front of the inn and outside, where Kirkland stood at the carriage door, ready to assist them inside.

Chapter Seventeen

Sitting across from each other to avoid wrinkling their gowns, Clarice tapped on the roof, signaling Kirkland that they were ready to go. The carriage rolled onward, and Clarice realized she had forgotten to ask Kirkland how long it would take to reach Ramsbury Ridge Farms. Thirty minutes later, they entered a queue of carriages on a tree-lined stone drive leading to a circular entrance and stopped in front of a grand, three-story stone house with wings extending out from each side.

Once the carriage rolled to a stop, a liveried footman opened the door and assisted first Clarice, then Letitia out of the carriage. The footman then escorted them inside the large estate, down a long corridor, and into a stunningly beautiful ballroom, decorated in cream and gold. Gold chandeliers hung from the ceiling, with hundreds of wax candles already lit. Beautiful, fragrant floral arrangements of all sizes and shapes were spread around the room.

As Clarice and Letitia made their way to greet their hosts, she looked around, her heart pounding with hope at seeing Samuel. Disappointment stabbed her when she didn't spot him anywhere. Yet she knew she was being silly. He was attending, and they would come face-to-face soon enough.

Her time had come to meet the hosts. She curtsied and said, "Baron and Baroness, it is a pleasure to make your acquaintance.

And I thank you for your invitation on such short notice."

"Lady Chesterfield," the baron said as he bowed, "welcome to our home."

"Yes, Marchioness," the baroness said with a curtsy. "Welcome. When our dear friend, the Duke of Stanton, asked if we would invite you and Lady Rutherford, we were honored to do so. I hope you enjoy yourself."

"I will, thank you."

Clarice and Letitia stood to the side of the dance floor and watched the musicians tune up their instruments. "Have you seen Greyson?" Letitia asked as her eyes moved through the guests milling about. It appeared everyone was getting their bearings.

"Not yet," Clarice answered. "But he's here, since I see Lady Anastasia talking with Mr. Hunter by one of the many double glass doors leading outside."

Letitia remarked, "Perhaps Greyson is with Stanton somewhere, since I don't see him, either." Letitia reached out and briefly touched Clarice's hand. "He's staying here, so he is here. It won't be long before you see him. I know how eager you are to lay eyes on him, but also how frightened you are at the same time because of your father's threats."

"I am. Even if I only get a few words with him to assure me he is fine, I will be appeased. And with the upcoming races, I know I will see him again." She didn't know what the owner did during the actual race. Did they have a designated area for owners only?

"Stanton and Greyson are coming this way," Letitia said as her cheeks pinkened. "I'm blushing, aren't I?"

"Yes, but so am I. My cheeks heated up so fast, I need to fan myself." She looked down at the closed parasol she was holding and her reticule, wondering how she had forgotten her fan back at the inn. By this time, Stanton and Greyson arrived.

"Lady Chesterfield, Lady Rutherford," Greyson said as he bowed. "It is a pleasure to see you both again today."

Clarice and Letitia both curtsied. "Wonderful to see you,

Greyson," Clarice said, trying to keep her eyes on the viscount and not the duke. She didn't succeed.

"Greyson," Letitia said. "I hope you enjoyed your luncheon at the inn?"

His green eyes sparkled as he took Letitia in from head to toe. The heat coming off them was spilling over to Clarice, making her truly wish she had a fan.

"I did, thank you."

By now, the musicians were playing a lively country reel, and Greyson and Letitia left hand in hand to join the dancing.

"Shall we dance?" Samuel asked. "Or shall we talk?"

Fan. She needed her fan. She probably made a face, because Samuel asked, "Are you unwell?"

"No," she sighed. "Just a little warm. Do you think it's wise to be together?"

"I don't believe it matters whether we're seen together or not. Your father has his plan in place, and nothing we do, or don't do, will stop him." He extended his arm. "Shall we? All the doors open onto terraces with pathways weaving through the intricate and lovely gardens. The air is much cooler out there than inside this stuffy ballroom."

She placed her hand on his forearm. "I would love to get some fresh air. Thank you."

As soon as they stepped outside, Clarice inhaled the cool, fresh air and felt better instantly. "Please accept my apologies if my letter and arrival in Newmarket caused you any discomfort."

He patted her hand that rested on his arm. "Your apologies are not necessary. I was thrilled when your letter arrived. Then dread settled in, but I've shoved it aside. When your father makes good on his threat about my father's secrets, so be it. I've got nothing to hide, and that's all that matters. The sooner we face your father's wrath, the quicker we can move on. Life's too short, and I refuse to let him ruin ours. My poor departed brother never had a chance to fall in love, to live his life as he saw fit. He never had a chance to marry and have children. We could be dead tomorrow, and I'm done waiting for your father to make his next move."

This was not what he'd believed when last they'd seen one another, and she was shocked. "What's changed?"

He sighed and ran his hands through his newly trimmed hair. "I'm not completely sure. Being away from London and spending time with my horses helps ease my worries and concerns. It helps me see things more clearly. Not that I wasn't seeing things clearly in London; it's just that I have a better perspective now. I'm a duke, and it's high time I acted like one. Of course, the biggest change came today with the post. I sent a letter to Prinny asking for his advice on the matter without revealing too much. He advised me to get a special license immediately and marry you, with his full blessing."

"You sent a letter to the Prince Regent?" Her mouth formed an "O," and she snapped it shut. "I had no idea you two were close."

"To answer your question, yes, I believe I just said so. We've spent time together, but I wouldn't say close. I advised him on his horseflesh."

"I see."

"I was thinking, though, I hate having to hurry or sneak our marriage. I want us to be free to celebrate with friends and get married at St. George's, Hanover Square."

"Do you mind if we sit down on that bench up ahead?" Clarice asked, suddenly feeling overwhelmed and warm again. Perhaps she needed something to drink? It had been warm today, and she was parched.

"Of course, my love." Once they sat, he turned toward her and took her reticle and parasol, placing them on the bench beside him. "Forgive me, I can tell I shocked you. I'm contradicting everything I said when we last spoke. But I hope Prinny has sent word to your father by now, telling him not to interfere. Even your father wouldn't be foolish enough to go against the Prince Regent."

Worry had her stomach clenching up tight. She wanted to believe Samuel, but something nagged her to be careful. Perhaps she was being silly. "I love the idea of a church wedding with our friends instead of sneaking off to Gretna Green or procuring a special license and marrying quickly and privately."

He leaned forward and brushed his lips across hers. "Even though I'm confident your father will not take action, I don't think we should flaunt our courtship out in the open. We can be seen together, but act casually, as acquaintances would, not lovers." His voice dipped low for the last two words, and the grin on his face and the sparkle in his dark eyes had her insides tingling with awareness.

"I understand what you're saying, but your expression is completely the opposite."

He brushed her lips with his again. "I'm sorry, I know," he said, kissing her more deeply. "All I can think about is taking you to bed and making sweet love to you all night long. Making love to you so often that neither of us has the strength to get out of bed the following day." He kissed her again, this time wrapping his arms around her, cupping her cheeks, and kissing her with heat, passion, and love.

A moan formed in her throat, but didn't escape as she joined her tongue with his. As the music inside her head beat faster and faster, so did the intensity of their kiss until she pulled back, gasping for air and smiling. "That was . . ." She swallowed the rest of her words as he caressed his hand down her arm. Most of her skin was covered by her short sleeves and long gloves, yet she felt his touch to the center of her being.

He nuzzled the skin beneath her ear. "You have the softest skin. I spent years hoping that one day I would get to touch you again, hold you in my arms, and cherish you. And now that I have, I won't let anyone take you away from me."

A sigh escaped her lips, and her head tilted to the side, giving him better access as he continued to place featherlight kisses down her neck. Each time his soft, warm lips touched her sensitive skin, heat flared low between her legs. She wanted more than anything to take his hand and slide it beneath her skirts. "I'm boiling up inside, Samuel."

He chuckled against her skin, and his hot breath had the same effect on her as his kisses. "If I put my hand between your thighs, will you be wet for me?"

Her head dropped back against the wooden bench, her lips parting in a deep sigh. "Yes."

He reached down, his hand creeping up the inside of her dress. She wantonly parted her thighs, waiting and waiting until he snatched his hand away and straightened her skirts.

"Someone is coming down the walkway."

Clarice sat up straight, her heart pounding erratically as she moved aside to put some distance between herself and Samuel. How had she not heard the crunch of gravel? She hoped it was only Letitia and Greyson.

CHAPTER EIGHTEEN

"HERE YOU ARE," Greyson said as he and Letitia came into view.

Samuel stood and waved to the bench, saying, "Have a seat, Lady Rutherford."

"Thank you, I will."

"I have some bad news to share," Greyson said, a frown marring his handsome face.

"The Jockey Club's betting book doesn't show good odds for Zeus, I'm afraid."

"I'm not surprised, nor does it bother me. I believe Zeus will place. Keep that in mind if you place a bet."

"Place a bet?" Greyson cocked a brow. "Of course I'm placing bets. And to hell—excuse me, ladies—with the odds. I'm betting on my friend."

Samuel was touched by Greyson's announcement about betting on his friend. As excited as Samuel was about entering his first racing season ever, he was equally nervous. As a new thoroughbred owner, his reputation going forward would be built on this season. Everything about starting a stud farm rested on how his horses performed during the upcoming races. He prayed all the hard work he'd done for the past three years wasn't for nothing.

"Where have you gone?" Clarice asked as three sets of eyes

focused on him.

"Sorry. My mind wandered." He held out his hand to her. "Shall we return to the ballroom? I should really join a conversation or two. Will you accompany me?" This was the part of the racing world he disliked. The socializing, making deals and business decisions. He loved horses, not business. What he needed was an equal business partner who could do those things and be trusted. Trust was a huge factor. He'd wanted Greyson and Hunter to join him. But he understood that until Greyson found husbands for his sisters, most of his free time was taken up. As for Hunter, he had been top of his class at Eton and Cambridge. His mind was made for business. He needed to speak to them, but timing was everything. And it wasn't the right time yet.

"I would like to. It will give me a peek into your world. I know most wives have nothing to do with their husbands' business dealings, but I want to understand your world. I love horses. And though I've never attended a race, from everything I've been reading lately, it sounds fun, invigorating, and totally different from London Society."

By now, they had reentered the ballroom, and Samuel made his way over to Ramsbury and Anna, who were talking with the chairman of The Jockey Club and several other owners with horses in the 2000 Guineas Stakes. "Shall we join Baron and Baroness Ramsbury?"

"Yes, it seems like a most interesting conversation. One of the gentlemen's faces is as red as a radish."

"Indeed. He is Viscount Thurston. His family has owned and still owns some of the fastest thoroughbreds ever to race. He and his brothers have built an empire. His two younger brothers will go head-to-head with anyone on the topic of racing. However, Thurston dislikes confrontation." Samuel looked around the ballroom. "I wonder where his brothers are tonight? It's the wrong night to abandon the man. People feel the need to attack him because of his family's history with the racing empire. Some feel the need to battle with those at the top, hoping to dethrone them. Many have tried, but the Thurston family has prevailed."

"Do you like the man?" Clarice asked as she watched Thurston interact with a gentleman she didn't recognize.

"It's not about liking or disliking. It's about respect or lack of it. Personally, I don't know him, but his reputation speaks for itself. I respect him for taking over the family empire and keeping it solvent, and their horses are some of the top contenders for winning this season. I've heard he is a fair man when it comes to negotiating his stud fees." Samuel chuckled deep and low. "I find talking about breeding horses a strange topic to discuss with you."

Clarice squeezed his arm. "It is a rather delicate subject. I imagine many of the older ladies attending would swoon talking about stud fees."

"You would be correct." Samuel, with Clarice still on his arm, moved their way to stand beside Ramsbury and Anna, joining them in the lively discussion about the chances of Thurston's newest horse, Moonlight, winning the 2000 Guineas Stakes.

"Nice of you to join us, Your Grace," said the chairman of The Jockey Club. "Who do you favor to win the first race?"

Samuel laughed, not nervously but confidently. "Zeus, of course."

Most of those gathered around laughed. Clarice could tell they weren't laughing at Samuel or his answer. They were laughing good-naturedly because what other answer could Samuel give?

"Of course you would answer Zeus," Ramsbury chimed in. "Any owner with a horse in the race would name their horse to win. Just as I would answer Thunder. Amongst this crowd, we all have winners."

Viscount Thurston spoke up. "Your Grace, I have heard good things about both Zeus and Clover. They come from strong bloodlines. I hope your jockey can handle them."

"Thank you," Samuel replied. "As for my jockey, Tobias, he has the magic touch. I'm hoping to shock the racing world this season."

"Good luck." Thurston nodded his head. "If you will excuse me, ladies and gentlemen, I will take my leave."

Clarice noticed he walked toward two men who had just entered the ballroom and looked similar. Each of the conversationists walked away, leaving Clarice and Samuel standing alone in a ballroom filled with people she didn't know. It made her realize how sheltered from society she had been, first by her parents and then by Chesterfield.

An older gentleman, well into his seventies, approached with a slightly younger lady on his arm and a cane in his other hand, which he leaned on with each step. They came right up to them. "Your Grace, Lady Chesterfield," the man said with a slight and stiff bow, while his wife slowly lowered into a curtsy, making Clarice realize how awkward it was to greet people when one was elderly.

"Lord and Lady Kendall," said Samuel. "What a pleasant surprise to see you. You are acquainted with Lady Chesterfield."

"Actually," Lady Kendall said, "we have never met, even though she was married to my brother."

Her brother? All the sounds in the room disappeared, and so did all the faces except for Samuel and Lord and Lady Kendall. They were vivid and overwhelming; she thought she might swoon. She closed her eyes briefly, inhaled and exhaled, and pulled herself together. She would not embarrass herself or Samuel by fainting dead away onto the floor. Why had Chesterfield never mentioned having a sister? He had been an enigma. A holder of many secrets.

"Lady Kendall," Clarice managed to find her voice. "I apologize. Your brother never told me about you."

Lady Kendall smiled, and her face softened, making her appear younger. "I should be the one apologizing for my brother. You poor thing, being married to that man. Oh, forgive me for speaking plainly, but Chesterfield distanced himself from his family when he inherited the title from my father. Besides occasionally seeing him in public, my family never spoke to him again. It was what he requested, and we abided by it. Sadly, I'm the only one left from my family. But when I heard word that you were attending this event, I had to approach you."

"I'm so glad you did," Clarice said as she smiled and began to get her bearings back.

"Pardon the interruption," Samuel said, and added, "I didn't realize you were related to Chesterfield."

"Yes, well," Lady Kendall said, "I hardly ever went around admitting to being related to a curmudgeon who didn't acknowledge his own family."

Lord Kendall grinned. "I hope it wasn't too forward of us to approach, but my dear wife just had to speak with you, Lady Chesterfield. Perhaps you would indulge us with a visit. We are staying at the Red Lion Inn."

Samuel met Clarice's eyes, smiled and nodded his head, giving her confidence. "Yes. I would like that very much. Lady Rutherford and I are staying there as well. We could meet for tea tomorrow afternoon."

"Wonderful," Lady Kendall said. "Will you be joining us, Your Grace?"

"I would enjoy that very much," Samuel said. "It's been a while, Lord Kendall, since you entertained me with your tales of when you had a filly racing."

He laughed. "Yes, my Queenie. She was a beauty. Won the 1000 Guineas as a three-year-old filly. Best race of her life and mine." He nodded his head. "Until tomorrow."

Her feet wouldn't move as she watched the couple walk away, looking happier than they had when they'd first approached. She had a sister-in-law she'd never known about. Life was full of surprises.

"Come," Samuel said, "let's get refreshments. I suddenly find myself in need of a glass of wine."

"I could use one, too," Clarice said as she took his arm. "I can't believe Chesterfield had a sister. That man had more secrets than the king's confidant. How do you know them?"

Samuel plucked two glasses of wine from a servant's tray. "I met the Earl of Kendall two years ago at Tattersall's. He has a love of horses as strong as mine. I learned a lot from our conversations there. His filly, Quennie, won the 1000 Guineas Stakes that year. Several weeks later, right before another race, she became sick and died. Kendall believes she was poisoned but couldn't prove it. His heart was broken, and he's yet to enter another horse in the races. Perhaps in time, he will."

"The poor man." She wasn't ignorant of the fact that thoroughbred racing was a business where people made fortunes and lost them just as easily. There were dishonest individuals willing to do anything to get ahead or become rich by eliminating the competition. Poisoning racehorses was nothing new. "Do you worry about that happening to you?"

Samuel's step faltered, and she had her answer. "Yes. I have a stablehand sleeping outside Zeus and Clover's side-by-side stalls. And during the day, they are never alone. I'm not risking someone poisoning them just because they are fast racehorses. I don't want to have to deal with what Kendall dealt with."

"I'm sorry you have this to contend with."

"Don't be. I knew when I got into this business that there were bad people. But there are a lot more good people than bad. I try to remember that when I worry about the lives of my horses." He paused and asked, "Would you care to sit outside in the gardens?"

She smiled and blushed. "Didn't we already spend time there?"

He chuckled. "Yes, but this time I truly want to sip my wine, resting on a bench with you by my side. I promise to behave."

She giggled. "Promise me you won't."

"Clarice," he groaned close to her ear, "Are you offering yourself up to me?" The low, deep timbre of his voice made her whole body come alive.

"Samuel," she said breathlessly. "I would do just about anything to be held in your arms."

"Then I will make it my duty to ensure we have enough time

alone, away from prying eyes and rumormongering ladies, to hold you close to my heart." Again with that tone. "And I will make it my goal in life to please you. Pleasure you. Worship your body. Love you every single day until my last breath."

She fanned her face with her free hand. "You have such a way with words. And when your voice gets all deep and throaty?" She shivered. "It does things to me."

"It does?" He wiggled his brows up and down, and his nearly-black eyes smoldered. She swore she saw red flames in his irises.

Before she could stop herself, she burst into laughter, then covered her mouth as several people frowned at her. "Perhaps we should head to the gardens before I embarrass myself further with any more laughing outbursts."

He extended his arm, "Perhaps we should."

Linking her arm with his, they made their way back out to the gardens. Clarice felt bad about leaving Letitia again, but she was in good hands, standing across the ballroom with Greyson and his sisters. She was quite positive that Letitia was where she wanted to be. Watching her in conversation with them and the way she looked at Greyson with adoration made her wonder if that was how she looked at Samuel. Most likely, since she had loved Samuel most of her life.

They relaxed on the same bench as before. Sitting close enough to touch everywhere, they both tilted their heads up to the sky. "The stars are in rare form tonight," Samuel said. "The North Star appears twice as bright as usual."

"Hmmm, it is. And the Plough is vibrant as well."

"Do you watch the stars?"

Clarice sighed and rested her head on Samuel's shoulder. "During my marriage, I spent many nights sitting outside in the gardens, listening to the nighttime bugs and watching the stars. It helped pass the time."

Samuel draped an arm across her shoulders, and she sighed, feeling the safety and comfort it provided. "I hate thinking of you being so alone and at his mercy for all those years," he said.

"Don't. Being alone was preferable to being with him. He was not a kind man."

"Did he ever hurt you?" The raw emotion in Samuel's voice brought tears to her eyes.

"He never laid a hand on me, though he used other ways to hurt me. His tongue was sharp, but I tried not to let his words unsettle me. I would focus on other things when he began to rant. Like remembering you and our times together. The mother rabbit and her bunnies nesting in the garden. The beautiful flowers and the bumblebees pollinating them." She paused and exhaled. "Have you ever truly watched a bumblebee up close? They have all the yellow pollen they've collected attached to the sides of their bodies, but if you truly look close, little yellow pieces of pollen stick to their faces; it's so adorable. I could watch them forever. That is what I would think about when he treated me abominably."

His arm tightened around her shoulder, and he pulled her closer. "Still. You shouldn't have had to suffer from his cruel words and unkind treatment."

Clarice swallowed the lump in her throat and ignored the tears in her eyes. They were having the perfect conversation to tell Samuel about their son. Unfortunately, they weren't somewhere more private. Yes, the gardens were relatively secluded, but not far away, hundreds of people were inside the ballroom. But she had an idea. "Do you think there is any way you could sneak into my room at the inn?"

"I would rather not give people something to gossip about." He stood and held out his hand. "Come with me. I know the perfect place where we can find privacy. We won't be long, though. I wouldn't want people to wonder where we are and draw their own conclusions. Even if those conclusions happen to be true."

She took his hand, and he led her through the gardens to another door, and they entered a small private drawing room. He approached the interior door and turned the lock, looking at her with such desire that the room's temperature rose, causing her heart to pound with excitement and her body to hum with desire. It was definitely not the time to talk about their son.

"This room is for family only. No one will disturb us here, and we can go back through the gardens and enter the ballroom. No one will suspect a thing."

Clarice wasn't convinced that no one would suspect anything. But they would believe they had been in the gardens the entire time. She wouldn't think of that now as she stood all jittery, waiting for Samuel's touch. As he walked toward her, his eyes drinking her in, her heart exploded with need. And when he pulled her into his arms and kissed her, she believed she would fly into the sky and explode into hundreds of sparkling lights.

The kiss was intense, with tongues dancing and tangling to an imaginary tune. Lips pressed hard against lips, and it took restraint to resist climbing up Samuel's chest, wrapping her legs around his waist, and never letting go. Trying to become one with him.

"Clarice," he gasped as he tore his lips away and rested his forehead against hers. "You drive me crazy with desire. With need. I can't believe it's as alive and intense today as it was all those years ago. I need you like the air I breathe to survive. I will wither and die without you. I love you so much it hurts when we're apart."

His words and the emotions he used to convey them caused her heart to reach out to him. "I understand. It's how I feel also. I love you and will not survive this life without you by my side."

His mouth took hers again, only this time he kissed her reverently. It was slow and succulent. He worshiped her mouth with his, worshiped her lips, her tongue. And then he moved his warm lips down her neck to the swell of her chest exposed by her low-cut dress. His hand tugged the front of her dress and chemise down, exposing her breasts to the cool air. He lavished the taut peak on one breast, then the other, and a moan escaped from deep within her chest. Heat burned at her core, and she needed to be touched there.

"Samuel," she breathed, her head having fallen back. "I need you."

"Yes, my love. I need you, too." He walked her back until she bumped the wall. "I'm ready to explode. I hope you don't mind that all my finesse has deserted me." He unbuttoned his trousers with one hand, while the other pulled up one of her legs and hooked it around his waist. When his hard member nudged against her womanhood, she held her breath, anticipating what would come. With one deep thrust of his hips, he was seated deep inside her. She moved her hands to his waist, and with each of his thrusts in and out, she pulled and pushed along with him.

The sounds of their strained breathing, moans escaping, and the slapping of their bodies echoed through the small drawing room. It was music to her ears. As her body began to quickly ascend toward euphoria, she buried her face in his chest to silence her screams. With one final thrust into her, Samuel's body tensed and then shook with his release.

They stayed where they were, intertwined and holding each other. Neither moved, and Clarice was afraid that if she let him go, she might lose him forever. Did he feel the same? She pushed the thought out of her mind. Nothing and no one would ever come between them again.

"Was I too rough?" Samuel's concerned voice murmured into her ear as, sadly, he pulled out of her body, taking a piece of her as they disconnected in body and soul.

"No," she replied breathlessly as her wobbly legs touched the floor and she was shocked they supported her weight. "You were perfect in every way."

HE STEPPED BACK and handed her his handkerchief. "I'm sorry, I made a mess of you." She took his handkerchief and wiped between her legs, smoothed out her skirts with one hand, pulled her bodice up, and held out the handkerchief, looking at him questioningly with a lovely blush staining her cheeks. He took the cloth and tucked it into the inside pocket of his jacket. "I'll take care of this later. We should get back."

Her blush deepened as she looked down at his waist, making him realize the placket on his trousers was still unbuttoned. "Oh, dear." After he fastened himself, he reached out and adjusted her bonnet, which he couldn't believe was still on her head. "There. You look perfect."

She giggled. "I highly doubt that. Not after what we did."

He kissed her cheek. "I promise, you look perfect. Now take my hand." Which she did, and they walked hand in hand back out to the gardens and down the path to the door leading into the ballroom. They came across several couples, but nobody took notice. They were too busy trying to blend in and avoid notice themselves. Samuel hated to be like them. He couldn't wait until they were wed. Enough of stealing off to be alone and share themselves with each other.

Not that he wouldn't keep doing that and enjoying it. Every minute he spent with Clarice was a gift in his eyes. He wouldn't take a second for granted. He knew too well what it felt like to have the life you always expected and the future you planned ripped away from you, through no fault of your own.

Life was too precious to squander even a moment. Nothing made that clearer than a fire that claimed your parents and your only brother. That was why tomorrow he would send a footman to the Archbishop of Canterbury, requesting a special license on his behalf. There was a perfectly good church and vicar who would be happy to marry a duke to his duchess in Newmarket. Suddenly, the idea of waiting and having a church wedding back in London frightened him. He couldn't see it in their future. The thought of waiting didn't sit right with him, no matter what he'd said to Clarice. The longer they waited, the more things could go wrong.

CHAPTER NINETEEN

WHEN THEY ENTERED the ballroom, Greyson and Lady Rutherford spotted them. "Back to the gardens, I see," Greyson said teasingly.

"It is a beautiful night and the stars are vibrant," Samuel replied, which had Greyson chuckling.

"Clarice," Letitia said, looking nervous. "I hate to ask this of you, but do you mind if we leave?"

Clarice touched Letitia's hand. "Are you unwell?"

"Not at all. Greyson asked me to attend a luncheon tomorrow with him and his sisters, and I want to be well rested."

"Then we shall go," Clarice said. She dipped a curtsy. "Good night, Your Grace, Lord Greyson."

Letitia did and said the same. Samuel and Greyson bowed, and the ladies exited the ballroom.

Samuel was puzzled by the abrupt departure of the ladies. "That was odd."

"What was?" Greyson asked as his eyes still looked to where Clarice and Lady Rutherford exited the room.

"The ladies' exit."

"Not really. Lady Rutherford expressed her desire to leave quite some time ago. But you and Lady Chesterfield had disappeared."

Samuel fought to prevent himself from blushing. Since when

did he start blushing? "I apologize for monopolizing Lady Chesterfield's time."

He patted Samuel on the back. "No apology necessary. I understand."

As he and Greyson moved along the outskirts of the ballroom to find their way to the game room, Samuel's heart felt heavy inside his chest. He could use some time alone. "You go on without me. I'm going to check on my horses."

"Very well," Greyson said. "Good night, then."

"Good night." Before he left the house, he took a lantern from the entryway table, and then he walked to the small stable where he boarded not only Zeus and Clover, but Smokey as well. When he approached the stable, all was quiet and as it should be, which quieted down his anxious heart. The stable lad was asleep, curled up with a blanket on a pile of clean hay right outside the stall doors. All three horses appeared at the small square openings at their doors, having recognized his footsteps and his approach. Or perhaps it was his smell? Either way, they were greeting him.

Samuel hung the lantern on a hook for safety and reached into a bucket hanging on a wall with apples and carrots inside for just such a visit. He took three carrots out of the bucket and made his way to open the top of each stall so they could poke their heads out. He went to Smokey first, rubbed his head, and fed him his carrot.

"How are you, boy?" After a few more rubs, he moved on to Clover and repeated the same. Then he went to Zeus, opened the lower stall door, and went inside. He rubbed him down and checked him over from head to toe. "You've got a big race coming up. Are you ready?" he said softly to his prized thorough-bred. His answer was Zeus blowing out from his nostrils and nodding his head up and down. Samuel laughed. He exited the stall, closed the horses' doors, and locked them. With one last glance at the sleeping stable lad, he retrieved the lantern, stepped outside, letting the bright stars guide his way back to the main house, where he went directly to his bedchamber and went to sleep.

ONCE THEY WERE inside their carriage, Clarice asked, "What's the real reason we left?"

"How well you know me. I suddenly got my courses when I visited the ladies' retiring room. I was unprepared and had to hunt down a maid for help."

"I hate when that happens."

"Thank God nothing got on my dress. I'm not sure what I would've done then." She looked at her inquisitively. "You were gone with Stanton a long time. Did you lose your way in the gardens? I didn't think they were that big or had a maze to get lost in."

Heat rose to her cheeks no matter how hard she tried to stop it. "I'm so sorry I disappeared. We were not in the gardens."

One of Letitia's well-shaped eyebrows lifted in silent question.

"I'm ashamed to admit we spent time alone in a private drawing room."

"Don't be ashamed. You deserve happiness. When you entered the ballroom, you were glowing."

"Oh my, do you think anyone noticed?"

"No. Only Greyson and me."

"Greyson?"

"Well, I'd be lying if I said he didn't because he said something like, 'Those two look relaxed and satisfied, don't they?'"

"How will I ever look Greyson in the eye again?" Clarice moaned.

"I'm sure you will." Letitia sighed. "Oh, to have been in your shoes tonight!"

"What?"

"Calm yourself," she laughed. "Not with Stanton, but with Greyson. I miss it."

"Your time will come soon, I just know it." Clarice had a feeling about Letitia and Greyson and wished them the best.

When the carriage pulled up to the Red Lion Inn, a footman opened the door and helped them as they exited the coach. They entered the inn's main entryway and made their way to their rooms. Clarice knocked on the door, and a sleepy Penny unlocked the door and opened it, rubbing her eyes. "My ladies."

"Please take care of Letitia first, Penny. I will wait."

"Thank you," Letitia said.

Letitia never let on that she was uncomfortable on the ride home, but she kept hugging her stomach, so Clarice knew she was in pain. It was the kind thing to do to let her prepare for bed first. Especially since she was spending the day tomorrow with Greyson and his sisters.

It didn't take long for Penny to enter her room, close the connecting door to Letitia's room, and help Clarice get ready for bed. When she climbed beneath the soft coverlet, she sighed and realized just how exhausted she was. As she relived her night with Samuel, she fell asleep with a contented smile on her face, dreaming of a future with Samuel.

Sooner than she could have believed possible, it was morning again, and Penny was entering the room carrying her breakfast tray. It felt as though she'd just gone to bed.

"Good morning, my lady," Penny said, putting the tray on the bedside table. "If you don't need me for anything right away, I'll help Lady Rutherford prepare for her outing today."

"I'll be fine. Go take care of Lady Rutherford." Clarice's day was free until afternoon tea when she and Samuel were meeting Lord and Lady Kendall. So she relaxed in bed, taking her time sipping her chocolate and nibbling her toast covered with cream and jam.

When Penny did return, she helped her prepare for her day. Then Clarice left her room and, for lack of anything better to do, she explored the inn's library, found a book of poetry on a shelf, and settled into a large wingback chair with a matching ottoman for her feet. She asked Penny to have luncheon served there, since she didn't want to go to the dining room and eat alone.

It seemed as though she had just settled down when a maid brought her a tray of food—a fried chicken leg, carrots, mashed potatoes, and a roll with sweet cream. There was also a delightful slice of apple pie and tea. Clarice could hardly eat it all, but she managed to eat quite a bit. Feeling sleepy, she closed her eyes, and the next thing she knew, someone was shaking her shoulders and calling her name.

"Clarice, my love, wake up."

"Hmmm. Samuel, is that you?"

"Yes, sleepyhead. Lord and Lady Kendall are in the salon waiting for us. Should I reschedule?"

"No, no. Give me a moment." She stood and stretched to work out the stiffness from falling asleep sitting up. "I can't believe I dozed."

"You must've needed the rest. Are you ready?"

"Almost." She smoothed out the skirt of her dark blue day dress, then patted her hair, hoping it still looked presentable.

Samuel kissed her cheek. "You look beautiful and perfect."

"Perfect is really hard to achieve, and you keep telling me I look perfect."

His face lit up with a wide smile that twinkled in his eyes. "To me, you will always be and look perfect." He held out his hand. "Shall we?"

"We shall," she said as she took his hand. They needed to go before she did something scandalous.

The inn's large salon, where guests could mingle and enjoy tea, was just down the corridor. It was a spacious, bright room, cheerfully decorated in yellow and blue, and they found Lord and Lady Kendall seated on the settee there, just as she and Letitia had sat yesterday afternoon. After exchanging pleasantries, Samuel and Clarice sat in chairs facing the settee.

"I hope we didn't disrupt your afternoon rest," Lady Kendall said, looking concerned.

"No. I'm embarrassed to admit that I fell asleep in the library while reading."

That brought a smile to Lady Kendall. "I do that sometimes, as well. Were you reading anything interesting?"

"A book of poetry. It was interesting until after luncheon when I fell asleep. Thank goodness no one but His Grace found me."

"Yes, indeed," Lady Kendall agreed. "Now tell me, my dear, how did you end up married to my dreadful brother?"

Clarice coughed, and shame and embarrassment swept over her. She didn't know where to start, and luckily, Samuel explained the events, leaving out some of the more personal details that had led up to her wedding with Chesterfield.

"Your father and my brother both seem to lack respect for others. I'm truly sorry for what both of them put you through. Do you mind if I ask how my brother died?"

Clarice clasped her hands together on her lap and fought the urge to fidget. "Since you are family, I don't see any reason not to share. He died in his mistress's bed."

"The blackguard," Lord Kendall said.

Lady Kendall added, "Once again, I apologize for what he put you through. Also, please forgive me for not reaching out to you sooner. There is no excuse except to say I didn't know what poison Chesterfield told you about me. Had I known he never mentioned me, I would have visited shortly after finding out about his death."

"Thank you. But it's over now. And there's no need to apologize for not making yourself known sooner. All that matters is that you have now."

"Has my great-nephew arrived from America to take over the title?"

"No, which worries me. He should have arrived by now. Maybe when I return to London, he'll be in residence. May I ask something of you both?"

"Anything," Lord Kendall replied.

"Is he a good man?"

The look they exchanged didn't look promising.

"He is neither a good man nor a bad man, or at least he wasn't. His father controlled every aspect of his life, which is why he fled to the colonies. Let us hope he returns as his own man, a family man and a good one at that," Lady Kendall said.

"My father threatened Samuel and me. He said if we didn't stop our courtship, he would talk to your nephew and force me into another loveless marriage."

"I don't believe they can force you to do anything. You're a widow and old enough not to need a keeper. Forgive me for asking such a personal question, but do you have any funds of your own?"

"Yes. I have my annual settlement as Chesterfield's widow— until I marry again."

Samuel reached over and put his hand on hers. "We plan to wed very soon."

Footsteps drew closer, and even before she turned to see who was there, every fiber of her being told her it was her father. He had found her.

"Stanton," he said menacingly, "get your filthy hand off my daughter. And don't think a letter from Prinny is going to change my mind on anything we talked about back in London."

"I don't know what you mean," Samuel said arrogantly.

Was he trying to purposely anger her father? Thank God, Samuel didn't obey her father and kept his hand on her because she needed the connection as her body began to tremble. It started deep in her core and spread out from there until it consumed her entire body.

"This is your father?" Lady Kendall asked, gazing frostily up at him.

He looked down his nose at her. "And you are?" Obviously, there would be no polite introductions.

"*We* are the Earl and Countess of Kendall. *I* was Chesterfield's sister, which makes the lovely Lady Chesterfield my sister-in-law."

Portsmouth chuckled. "He had no family except for his great-nephew, the heir."

Lady Kendall appeared annoyed and glared at her father. "Just because he didn't tell you about me, doesn't mean I don't exist. I can assure you, I am his sister."

"Very well," her father spat, looking bored, "Chesterfield had a sister." He bowed, barely folding at the waist. "Lord and Lady Kendall. How very nice to make your acquaintance." He stood straight and glared once again at Samuel. "I told you to take your vile, filthy hand off my daughter."

"I will not," Samuel growled. "She is a grown woman and doesn't answer to you. Nor do I."

"Clarice, daughter of mine, may I have a private word with you?" her father asked impertinently.

"She's not going anywhere with you," Samuel practically growled.

"He's right," Lady Kendall remarked. "You don't deserve time alone with her."

Clarice witnessed her father's face turn deep red and the veins in his neck and forehead bulge. She could see the scene unfolding in front of her eyes if she didn't appease her father. She could handle a little gossip, but she'd rather not have her father air their dirty secrets in a hotel full of guests with nothing to do until the first race began. She had no desire to hear anything he had to say, nor be in the same room with him, but she would do so to keep the peace and hopefully convince her father to leave.

She patted Samuel's hand. "I'll be right back." She stood and spoke to Lord and Lady Kendall, "Please excuse me. I will return shortly." Then she turned to her father. "You have ten minutes."

She walked away without even bothering to check if he followed. She knew he was by the sound of footsteps pattering behind her. As she walked, she tried to breathe evenly to ease her racing heart and trembling body. She would not give her father the satisfaction of seeing her squirm. When they reached the library, where she had read, taken lunch, and napped earlier, she entered and sat in the same chair. Her father didn't sit; instead, he loomed over her, hoping to intimidate her. It wouldn't work. At least she would try not to let him succeed.

"What is it you want, Father?" She struggled to appear casual and unaffected by his presence.

He laughed. "That is a funny question. I believe I discussed with you what would happen if you insisted on seeing Stanton again."

"Yes, well, you see, you have no say in what I do or don't do. I am old enough to handle my own affairs. Nobody is in charge of my life or what I do with it but me. You no longer have the authority to marry me off to someone of your choosing."

His brows furrowed, and he looked displeased. Perhaps he had finally come to terms with the situation and understood that he had no control over her. "I see. Well, you do know there are other ways to get what I want." He placed his hand on his chin, rubbing his index finger across it. "Perhaps Staton would prefer to keep his father's secrets hidden and walk away from you. If not, I'll enjoy tarnishing my old friend's reputation. Not to mention the gossip I can spread about Samuel starting the fires that killed his family to inherit the dukedom."

She jumped up and practically growled at him like a mama lion protecting her cub—or in this case, the love of her life. Her soon-to-be husband. "Go right ahead. There are plenty of servants who witnessed Samuel going into the stables long before the fires started. He had nothing to do with it."

More laughter from her father. A laugh that sent icy talons scratching her exposed skin and a numbing chill through her veins. She waited, breathing heavily, for him to say something—anything—to make this craziness go away.

"It doesn't matter whether it's true or not. Members of the *ton* pay close attention to rumors. They love to believe that everything they hear is the truth. Some members take pride in spreading rumors, no matter how ridiculous they seem. As for Samuel setting the fire, it's plausible enough. His reputation will be ruined regardless of the actual truth. And if you marry him, you and your children will be shunned by Society. Enjoy your lonely, isolated life. I hope you find Samuel worth it." He bowed, the blackhearted man. "Until we meet again, daughter."

He walked out without looking back. The man had no conscience or morals. He just expelled words without a care as to how they hurt or upset her or anyone else. She hurried back to the salon to warn Samuel about what was to come.

When she arrived, she found him alone in the same chair she'd left him sitting in. She plopped back down in her chair. And she meant plopped. She had no energy or desire to sit all ladylike and proper. "Where did Lord and Lady Kendall go?"

"They said they wanted to rest before dinner and hoped to see you either tonight or tomorrow. They're in town for a while, so you'll have plenty of time to get to know them."

"But what if I won't be here for long?"

He appeared shocked by her words. "And why not? Now that your father knows where you are, there's no need to go back to London."

"True, but he intends to follow through on his threats. He plans to spread rumors about your father and accuse you of killing your family for the title."

Samuel reached over and linked his hand with one of hers. "If and when the rumors start, I will address them. Or ignore them. I hardly see that it matters what I say or don't say. The damage will be done." He exhaled. "To be honest, I don't care what comes of your father's threats, as long as the two of us are together."

She thought about what he said, and he was right. If they cared about each other, what did the rest matter? "I agree with you."

He raised his eyebrows and grinned. "You do?"

"Yes, and this is not the time for teasing."

He cleared his throat. "Yes. You are right. On another note, I apologize for not discussing this with you, but I have requested a special license. When it's issued, I think we should go to the local vicar and his quaint stone church and get married."

"Samuel Radcliff, you tell me this now? In a room full of onlookers. I'm going to have to sit on my hands to keep from pulling you into a hug and kissing you into tomorrow."

He answered her with a chuckle and a blush. Good Lord, he blushed. "I have something better. Would you accompany me to Ramsbury Ridge Farm so I can show off Zeus and Clover?"

"I would love that. But don't you have a social engagement tonight?"

"I do. But trust me when I say I'd much rather spend tonight with you. Skipping one gathering before the 2000 Guineas Stakes isn't going to hurt my chances."

"Why is that?"

"Well, I have acquired membership in The Jockey Club, thanks to Baron Ramsbury. I am making connections regarding my stud farm." He stood up and extended his hand. "The only thing left to do is to win a race or two or three!"

Clarice giggled. "Is that all?"

"Pretty much. I'll take you to your room and wait outside while you gather your things.

With her hand entwined with his, she focused on the path to her room and not on any people they encountered along the way. She would not let condescending stares or looks rattle her. "This is my room." She turned the knob. "I'll only be a minute."

"Take your time. We've got all night."

Slipping inside and shutting the door behind her, Clarice found Penny sitting at the dressing table, drawing with a piece of coal and parchment. The maid was lost in her sketching. "Penny?"

She finally looked her way, then jumped up quickly and curtsied. "My lady. How may I help you?"

"I'm accompanying the Duke of Stanton to Ramsbury Ridge Farm to meet his racing horses. I need a cloak, a hat, and my boots."

"Right away, my lady."

As Penny went through the wardrobe, Clarice curiously

approached the dressing table and picked up the drawing Penny was working on, along with several others. Her eyes widened. "Penny, did you design these?" The pages featured clothing designs, mostly for ladies.

"Yes, my lady."

"These are incredible. Even in black and white, I can picture the vibrant or pastel colors you must be envisioning when you create these. You are very talented. Have you ever tried to sell your designs to a modiste?"

"No, my lady."

Clarice sat in the chair while Penny put on her boots. She immediately stood to receive her cloak and hat. "Well, I think you should. When we're back in London, Lady Rutherford and I will introduce you to Madam Serena. She is so busy with all the *ton* crowding her doors for her newest creations that she can't possibly be doing all her own designs. Perhaps she would be interested in yours."

Poor Penny. Her mouth opened and closed several times as her eyes widened, and then tears fell from her eyes. "That is very kind, my lady, and I thank you."

"Lock both outside doors when I leave. I don't want any guests who have overindulged in spirits to think these are their rooms. Also, please inform Lady Rutherford where I went and that I don't know when I'll return."

Just as Samuel said, he was out in the corridor, leaning against a wall, waiting for her. His face lit up with a smile when he saw her. "My dear, you look lovely." He took her gloved hand, raised it up, and brushed his lips across her knuckles. "Not just lovely, enchanting. You have enchanted me since I was a boy."

A blush warmed her cheeks as she pulled her hand away. "Samuel, you are being silly."

He took her hand again, this time wrapping it through his arm as they started walking down the corridor. "Not silly. Serious. You are lovely, enchanting, beautiful, kind, considerate . . . should I continue?"

His words, which had seemed to come straight from his heart, warmed hers. "Thank you. And forgive me for thinking you were being silly."

"Not at all." He nodded to the doorman as they approached the front doors. Once the doors opened, they swept through and out into her waiting carriage with Kirkland in the driver's seat.

"Before you ask, I sent word to have your carriage brought around. I rode Smokey here, and here he will stay. When I return you to the inn, I can ride Smokey back again to Ramsbury Ridge Farm."

"Very ingenious of you to think of that all by yourself." She jabbed her elbow into his side teasingly.

"Now who's being silly?"

"Me." They sat side by side in companionable silence, holding hands for most of the ride. Clarice had a lot on her mind, and she knew Samuel did, too. He had his first horserace of his life coming up in just a few days. She was amazed he was so composed. At least on the outside, he was. She could only imagine what was going on inside. These next five races would make or break his dreams of owning a stud farm.

"I recommend you take off your pristine white gloves before entering the stables."

"You are right." She took off her gloves and put them beside her.

Samuel leaned forward, pushed the curtain aside, and said, "We have arrived."

CHAPTER TWENTY

"**A**RE THE BARON and baroness home?" Clarice asked, looking worried. "I don't want to impose."

"They informed me they would be gone all day, only return-ing at dinnertime. So you need not worry."

"Then we have plenty of time."

"Even if they return early, you are my guest. They will be happy to welcome you into their home again. Please don't worry."

"Fine. I won't. If you say I am welcome, then I will believe you."

The driver, a nice fellow named Kirkland whom Samuel met that day, opened the door and lowered the stairs. Samuel exited, leaning back in with his hand out. "My dear lady, are you prepared to fall in love with my equine family?"

She took his hand and stepped out of the carriage with more grace than anyone else he knew. "By all means. From the way you brag about them, I expect them to have wings and be able to fly."

Chuckling, Samuel replied with a lightness in his heart, "Some days when they race, I believe they have invisible wings." Still holding her hand and leading her away from the main house, he said, "This way. The property is huge. I don't know how many acres, but the walk to my stable isn't far. When you own valuable livestock, it's best to keep them close to the main house. I'm glad to see you wore boots since I forgot to mention it."

"Yes, well, I figured there would be walking involved, not to mention whatever's on the floor of the barn." She exaggerated a full-body shudder. "No pair of slippers of mine would survive such abuse."

"Probably not." He paused and cleared his throat to broach something they needed to discuss. "I spoke to you about getting a special license. Because I couldn't leave Newmarket with the first race happening in two days' time, I sent my valet to the archbishop with a note from me. He should arrive back in Newmarket sometime tomorrow night or the following morning if he rode straight through, only stopping to change his mount."

"I see."

Nerves, something he didn't usually suffer from when in her company, appeared in the form of sweating. He removed his handkerchief from his riding jacket and wiped his brow. "If you wish, we can marry the day after the 2000 Guineas Stakes. I sent word to the local vicar, and he is looking forward to marrying us. We could keep it simple: Lady Rutherford, Greyson, his two sisters, and Hunter." He exhaled. "However, we must invite the baron and baroness since I'm staying with them." He wiped his forehead again as his nervousness intensified. "Please say something? If this isn't what you want, I need to know before I keep rambling on, making an utter arse of myself."

Her feet stopped. She turned and took his other hand in hers, her fingers rubbing across the tops of them. "I'm just now realizing how freeing it is to hold your hands without gloves as an impediment. To feel your warm hands. And even though you are a wealthy duke and could live a pampered life, never working or getting your hands dirty, you choose the opposite. You have the strong hands of a man who knows what he wants and sets out to get it. You are the furthest thing from a lazy, pompous aristocrat. You inherited this need and desire to accomplish something from your father, who I remember spent hours in his gardens. He also loved to get his hands dirty and become one with nature. His nature was the flora, and yours is the fauna." She leaned up on tiptoes and kissed him soundly on the mouth, then lowered back to her normal height. "I'm sorry if my silence worried you. I was too in awe of you and how you think of everything when it comes to me. I love you so much, Samuel." She wrapped her arms around his waist and rested her head against his heart, which she noticed was beating wildly. "Everything you said pertaining to our marriage is as I would wish it to be."

"I'm not sure I heard much after you said, 'I love you so much, Samuel.'" He wrapped his arms around her, too, and they stood there, their bodies swaying gently as if the wind moved them. After a moment, Samuel stepped back and again took her hand, and they kept walking toward the stable, which was not far from Ramsbury's large main stable where he kept his prized thoroughbreds. Ramsbury's horse, Thunder, was going to be Zeus's toughest competitor. Samuel wished Ramsbury all the best and wanted him to win, but he wanted to win more. "Here we are."

"I hear them. Do they recognize you, even from out here?"

"Yes." No doubt his scent drifted their way with the main barn doors wide open. It was common to leave them open to give the horses, stablehands, his jockey, and horse trainer inside, fresh air and the all-important daylight. Lanterns and candles didn't mix well with hay.

They entered the stable, and Samuel noticed the floors had been swept clean recently, and the scent of fresh hay filled the air, also mingling with leather and polish. "Prepare to fall in love," he said, grinning—no doubt looking like a silly fool. He opened the tops of both stalls, which were side by side, and immediately Zeus and Clover made noises and shook their heads, seeking attention. "You need a stool." He hurried to the corner, grabbed a three-legged stool, and helped Clarice stand on it in front of the animals. "Stay here."

"Where would I go?" she said, laughing.

He brought back the pail that stored carrots and apples that were too bruised for the kitchen. He handed Clarice an apple. "Clover loves apples. She will be your best friend forever if you feed her one."

Once again, Clarice laughed. "That is good to know." Samuel watched as she held out her hand with the apple cradled in her open palm. Clover, using her lips, took it gently from Clarice's hand. "Do you know that I've never had a horse of my own?"

"I don't think I ever knew that. You ride well, that I do remember."

"Yes. I trained on my mother's mare, Goldie. She was more or less mine as Mother didn't ride much."

"Do you think she rode Goldie to meet my father for their tête-à-têtes?"

Clarice grabbed the wooden door as she wobbled on the stool, steadying herself before Samuel could react. "I'm sorry. That was insensitive of me." He took a carrot from the bucket and fed it to Zeus. "It really doesn't matter. What's in the past is behind us. The future . . . our future is what matters."

"You are right. There's nothing we can do to change the past, but the future is wide open and ready for the taking." Clover nickered and moved her head up and down as if she understood what she said and agreed. "You were right. I'm in love with this sweet filly."

"Let's switch so you can meet Zeus."

Clarice hopped off the stool. Samuel moved it several feet to the right, and she stood back on it. As she petted Zeus, she said, "Shouldn't they be on a special diet for the upcoming races?"

"Guilty, yes. But the one treat they get a day shouldn't hurt."

"You haven't said anything about your silks and your colors. Are you keeping them a secret until the first race?"

"I am. They are locked away in my chambers. Would you like to be the first—besides my jockey and The Jockey Club, who needed to approve and record them—to see them?"

"Can I give Zeus a carrot first?"

Samuel chuckled as he handed her a carrot. "If not, I think he might eat your long strands of hair."

"Now, you be a good boy, Zeus, and win that 2000 Guineas Stakes for your owner. As you know, he's a wonderful, loyal, and kind man. I have it on good authority that if you win, you can eat all the carrots you want."

"You listen to Clarice, Zeus. She knows what she's talking about. I can plant a row of carrots in the pasture, and you can dig them up whenever you want. I'm leaving the top door open, as Tobias comes by this time of the day." Laughing, Samuel held out his hand, his eyes filled with amusement. "Come. I would love to show you my silks, but you must swear yourself to secrecy."

She took his hand, stepped down from the stool, and giggled. "Be careful what you say. One might think you're showing me your silk bedding."

Samuel couldn't help it; he burst out laughing. He couldn't be more in love with Clarice if he tried. "I never thought of it like that." He tugged gently on her hand to hurry her along. She had given him a very salacious idea. He may not be sleeping on silk bedding, but the cotton was soft, and he definitely wanted to show it to her.

They entered through the front door and were greeted by the butler, who bowed in greeting. "Your Grace, Lady Chesterfield."

"Sullivan, are the baron and baroness in?"

"They have not returned yet."

"Thank you. When they return, please inform them that Lady Chesterfield will be joining us for dinner. Also, send a message to Mrs. Mather. I don't want her to panic when she sees an extra place setting at the table."

"Yes, Your Grace."

Samuel, still holding her hand, led them up two flights of stairs and down the hall to the room he used when in Newmarket. He always wondered how he could repay Ramsbury and Anna for their kindness. Not just for housing him and his horses, but also for their friendship and sharing their deep knowledge of the racing business. He didn't know what he would do without them, especially Ramsbury.

"Here we are."

"It's nicely decorated with masculine colors. I love the navy and brown. And you have a nice sitting area in front of the hearth. You would think the room would be dark, done in deep colors, but with light from the windows, it's not."

"There's a dressing room through that door." Samuel pointed to the right. "It's comfortable and I feel at home here."

Clarice wandered over to look out a window. "You mentioned buying property somewhere near here. Have you found anything to your liking that meets your needs?"

"I have a business agent looking for me, but so far, nothing is for sale that meets my approval. There is land for sale, but it would take too long to build a house and stables. The perfect property needs a large house and stables already built and in good condition. If nothing becomes available soon, I'll set up my stud farm at my country estate in Hampshire. That is where I spend most of my time anyway." He moved and now stood beside her. "I just thought if I had a farm close to Newmarket, it would be more convenient for buyers to visit. Although, to be realistic, I can always use Tattersall's."

She turned to look at him, and he could see her thinking. "Forgive me if I overstep, but I believe you said funds were tight and you were looking for investors. Perhaps you could start the stud farm in Hampshire, and when you have the money, you could then buy property here."

"Hmmm. I've thought about that. Truthfully, I'm waiting for the perfect moment to speak with Greyson and Hunter and ask them to invest. I'd rather have them as partners than anyone else. With them, I know I'll get hard work and honesty." He paused and considered another option. "I could always give up my dream of owning a stud farm and just enjoy the ride as far as it goes with Zeus and Clover. It would be the safest and wisest path. I could spend more time dealing with obligations to the dukedom. I would feel less guilty if I did that."

She moved closer, wrapped her arm around his waist, and leaned her head against his shoulder. "What would make you happy?"

He exhaled and ignored the knot in his stomach. "Perhaps when one is a duke, one is not meant to be happy. I have obligations to my title. I try. I really try to manage it all, but I don't always succeed. I have this undeniable draw and connection to my horses—actually, all horses in general—I can't always ignore it. I know this might sound perplexing, but they know me and I know them on an elemental level. We connect. Both Greyson and Hunter say I'm part Arabian horse myself."

"Regarding dukes or gentlemen with titles, I'm unsure how truly happy anyone is. But for daughters born into the aristocracy, we learn early on that our success, our hoped for happiness, depends on the talents we can share—embroidery, musical instruments, painting, and other art forms—things a potential husband admires in his bride. And, of course, there is the amount of our dowry. But our parents will plan the match for most unwed young ladies. Whether it's a father, mother, or legal guardian, they have complete control over us." She sighed. "Our years together, Samuel, knowing we were meant to marry and spend our lives together, becoming friends and then lovers, is most unusual. Most girls and young ladies are made to feel that their only purpose in life is to secure a good match for their family. And then produce heirs for her husband. If that match leads to friendship, common interests, and perhaps love, they are considered lucky. That is the only happiness a woman can hope for or expect."

"You are correct. But it's sad to hear it said aloud." Because he and Clarice had had a wonderful time growing up and falling in love, he'd never thought of how little input a young lady had when it came to marriage.

At least he hadn't thought about it until Clarice married Chesterfield.

CHAPTER TWENTY-ONE

S AYING THOSE WORDS was sad but true. Her father's decision to sell her to Chesterfield nearly broke her at the time. And when Chesterfield stole her and Samuel's son away, it left her crushed with grief for a long time, but now, she was her own woman, able to make her own decisions, do what she wanted within the rules of Society if she wanted to stay welcome in it. It was freeing. "Perhaps you should show me those silks."

"Yes. We veered away from our original conversation. And as for making any decisions regarding the stud farm, I can't decide until after the upcoming races. After that, I'll have a better idea of the future. Why don't you sit down, and I'll be right back."

Samuel walked away and entered the dressing room. Clarice sat down on a navy-blue tufted-back chair. Moments later, Samuel returned with a box, which he placed on the chair next to hers. "Are you ready?" he asked, his eyes bright with excitement.

"Whenever you are."

He removed the cover from the box and set it on the floor. Pushing aside tissue paper, he took out a shirt, which must be the jockey's, and held it up.

Her eyes were fixed on the mixture of colors. The only thing she knew about silks was that they required two colors, but no more than four. They could be a pattern or a solid. The Jockey Club had to approve and document the design and colors so no other owner or jockey could have the same.

"You're quiet."

"Sorry, I'm taking it in." She stood up and reached out her hand to feel the fabric, soft and silky as it looked. "I love the peacock blue as the main color. Adding the vertical, vibrant yellow stripes on the front and back of the body really makes it stand out. What does the jockey's hat look like?"

Samuel pulled out a riding cap. It was blue with a yellow visor.

"Very nice."

He wrapped them back up in the tissue paper and replaced the cover. "Forgive me for a moment." He disappeared into the dressing room again, and Clarice took that opportunity to walk over to the table beside the bed. She picked up a book that was upside down and open. She looked at the title, then laughed.

"What's so funny?" Samuel asked as he walked out of the dressing room.

"I should have known you would be reading a book about the origins of thoroughbred horses in England."

He shrugged his shoulders. "Is there anything else to read about? Did you know that in the late 1600s and early 1700s, three horses arrived in England and were bred with our large English mares, and the thoroughbred breed was created?"

Her eyes widened as she absorbed what he said. "Does that mean Zeus and Clover are descended from one of those horses?"

He chuckled as he moved to stand beside her. He put his hands on her waist and gently guided her to sit down on the soft bed. "You catch on quick. Yes. Both Zeus and Clarice descend from the Darley Arabian." He stepped back and his intense eyes met hers. "I think we've talked enough about horses." He began removing his riding jacket and waistcoat. "It's hot in here. Perhaps we should shed some clothing." His long, capable hands and talented fingers began to untie his cravat, slowly and steadily. The top buttons on his fine linen shirt were next. He reached behind his neck with both arms and pulled it up and over his head, exposing his chiseled chest, which was worthy of being a sculptor's model. He sank onto the bed beside her, tugging off his boots and hose. "Are you going to let me be naked alone, or will you join me?" He leaned and kissed her neck. "I promise you will enjoy yourself if you get naked."

She shifted to turn her back to him. "I knew you had other things on your mind when you brought me up here under the pretense of seeing your silks," she said through her laughter. Then she moaned as his fingers, having quickly loosened her ties, slipped her dress off her shoulders, and his warm lips moved across her skin as softly as butterfly wings. Heat burned where his lips tantalizingly traveled across her neck, shoulders, and back. His large, warm hands replaced his mouth as he rubbed and caressed her exposed skin, making her entire body melt. She nearly fell back on the bed in utter contentment.

"You have the softest skin. I could stroke it all day and night and never get bored." He released her bodice even more, slipped her arms out of her short sleeves, and let the top of her dress and thin chemise fall to her waist. "What is this? No stays today? What a fashion rebel you are!" He chuckled as his arm came around from the back and cupped her breasts. Another moan escaped her lips, and she leaned back into his bare chest. Skin against skin. "Stand, so we can get you out of this dress."

Clarice stood as Samuel tugged her clothing over her hips until it pooled on the floor. Wary of wrinkling it, knowing she would be dining with the baron and baroness, she picked it up, hurried across the room, and draped it over a chair. It wasn't until she turned to join Samuel back on the bed that she became aware of her nakedness and felt her entire body blush.

By now, Samuel had removed his breeches, stood naked and fully aroused with his hand out. "Come. Let me worship you and prove my love."

A lump formed in her throat, and tears threatened to fill her eyes as his hand, which might as well have been his heart, reached out to her. She took several steps toward his outstretched hand, clasped it, and let him lead her away. They fell onto the bed on their sides, arms and legs entwined. You couldn't tell one body from the other as they were wrapped up as one.

"I'm afraid to move and spoil the moment," Samuel said as the tips of his fingers gently traced circles along her back.

"I know what you mean." Her lips went on a quest, kissing his neck and cheeks, before finally settling on his decadent mouth. The kiss intensified quickly. She couldn't seem to get enough of his taste, nor he of hers.

Abruptly, he tore his mouth from hers, rolled her onto her back, and took one of her nipples into his mouth and sucked hard. The instant connection with her core had her hips rubbing against his erection, and a deep guttural moan escaped his mouth as he moved from one breast to the other. He repeated the sucking, and she nearly screamed out. As his hand moved between their bodies, opening her folds, his thumb circling her nub, she thought she was going to explode. Then he slipped a finger inside and out several times, and she did scream out. Samuel continued his sweet torture until she shut her legs tight, trapping his hands.

He chuckled. "Why did you stop me?" He pulled his hand out from between her thighs. He nudged her legs apart with his knee, and she sighed as his manhood pushed against her opening. "Is this what you want?"

"Stop teasing me with words," she gasped as he pushed and seated himself deep within her.

"Is this better?"

"Yes," she cried out as he pulled one of her legs up over his shoulder.

"Better?"

"Yes," she cried, feeling him deeper inside her than she ever thought possible.

His hips moved fast. She tried to keep up, but her body was reaching that pinnacle. She felt it first, tingling in her breasts, then her lower belly as it traveled down to her core. Her legs began to tremble and weaken. The sounds of their heavy breathing, the bed squeaking, and their hips slapping hit her oddly, and she almost laughed. Except at the precise moment Samuel thrust inside her and stopped. His hands gripped her hips, holding her and keeping her from moving. He looked her in the eyes, and she couldn't look away. Not when he looked at her with a raw intensity and animalistic need.

"Come with me," he said as his eyes glazed over, his body bowed back, and he moaned and groaned. It was the most magnificent sight she'd ever seen. Samuel at his most vulnerable, surrendering himself to her, body and soul. It was then she realized the euphoria Samuel was experiencing was happening simultaneously with her own. She felt her insides pulsing around his manhood, witnessed darkness descend and stars shoot across the room. All while her body shook until her legs collapsed on the bed, her arms flung out to the side, and she inhaled shakily, trying to return to her body. Samuel collapsed beside her and pulled her close to the front of him. He kissed the back of her neck and sighed. "I think a little nap before dinner is warranted."

"My sentiments exactly." She shivered, and without a word, he pulled up the counterpane that somehow had been pushed to the foot of the bed.

He wrapped his arms tighter around her and lightly brushed his lips across the top of her head. "Sleep. We have time before we need to get ready for dinner." Words she wanted to say stayed unsaid as she drifted into a deep sleep.

Pain like she had never experienced or expected tore through her belly. Her belly with her and Samuel's baby inside. Her time had come, and she had two women attending her who hated her and did anything her husband told them. Mrs. Johnson, her dour-faced maid, and Mrs. Fitzhugh, the nasty housekeeper. They shared no words of encouragement each time the contractions overtook her. How many hours had she labored? If only a midwife had attended her, she would know if the labor was progressing normally or even what to expect. Clarice was so frightened. She thought she and the baby might be dying. How could the miracle of birth hurt so much? Sweat poured off her, soaking her nightgown, which made her shiver. Was she supposed to sweat and be cold?

She wanted her mother, which brought tears to her eyes and heaviness to her chest. Why couldn't she have come to her? She knew why. Chesterfield didn't want a scandal, nor did he want to acknowledge this child as his. So what was going to happen to her baby? Another wave of pain and a hard tightening of her belly came, and this time she felt the need to push; she could feel the baby coming. The hardest thing was staying quiet and not screaming out. It went against nature not to scream at such pain piercing one's body, but she refused to make a sound and be called weak by Mrs. Johnson and Mrs. Fitzhugh.

"I see the head," Mrs. Johnson said as she moved her head between Clarice's legs. "Open those thighs wider, like you did for your lover, so your bastard can be born." Anger flared through Clarice, so when the next contraction came and she felt the urge to push, she bore down hard and long until she experienced instant relief, and the cry of a baby reached her ears. At the sound of the crying, she tried to get up.

"Stay down, you stupid girl. The afterbirth needs to come out. Unless you would rather it stay in and kill you?"

"I want to see my baby."

Mrs. Fitzhugh said, "Per Lord Chesterfield's orders, you may not see nor hold the bastard."

Out of the corner of Clarice's eye, the housekeeper held the baby, and as she wrapped it up in a blanket, Clarice saw that it was a boy. Her heart soared. A boy. Samuel had a son. She gasped with surprise as something came out of her body. The afterbirth. "Please let me see him?" she begged, though she hated to do so.

"No," Mrs. Fitzhugh snarled and exited the room, taking Clarice's son with her.

"Come back! Come back, I want my son," Clarice begged repeatedly until she had no voice left. She was alone in her chambers, in a bed that needed changing, wearing a blood-stained and wet night rail. The only light in the room came from the smoldering remains in the hearth. Clarice rolled onto her side, holding her stomach, and somehow managed to roll off the bed and land on her shaking legs. She shuffled across the room to the washstand, removed her night rail, and stuffed it between her legs when she felt a gush of blood. Using cool water, soap, and a

piece of linen, she bathed herself as best she could.

In her wardrobe, she found strips of cloth, ones used for her monthly courses. She dressed in a clean, warm night rail and robe. She took the coverlet that had been removed from the bed so it wouldn't get ruined and spread it out on the floor in front of the fireplace. She swayed from weakness but focused and managed to place several logs in the hearth before she collapsed on the floor, rolled herself up in the coverlet, and blackness descended.

"Come back!" she yelled as she abruptly sat up in bed, her body trembling and covered in sweat. She scanned her surroundings and was stunned by what she saw. She'd swear she was back at Chesterfield Manor in her old chambers, reliving the labor and delivery of her son.

"Clarice." The bed dipped as Samuel, fully dressed, sat down and looked at her with concern. "You were dreaming, and from the sounds of it, it was a nightmare. Do you want to talk about it?"

"Did I say anything?" Dear God, she hoped not.

"Mostly moaning and groaning, and right before you woke up, you yelled, 'Come back.' If you're not up to dinner with the baron and baroness, I can send our regrets and have our meals brought to the room."

"No. I just need some time to get ready." At that moment, she realized she was naked and exposed. She clutched the covers to her chest, which made Samuel smile. "It's too late for modesty, my dear. There is no part of your body I haven't seen or touched."

She nudged him. "Stop it. Could you please bring my things over?"

"Already done," he said, then his eyes shifted to the foot of the bed, where her gaze followed and settled on her clothing.

"Thank you." It was one thing to be naked and in bed together, and quite another for him to be fully clothed while she was not. She reached for her chemise, pulled it over her head, tossed the covers aside, and stood as the fabric fell just below her knees.

She tied up the laces while Samuel picked up her day dress and helped her into it. His hands adeptly laced up her back.

"Your stockings and boots are by the chair. I had the housekeeper bring a brush and some pins for you. They're in the dressing room, where you'll find a table and a mirror."

"Thank you." She moved to the chair, sat down, and pulled up her stockings to tie the ribbon around her thigh. Then she slipped on her boots and laced them. She entered the dressing room and sat at the table. She removed the remaining pins that hadn't fallen out in bed from her hair and brushed it. Free of tangles, she gathered her hair and twisted it into a simple knot, securing it with several pins. With one last look in the mirror, she decided she was ready for an informal dinner. She covered her stomach with one hand as it tumbled around. Would the baron and baroness be able to guess what they were doing? Would they think less of her if they did? Oh dear, she hated all this uncertainty nagging at her. With luck, she and Samuel could be married by this time next week.

Except the memory of her dream troubled her. Was it her mind's way of telling her she needed to confess everything to Samuel? Had the guilt of keeping it from him caused her nightmare? Tonight, after dinner, she would tell him. Taking a deep breath to gather her courage, she stood, smoothing out any creases in her dress as best as she could, and then walked out of the dressing room. The moment her eyes met Samuel's, her entire body relaxed. Everything about him brought her comfort when she needed it most.

His dark eyes swept over her. "You look beautiful."

"Thank you."

"Come." He held out his hand. "The dinner bell just rang and I'm famished."

They held hands all the way to the dining room, where the baron sat at the head of one side of the table, with the baroness on his left. Samuel waved off a footman and helped Clarice into her seat beside the baroness. Then he walked around the table and took a seat opposite her.

Ramsbury, the baron, smiled at them. "Lady Chesterfield, we are very fortunate to have you dining with us tonight."

"Thank you for welcoming me on such short notice. And please call me Clarice."

"Only if you call us Ramsbury and Anna," he said as he picked up a goblet of wine and took a sip. "While Samuel stays with us, his friends are our friends and always welcome."

"Once again, thank you for your generosity and kindness." As she spoke, warmth flooded her cheeks.

Dinner passed surprisingly quickly once Clarice relaxed and enjoyed the lively conversation, mostly about the upcoming races. Anna was softspoken and close in age to her. Clarice learned that she and Ramsbury rarely spent time in London, except during Parliament's season. Even then, they kept to themselves. Their stud farm was their whole world, and it made Clarice wonder if, when Samuel started his stud farm, their lives would be similar. But she didn't mind. She would be happy and content living anywhere as long as she was with Samuel.

IT HAD BEEN a long day for Ramsbury and Anna, and they excused themselves right after dinner, leaving Clarice and Samuel sitting in the drawing room, sipping sherry. Samuel put his arm around her shoulder as they shared the settee and said, "Would you like to tell me about your nightmare? I didn't push you earlier because dinner was ready, but I have this feeling it involves me." He couldn't explain why he had the feeling; he just did.

"There is something I've been wanting to tell you, but there's never been a good time," she sighed and rested her head on his shoulder. "First, let me tell you how truly sorry I am. I tried. I really did, but I was a prisoner, locked inside my chambers for eight months. Looked after by two dreadful servants. I was only allowed the freedom to roam the house and grounds after the night my . . . our son was born."

He knew, somehow, he knew before she spoke the words. The moment she said she was sorry, deep inside where things cannot be explained, he knew what she had to say. His throat burned, and he struggled to breathe. His body shook from within. He wanted to scream, pull his hair out, and punch a wall. It wouldn't solve anything, and from the soft crying sounds coming from Clarice, it would only make things worse. She needed him as much as he needed her.

"I could never blame you. *He* did this to you, to us. I'm sorry for what you went through." Tears streamed down his cheeks, and he didn't bother wiping them away. Both of them could use a good cry over losing their son. Then it occurred to him, "What happened to him?"

A sob tore from Clarice. She shifted her position so her head rested on his lap, and her legs curled up on the settee. "I don't know. I don't know if he's alive or dead."

He stroked her hair, his heart pounding with excruciating pain. Pain he didn't believe would ease until he'd learned what happened to his son. Christ, what Clarice had endured all on her own. What that cruel, blackguard of a husband did to her, all because of her vengeful father. He had started the chain of events that had led them here. His poor Clarice, having her baby taken away. How had she survived?

"I love you. And I promise we will find out what happened to our son. I will hire an investigator to locate the two servants, bribe them for the answers we seek, and threaten them with kidnapping charges. I swear, we will find him."

"Th-thank you. I just want to know that he's safe. Perhaps he's living in a loving home."

"We will. Meanwhile, if you're ready, I should take you back to the inn."

The ride to the Red Lion Inn was quiet, each lost in their own thoughts. Samuel held Clarice's hand, trying to comfort her heartbreak as best he could. No doubt, it had broken her the day she'd brought the baby into the world and only worsened year after year. How did she manage to carry on with all the uncertainty and unknowing? He had always known she was strong and brave, and thank God she was. A lesser person might not have endured the loss.

He saw her safely to her room and kissed her on the cheek. Now that he knew about her loss, she wasn't hiding her sadness, and it tore at his insides. "My schedule is brutal for the next two days until the race." He brushed his lips lightly against hers. "I'll find you at the racecourse. Goodnight."

After she entered her room and closed the door, Samuel leaned against the wall to steady himself. He didn't want to fall apart in front of Clarice. Not because he wasn't devastated by the news of a son, but because he didn't want to cause her any more pain or guilt. Not that she had any reason to feel guilty, but he could see it in her eyes that she did. He could hear it in her voice when she'd talked about the birth. As footsteps approached, he composed himself, so no one seeing him would ever know what he was going through.

CHAPTER TWENTY-TWO

IT WAS THE day of the 2000 Guineas Stakes, and Samuel was pacing outside Zeus's stall at one of several stables at the Newmarket Racecourse, with a knot in his stomach the size of London. He hadn't seen Clarice since he'd returned her to the Red Lion Inn after dinner with the baron and baroness.

Also the night he'd found out about having a son.

Something he could not allow himself to dwell on today, as it was race day and he needed to focus on one thing only: Getting Zeus to the starting gate and running the Rowley Mile.

At the end of this row of stalls was Ramsbury's horse, Thunder, which was being watched over by his trainer. Since this was Samuel's first race with Zeus, he didn't trust anyone else to stay with him. Once Tobias mounted Zeus and Albert, his trainer, led them to the starting line, Samuel would hurry to find Clarice, and hopefully watch his thoroughbred win—or at least show.

"Your Grace," Tobias said as he entered the stables and approached him. "It's time."

"Relax, Your Grace," Albert said, having arrived with Tobias. "We will take it from here. Tobias is ready, and Zeus has been trained for this day."

He heard their words and knew they were true, but Samuel still found it hard to leave Zeus. Did all owners feel this way? The three of them had spoken earlier in the day, so there was nothing more for Samuel to do or say. "Take care of Zeus," Samuel said as he walked away from the stables, stepped into the filtered sunshine, and inhaled the fresh air. He paused to brush dust and hay particles off his black jacket and trousers. When he started toward the course, he had to weave around spectators on horseback and in both open and closed carriages as they searched for a spot to watch the race. Not to mention all the people walking around. He wondered if he would ever find Clarice in this crowd.

Just when he was about to give up hope of ever finding them, he heard Greyson yell, "Stanton, over here!" Greyson was standing up in an open barouche with Lady Rutherford, Lady Aurora, and Lady Anastasia. Hunter was in another barouche parked beside theirs with Clarice, who waved enthusiastically.

He sighed with relief upon seeing Clarice happy. The tension in his shoulders relaxed, and the nerves plaguing him earlier turned into excitement as he headed toward his friends.

"How are you faring?" Greyson asked.

"Better now than I was," he replied as he climbed into the carriage with Clarice and Hunter, taking the seat beside Clarice and immediately holding her hand. He took his timepiece out of his jacket pocket and set it on the seat next to him.

"It's going to be a great race. Zeus will do well. He had good times during practice runs on the course," Greyson shouted to be heard over the ever-growing and overly passionate crowd.

Samuel removed his black top hat, ran his hands through his hair, and placed it back on his head. The brim would help block the sun's glare when the race started. His eyes fixed on the wide, flat grass racecourse. In less than thirty minutes, Zeus would either win or lose this race. Since the stables were near the finish line, the spot Samuel needed to be, Hunter and Greyson had found the perfect place to watch the race's end. Looking down the straightaway, he could see the "Dip" in the distance. During the trials, Zeus handled the dip well.

"Here they come," Hunter said, pulling him out of his introspection.

And they were coming, but not yet racing. The horses were being led by their jockeys and trainers down the track, a mile away from the starting line.

"Samuel," Clarice squeezed his hand. "Your silks stand out. The yellow stripes were a perfect choice."

She spoke the truth. Tobias was easy to identify.

"I can't believe I never thought to ask about your silks," Greyson bellowed from his carriage. "You did well with the design and colors."

"Yes, you did," Hunter said in agreement.

Samuel struggled to contain his excitement now that he saw Zeus heading to the starting line. It made everything feel real for the first time. He had known the race was coming up, but it had seemed like a dream. It had been hard to think it would all actually come to fruition.

"How are you doing?" Clarice's voice interrupted his thoughts.

"Better, now that the race is here and you're by my side."

"Me too," she said as she looked at him and smiled. "All I could think about was you the past two days." She lowered her voice so Hunter couldn't hear. "I should never have burdened you with our conversation the other night, knowing how much strain you were under because of the race. I should have waited. And this morning, I tried to imagine what you were going through. The anxiety, the excitement, the nerves. Time couldn't go by fast enough so I could be with you."

He raised her hand to his lips and kissed her fingers. "I'm glad you told me, so we can share the pain and loss together." He grinned and winked, burying the ache inside for today. "I want to pull you into my arms and kiss you, but this will have to do."

Hunter heard his last comment and chuckled as he sat across from them. Samuel ignored him while he picked up his timepiece. His eyes widened, his stomach dropped, and his heart pounded even harder than before. "The race has begun."

He stood up on trembling legs, and his friends did the same, all straining their necks to see down the track. Samuel heard the thunder and felt the vibrations of the horses running long before he could see them. When they finally came into view, it was so fast—happening quickly—that everything was a blur of horses and colors. Samuel's eyes fixed on Tobias. He was neck and neck with two other horses, one of which he recognized as Ramsbury's horse.

Screaming and cheering nearly deafened him as the horses reached the finish line. Having no idea who won, he jumped down from the carriage and held out his hand for Clarice. "Come. We need to hurry to the finish line."

As they quickly weaved through the crowd, spilling onto the track, they reached Tobias, who yelled over the crowd, "We won! We won!"

Samuel turned to Clarice, lifted her up, and spun her around while shouting, "We won! We won!"

"Samuel, I'm dizzy," she laughed out.

He stopped spinning and gently set her down, keeping his arm around her until she was steady on her feet. Not that he felt steady himself. He was lightheaded, and his knees were weak. Not only had his dream of owning a thoroughbred racehorse come true, but Zeus had won a race. And not just any race—the 2000 Guineas Stakes. The opening race of the 1817 racing season.

The rest of the afternoon was spent being congratulated and envied at the celebration party at The Jockey Club. He enjoyed the praise, but what he really wanted was to go back to Ramsbury Ridge Farm and spend private time with Clarice. However, since the Winner's Ball was being hosted by Viscount Thurston, their time alone would have to wait.

WHEN CLARICE HAD arrived at the Newmarket Racecourse on race day, excitement had coursed through her body. The ladies were dressed in their finest day dresses with elaborate hats and parasols. She and Letitia were dressed equally so. Gentlemen were expected to wear black. Some wore formal wear, while others sported black riding clothes. It shouldn't have surprised her that so many people were in attendance to watch the race. After all, Newmarket was the racing town. Many people lived here for the races.

When Samuel had finally joined her in Hunter's open-air coach, and she convinced herself he was doing well after their delicate conversation from two nights ago, she had been able to breathe easier. And when she'd stood in the carriage and watched all the horses stampeding down the track, giddiness had set in. Then when they'd learned Zeus had won and Samuel picked her up, swinging her around, it was the happiest moment. She was so proud and thrilled for him. And the day after that was simply a blur of activity.

"What a day," Clarice said hours later, once she and Samuel were in her hotel room. Dressed only in her night rail, she nibbled on some cold chicken, grapes, bread, and cheese that a chambermaid had brought to her room moments ago. With all the excitement of the day and the whirlwind of social events and the Winner's Ball they'd attended, they had hardly eaten, and she was famished—the noises her stomach made proved it. "You should eat something."

Samuel stood, looking out the window at the dark night sky. "I will." He'd shed most of his clothes except for his lawn shirt and breeches.

"What's troubling you?"

He turned and met her eyes. "Nothing. Everything. You know what they say about being on the top?"

"I believe I do."

"There's only one way to go, and that's down. I'm not ready for that. I want to savor the exhilaration of being a winner for a little longer."

"Nonsense. You and Zeus hold the title for a year until the

next race, no matter what happens in the other upcoming races. Plus, it will be documented forever. At least, I think it will. Well, it should be, if it's not."

He chuckled and moved to her side, plucking a piece of cheese off the tray and nibbling on it. "You should be an advisor at The Jockey Club."

Laughter burst from her. "Oh, please, as if they would ever let a woman into their sacred club."

"You never know." He ate a few grapes. "The 1000 Genius Stakes is coming up and Clover will be making her debut. Just when I think I can relax, I start worrying again."

"She's a beauty. I predict she will—"

"No, no, no," he interrupted as he shook his head. "You can say you hope or wish she wins, but you can't come right out and say she will do anything."

She laughed again. "That's the silliest thing I've ever heard."

"Superstitions and all that."

"In that case, I hope Clover wins," she said. "Is that acceptable?"

He wrapped his arm around her waist and pulled her close. "It is." His eyes shifted to the bed, and she understood what he was thinking. Her body responded accordingly. "Would you like to go to bed?" he asked.

"Yes." Before she could move, he swept her up into his arms and gently placed her on the bed with his body coming down beside hers. Thankfully, Penny had drawn the covers down, and they slipped right in, pulling the counterpane over them.

Turning on his side, facing her back, Samuel nuzzled her neck. "Today was the best day of my life because I got to spend it with the woman I love."

Her skin tingled from his warm breath. "I believe it was the best day of mine, as well." She waited for him to say something else. When she heard soft snoring, she smiled. Poor Samuel, he probably hadn't had a good night's sleep in a long time. She closed her eyes and wished they could fall asleep like this for years and years to come.

CHAPTER TWENTY-THREE

A LOUD POUNDING on the door early in the morning made both Clarice and Samuel jump out of bed. "Stay behind the door, so nobody sees you," she said as she slipped on her robe and moved toward the door. Before opening it, she asked, "Who is it?"

"My lady, it's Kirkland. I need to speak with you privately."

She opened the door. "Come in quickly." After he stepped inside, she shut and locked the door, and she noticed Kirkland wasn't surprised to see Samuel.

"Pardon the intrusion," he bowed, "but I thought His Grace would want to hear what's being said about him."

She and Samuel looked at each other, both knowing her father had done something.

"Tell me, Kirkland," Samuel said as he leaned against the door, his arms crossed, prepared for a confrontation.

"Rumor has it that you torched Stanton Hall, killing your family so you could inherit the title." Kirkland shifted his weight from one leg to the other. "I'm sorry. I know it's not true. You're an honorable man."

"Do you know who started it?"

"A former Stanton Hall stable boy who now works somewhere as a stable hand in Newmarket said you started the fire, then went to the stables so you'd look innocent."

Clarice swiftly pressed her hand over her mouth to quiet her gasp.

"Thank you, Kirkland."

He bowed. "Your Grace, my lady."

After he left, Samuel locked the door again and started pacing the room, looking worried. Clarice didn't blame him. She couldn't imagine what he must be thinking, knowing people believed he murdered his family.

"Your father must have bribed him. Whether he worked at Stanton Hall or not doesn't matter. The damage is done. I need to think. Can you ring for a breakfast tray? I need strong coffee."

Clarice went to the door between her and Letitia's room and knocked. A moment later, Penny opened it. "My lady."

"Can you please send for a breakfast tray? In addition to tea, I want strong black coffee."

"Right away, my lady."

Clarice shut the door, and when she turned, Samuel was dressed, which made her think she should be as well. She pulled a chemise and a day dress out of the wardrobe and dressed behind the screen in the corner. When she came around the screen, she asked, turning her back to Samuel, "Could you please lace up my dress?" Samuel, seeming lost in unhappy thoughts, had her asking again, "Could you lace up my dress?"

"Oh," he said, coming to himself. "I'm sorry." His fingers worked the laces. "I keep hearing Kirkland's voice in my head. Your father finally got what he wanted. He ruined my victory with Zeus and has everyone in Newmarket and all of Suffolk, no doubt, gossiping about whether I did or didn't start the fire."

"I'm sorry."

"Don't you dare apologize for what he did," he bellowed and grimaced. "Forgive me. I'm just frustrated and angry that your father hates me so much that he would do this. Making threats is bad enough, but to act on them and purposely try to ruin my life is beyond reprehensible."

"I agree. How do we make it right?"

"We find the rumormonger. Or rather, Kirkland does. He shouldn't have too much trouble locating a former stable boy who recently came into coin." Samuel walked to the door. "I'll be back soon. Actually, meet me outside the inn doors in thirty minutes. I want to go to Ramsbury Ridge Farm and find out from Ramsbury how bad the gossip is."

"What about breakfast?"

"I can't eat now," he said as he went out the door.

She didn't think she could eat either, but a cup of tea would be nice. Just then, Penny entered through the adjoining door with a tray. Clarice asked, "Is Letitia up?"

"Yes, my lady. She'll be right in to join you now that His Grace has left."

"I'm here," Letitia said as she swept into the room, already groomed and dressed for the day. "What is happening?"

Clarice told her everything.

"I can't believe Portsmouth did this. I knew something was off with him when he called on me."

"Sometimes he hides it well. For most of my life, actually. At least until I turned eighteen." She sat down at the dressing table. "Penny, will you please do my hair?"

"Yes, my lady."

While Penny brushed and styled her hair, she said to Letitia, "I'm going with Samuel to Ramsbury Ridge Farm. He wants to speak to the baron. We are both hoping Kirkland finds this former stable boy. And if he was in fact working at Stanton Hall at the time, he would be a grown man now. My father, no doubt, bribed the first likely person he came across, knowing it didn't matter if he was at Stanton Hall or not. Once the rumor was spoken, it would spread like a forest fire. Samuel is already being talked about after winning the race yesterday. And today, his competition on the racing circuit will be all too happy to see him fall from grace."

"Is there anything I can do?"

"Can you send word to Greyson and Hunter and ask them to

come to Ramsbury Ridge Farm? I have a feeling Samuel will be keeping a low profile until he can clear this up. Even if he gets the person to recant what they said, the damage will be done. But still, it's better than doing nothing."

"I can do that."

"Thank you," she said as she hugged Letitia. "I'm meeting Samuel outside the inn. I'll see you later."

"Be careful."

"Thank you. You too."

Clarice entered the quiet corridor and made her way to the inn's main entrance, keeping her head down and listening for Samuel's name.

"Lady Chesterfield."

Her feet came to a halt as she looked up to see Lord and Lady Kendall, their faces worried. "We heard the rumors about Stanton," Lady Kendall said with a tense frown. "So your father went through with his threats? The blackguard. I'll see him ruined if it's the last thing I do."

"Thank you."

"Is there anything we can do?" Lord Kendall asked.

"If you see my father, send word to me at Ramsbury Ridge Farms. I'll be with Stanton."

"We will. Tell His Grace that he can count on our support," Lady Kendall added.

"Thank you. I will. I must go."

Clarice hurried outside and found Samuel standing by a hackney. "Kirkland is otherwise occupied, so we're traveling in this." He opened the door and assisted her inside, then he joined her on the bench.

"What did Kirkland say?"

He said he would tear apart every stable and mews until he finds the stable hand. He said it wouldn't be too hard. Other servants will not appreciate one of their own suddenly having money to spend. Or at least more money than they earn. More likely, he's bragging about how he got the funds, and all he had to do was tell a lie.

"Yes. Most likely."

They arrived at the farm and found Ramsbury and Anna in the breakfast room having their morning meal. Both looked up with concern when they entered.

"Help yourself to breakfast. There's plenty," Anna said. "And strong coffee, just the way you like it, Samuel."

"Thank you."

She and Samuel filled their plates with food from the sideboard and sat next to each other, joining the baron and baroness at the table. A footman poured Samuel a cup of coffee and Clarice a cup of tea.

"Now that you're settled," Ramsbury said, his brows furrowed, "we heard. A new stable hand I recently hired told me and was quite vocal about wanting to throw you out before you burn Ramsbury Ridge Farms to the ground."

Clarice reached over and squeezed Samuel's hand.

"Don't worry, I relieved him of his duties and sent him on his way. No one in this household believes this nonsense, and if they do, they will also find themselves packing their things."

"I don't want to cause you any trouble," Samuel said, his voice cracking with emotion.

"You aren't. I pride myself on hiring good people who don't listen to gossip."

"Everyone talks about gossip at some point," Clarice said.

"I stand corrected. Listening to gossip and believing it are two different things," Ramsbury added.

"Clover races in five days. What am I going to do if things don't settle down?"

"You act as if nothing happened," Ramsbury said. "You have nothing to hide, so you have nothing to worry about."

Samuel went on to explain Kirkland's search for the stable hand who leaked the gossip. Clarice told them that Lord and Lady Kendall would send word if they saw her father.

"Oh, I forgot to tell you, Samuel," she said. "Lady Rutherford asked if there was anything she could do. I hope you don't mind, but I asked her to get word to Greyson and Hunter, and have all three of them meet us here."

"Thank you. Seeing Greyson and Hunter will make me feel better. I hope Tobias and Albert don't buy into the gossip and quit, leaving me high and dry for the rest of the racing season."

Ramsbury chuckled. "Forgive me for laughing. Tobias and Albert would be insane to leave your employment after Zeus won yesterday. One doesn't leave a winning horse and its owner for gossip."

Samuel leaned back in his chair, cradling his cup of coffee in his hands and sighed. "I think the only thing I can do is spend time getting Clover ready and stay away from any members of the *ton*." He paused, taking a sip of his coffee. "Do you think The Jockey Club will revoke my membership? They pride themselves on the pristine reputations of their members."

Ramsbury looked thoughtful, then shook his head. "I can't say. But they would be fools to believe a stable hand over a duke."

Samuel shrugged his shoulders. "I can only hope. If they cancel my membership, I'll get a letter today. Meanwhile, I'm going to see Clover. Tobias and Albert should be with her in the paddocks. No better time than now to find out what they have to say. And Zeus, well, that boy deserves some carrots."

"I'll accompany you," Ramsbury said.

"Lady Clarice," the baroness spoke up. "Would you care to join me in the drawing room? We can find something to pass the time while we wait for Lady Rutherford, Viscount Greyson, and Mr. Hunter."

"I would like that very much."

Samuel and Ramsbury left, and Clarice found herself in a pretty burgundy drawing room, sitting on a chair facing Anna, who was sitting on a settee with an embroidery hoop on her lap. "Do you mind if I work on this?"

"Not at all. I'm happy to sit and wile away the time pretending nothing is amiss."

"This must be difficult on you, knowing your father is responsible for what is being said about Samuel."

"It is. Except he warned both of us it was coming. We didn't think he would go through with it, though. And if he did, Samuel believed it was better than granting him what he wanted."

"Forgive me for prying, but what does your father want?"

"I assumed you knew. That perhaps Samuel told Ramsbury. Anyway, he wants to keep us apart and force me to marry a man of his choosing . . . again."

"Does he realize he doesn't have that type of control over you anymore?"

Clarice found herself laughing. "Yes. He chooses to ignore it. There is more to the story of why he hates Samuel and forced me to marry Chesterfield instead of him seven years ago. But I'm not at liberty to say."

"I can't imagine my father forcing me to marry anyone other than Ramsbury. You must have been truly devastated when this happened."

"I was. I'm glad it's all behind me now. And no matter what my father tries to do now, Samuel and I will prevail and get married."

"Ramsbury and I will help you in any way we can."

"Thank you."

A footman entered and announced, "Lady Rutherford to see you, my lady."

"Thank you," Anna said.

Letitia entered the room and said, "Baroness, I hope you don't mind the intrusion. I just had to come with Greyson and Hunter, who have joined Stanton and your husband at the stables."

"Not at all. Please sit," Anna said, and Letitia sat on the settee with Anna. "Clarice explained what was going on and said you'd be coming."

Letitia looked at Clarice and sighed in relief. "Oh, good. Have you heard anything new?"

"No," she said as she clasped her hands together on her lap. "Hopefully, Kirkland will have word soon. Until then, I'm going crazy with worry. I just can't understand why my father can't let it go. He already got his revenge once." She had a terrible feeling that her father would forever, until the day he died, cause strife in her and Samuel's life.

CHAPTER TWENTY-FOUR

Ramsbury and Samuel examined every horse in both stables. Mr. Harrington, the lead stable hand, explained that he had heard something outside the night before. Since he slept in the main stable where Ramsbury kept his horses and thoroughbreds, it was cause for vigilance.

"Nothing seems disturbed inside or out," Ramsbury said as they walked the perimeter of both buildings, inspecting the dirt.

"I know," Samuel replied. "There are footprints all over the place, but they could belong to anyone. With Zeus and Thunder racing yesterday, trainers, handlers, jockeys, and stable hands were all over this area."

"In addition to extra stable hands, I'll have several footmen watching tonight as well. If someone was snooping around, they might come back."

"Good idea," Samuel said as Greyson and Hunter approached.

Greyson spoke first, "Stanton, Lady Rutherford told us what happened, although we heard people talking about it at the Red Lion Inn. Anyone would be crazy to believe such nonsense." He nodded to the baron. "Nice to see you, Ramsbury."

"You, as well, Greyson," Ramsbury said.

"Stanton, Ramsbury," Hunter greeted them. "Have you heard anything from Kirkland or from the blackguard, Portsmouth?"

Samuel shook his head. "No. Nothing. I would've thought Portsmouth would want to gloat in my face."

"How's Lady Chesterfield taking it?" Greyson asked.

"She's shocked and angry at her father. I wouldn't want to be him when she catches up to him," Samuel said.

Ramsbury said, "We should join the ladies in the drawing room. There's nothing else we can do but wait."

The rest of the day went by slower than slow, and Samuel thought he might lose his mind from boredom and worry. When afternoon tea concluded, Greyson, Hunter, and Lady Rutherford traveled back to the Red Lion Inn, promising to look for Kirkland and send word with any news.

Dinner was a somber affair. He noticed Clarice had very little appetite, as did he. Right after finishing eating, Clarice made it clear she was not leaving him until they had some answers, and they retired to his room. Anna kindly lent her a night rail, a robe, a chemise, and a day dress for the morning, as they were of similar size and height. Samuel appreciated how understanding Ramsbury and Anna were being about their unusual situation. He could never thank them enough for making Clarice feel welcome.

Samuel requested that a fire be lit in the room, since a chill had settled in the air or perhaps in his bones. He occupied one of the tufted chairs facing the hearth and pulled his robe tighter around his chest. Clarice, dressed in her night clothes, had a blanket on her lap and sat in the other chair.

"Is it just me, or is it cold?" he asked.

"It's chilly," she replied as she adjusted her blanket. "Do you want a blanket?"

"No. As soon as the fire warms me, I'm going to bed." He sighed, letting his head fall back against the chair. "I'm fatigued. My body aches, and my mind hurts from thinking all day. I'm worried about Kirkland. We've heard nothing."

She reached between the two chairs and rested her hand on his arm. "I'm exhausted, and I did nothing today. Worrying does take a toll on you. Let's hope we receive word from Kirkland tomorrow."

"Yes. Let's hope." He took her hand off his arm and held it. "Ready for bed?"

"Yes, but my legs are so tired I don't think I can make it that far."

Samuel, for the first time that day, felt a brief lightness in his chest, and he smiled. "I can carry you."

By now, she was standing. "I can make it."

They both discarded their robes and slipped under the coverlet. He lay on his back, one arm around Clarice, holding her close. Her head and hand rested on his chest, and one of her legs covered one of his, causing his body to awaken with desire. After the day they'd had, he was shocked.

The hand on his chest moved lower down, and lower still until she cupped him and he moaned. "Clarice, you little devil." He laughed, then gasped when she wrapped her soft hand partly around his hard manhood and slid it up and down, gently at first, then harder and faster.

"Let me give you pleasure." She removed her hand and slithered down his body. All the air in his lungs deserted him.

"What are you doing?" he croaked.

Her warm lips against his lower abdomen curved into a smile. "Come now, Samuel, use your imagination."

"Christ," Samuel's body arched when she took him into her hot mouth. Then he forced himself to relax and enjoy Clarice's mouth on him. One of her hands squeezed his bollocks. "Bloody hell, Clarice, I'm going to . . . Clarice . . ." he moaned. She didn't stop, and he spilled his seed into her luscious mouth.

She moved up his body and kissed him deeply. Then she returned to her original position and whispered, "Go to sleep, my love."

"But . . ."

She kissed his chest. "Sleep. You always put my needs before yours. Now I'm returning the favor. Sleep. I promise tomorrow will be a better day."

"Thank you. I love you."

Samuel preferred Clarice to fall asleep before him, but he could no longer keep his eyes open. The pleasure she had given him melted every muscle and tendon in his body, and sleep pulled him in.

What seemed like a moment later, Samuel yelled, "What?" hearing what he thought was someone pounding on the door. Now that he was wide awake, he realized the sound wasn't knocking; it was crackling and popping. The smell of smoke hung heavy in the room. He extricated himself from Clarice, jumped out of bed, threw on his robe, and looked at the hearth—only ash and coals remained.

"Oh, God." Fire, the house was on fire. "Clarice, wake up. There's a fire."

She sat up, rubbing her eyes. "Did you say fire?"

"Yes. Get up!"

He handed her her robe and took her hand. "Whatever you do, don't let go."

Pausing at the door, Samuel felt the wood. Warm, but not hot. He opened it a crack, then wider, making sure they weren't walking into flames. No flames that he could see, just smoke everywhere. As they headed toward the main stairs, they bumped into Ramsbury and Anna crawling on the ground.

"We need to alert the servants," Samuel bellowed.

"Already did. The servants' stairs were clear, they all got out. We were coming for you. We can't go down the main staircase," Ramsbury yelled. "We need to go down the servants' staircase at the end of the east wing hall. Let's hope the fire hasn't spread there by now. Come, it's back this way. Stay low so you can see and breathe."

Samuel, knowing he was wearing undergarments beneath his robe, removed it and tossed it aside. When he saw Clarice crawling before him, struggling, he yelled, "Pull the fabric up to your waist so you can move faster."

She complied, and before long, they reached the servants' stairs at the end of the hall. The stairs ran along the outside wall of the house, and Samuel prayed they were still clear of flames.

Nausea washed over him. Had his parents and brother tried fighting their way out of Stanton Hall only to be met with flames and smoke at every turn? Did they know they were going to die? Did they burn to death, feeling every excruciating lick of the flames?

"Samuel, Samuel," Clarice was yelling at him. "Hurry."

He hopped to his feet and followed her onto the servants' stairs. The smoke was thick and stung his eyes. He used his hands to feel for the walls, praying that Ramsbury, Anna, and Clarice were still ahead of him. He tried to hold his breath, but when he felt his eyes bulging, he instinctively opened his mouth and inhaled a lungful of smoke-filled air, which made him cough. Still, he continued feeling his way down the stairs. Two flights. They were only up two flights. The smoke cleared. He saw darkness and fell outside the door, inhaling a lungful of clear air.

Ramsbury and Anna stood, holding each other as they cried, their eyes never leaving the ghastly scene of the east wing burning. Every available hand was throwing water where the east wing met the main house. The outside was stone; only the inside would burn, but they had to keep the fire from spreading.

He got up with Clarice's help. They moved next to Ramsbury and Anna. Tears ran down his face as he mumbled, "I'm sorry."

Clarice held him tightly and whispered into his ear. "Do you think my father . . .?"

"No." But as he said the word, he wondered. His parents and brother died in a fire. He never once thought it was set intentionally. Never suspected Portsmouth of having anything to do with it. But now, his mind screamed and wouldn't be ignored.

"Did everyone get out?" Ramsbury yelled to the butler.

"Yes, my lord."

"Thank God." He turned to Samuel, "We need to water down the stables. We can't have any flying embers igniting them, and we need to get the horses to the paddock for safety."

"Already moving," Samuel said as he and Ramsbury hurried off. Anna and Clarice followed close behind.

Approaching the main stable, they saw stable hands wetting down the barns, and all the horses were already in the paddocks. Mr. Harrington, the head of the stables, approached them, escorting a boy, perhaps sixteen or seventeen. "Baron, I found this trespasser trying to torch the stables." He shoved the boy to his knees. Mr. Harrington had tied his hands behind his back.

"Send for the constable."

"Yes, my lord."

Ramsbury moved until he stood right in front of the boy. "Who hired you? And don't lie to me, boy, because you had no reason to burn my life down."

"N-n-no one."

He grabbed a fistful of his hair and forced the boy to look at him. "I said, don't lie to me. You're going to pay for your crimes. Don't you want the person who hired you to pay for his? I'll say it again. Who hired you?"

The boy broke down and sobbed. "My ma's sick. My pa's dead. It's just me and my ma. I needed the coin."

"If you tell me, I guarantee you that your ma will be taken care of." Ramsbury pulled his head up again. "So what will it be? Confess or lie?"

"The same lord who paid me to spread the gossip about the duke. He told me what side of the house to burn."

Samuel heard Clarice gasp beside him. He entwined his hand with hers and squeezed, hoping to give her strength to face the truth.

"I only know his name because I overheard someone call him. It's Port something. That's all I know."

"Portsmouth," Samuel spat out.

"That's it," the boy hissed.

Ramsbury said, "I'm going to lock him inside one of the stalls and have someone watch over him. We need to talk to the constable."

Clarice approached Anna and took her hand to offer support. "I'm so sorry for what my father did."

Anna took a deep breath and cleared her throat. "You had nothing to do with it. Your father did."

Samuel approached Anna and Clarice, both shivering in their nightclothes. He knew how they felt—he was chilled to the bone, not only because he wore nothing but underclothes but also from the realization that Portsmouth was responsible. The more he thought about it, the more convinced he was that the man had also killed his family. He may not have been the one to hold the torch that had ignited that fire, but he was growing more and more certain that he'd hired them. It was too much of a coincidence. He'd failed to kill him with his family, so he'd tried again. Oh, dear God, what kind of person would risk killing others to reach the one he wanted? What about his own daughter? Had she ever meant anything to him?

If Samuel had had any substantial amount of food in his stomach, he knew it would have come up. "Come, let's get you ladies to the house. It may be smoky and smell of burning wood, but there must be a room in the west wing that we can go to and be safe."

"There is a small salon there," Anna said. "There's a door at the beginning of the wing. We can enter there."

"With any luck, the kitchen is not in danger of fire, and the cook can prepare a tray with hot coffee and tea while we wait for the constable's arrival," Samuel remarked.

Anna followed Samuel and Clarice through the door she mentioned. All three of them paused and looked down a long hall, which eventually opened into the main entry, trying to see any damage or any sign of fire. Smoke hung in the air. Samuel would be alert in case the fire spread. "Which door?"

"Second on the right."

The room was shut, so when they entered, it was smoke-free and had only a slight smell. Or that could just be the soot and smoke stuck in his nasal passages.

"If you see or hear any sign of fire, get out. I'll be back as soon as I can." He left them on the sofa together, wrapped in a throw he found. He picked up a discarded shawl and draped it across his shoulders to cover his chest. He carefully made his way down the long corridor to the main entry. He didn't dare to go down the corridor to the entrance to the east wing. But so far, he hadn't come across any fire damage. Instead, he made his way to the back of the house to the kitchen. The cook and several kitchen maids were already preparing the morning meal, heating water, and steaming coffee as if nothing was amiss, though a bit early to be sure. When Mrs. Mather saw him, she clutched her chest and gasped. "Your Grace. Thank Christ you all escaped the fire unharmed. What can I get you?"

"Forgive my appearance. Could you prepare a tray? We are expecting the constable."

She bobbed a curtsy. "Yes, Your Grace."

"Deliver it to the salon in the west wing. But mind you, the fire is still smoldering in the east wing. Be safe and aware. Get out if you see any sign the fire is spreading this way."

"Yes, Your Grace."

Samuel, clutching the shawl, hurried from the kitchen and rushed to the salon. He laughed when he thought about the look Mrs. Mather gave him when she saw his lack of clothing and the green and pink shawl he used to try and hide what he could.

Entering the salon, he found Ramsbury, who wore clean breeches and a shirt—but by the baggy fit, definitely not his—comforting Anna on the settee. Clarice had moved to a chair, and he sank down in the one next to her and looked at Ramsbury. "I don't suppose you and Anna had clothing in any other rooms in the house besides the east wing?"

Ramsbury managed a brief grin. "I already sent my valet and Anna's maid to the attic where we store our out-of-season clothing. And of course you must both borrow whatever you need."

"Thank you," Clarice said, still shivering.

"Did the boy confess anything else?" he asked.

"Just what he told us the first time. Oh, but yes. There's one more thing. When Portsmouth approached him at the Pheasant Inn stables, where the boy works, about setting the fire, he recognized Kirkland, hit him over the head, tied him up, and left him locked inside an empty horse stall. I sent one of the footmen to free him, take him to the Red Lion Inn, and have them tend to his injuries and ensure his safety."

Well, that explained why they had never heard from Kirkland. He hoped the man hadn't sustained a head injury.

Samuel looked over at Clarice. He was worried about how quiet she was, listening to them talk about her father and what he had done as though she weren't in the room.

"My lord," Ramsbury's valet said as he entered the room and bowed. "Chambers in the west wing have been prepared for you and the baroness and another for His Grace and one for Lady Chesterfield. Clothing has been laid out."

"Thank you, Hennesey. We should make ourselves presentable for when the constable arrives."

Samuel and Clarice followed Ramsbury and Anna, who followed Hennesey as he led them past the salon they had been in earlier and down the hall to the prepared rooms. Clarice's room was across the hall from Samuel's. When she opened it, he was surprised to see a maid waiting to assist her. "I'll be right across the hall. I'll knock when I'm ready."

Instead of speaking, she nodded her head, her eyes resembling those of a lost puppy. He fought back the guilt trying to swallow him. He entered his room and found Wallace waiting for him. Thankfully he had been sleeping in the servants' quarters on the top floor of the main part of the house.

"There is hot water, soap, and linens to wash with, Your Grace."

Samuel dropped the shawl he still had wrapped around himself and began to wash away the ash and smoky smell from the fire.

"The baron is not as tall as you are, I'm afraid, so the breeches, waistcoat, and jacket might be a bit short. The good news is, you have the same shoe size, and I found boots for you."

"I don't care, Wallace. I just need something to wear." He paused, then hurried on. "I also want to ask you something about the night Stanton Hall burned down. Did you hear or see anything out of the ordinary? Or did anyone else who was also in the house and survived?"

Wallace frowned. "No. Not that I remember. It was very windy that night, thunder and lightning, but no rain. Everyone believed the house had been struck by lightning. And with the wind, it spread so fast. If I had been in your chambers instead of the kitchen having a drink because I couldn't sleep, I'd be dead."

"Christ, Wallace," Samuel moaned. "I'm glad you couldn't sleep."

Dressed in respectable clothing, he exited the room and knocked on Clarice's door. It opened, and she slipped out wearing a pretty yellow day dress with matching slippers. Her hair was combed and styled into a neat chignon.

"How are you feeling?" he asked as he took her hand and they started walking.

"Better. I smell better, and my skin isn't tinged with ash and soot."

"You don't need to be there when Ramsbury and I talk to the constable."

"I understand that. But I have to," Clarice said, exhaling.

"You must be exhausted after the ordeal, and the sun still hasn't even properly risen."

"I'm not so much as exhausted as anxious to get this visit with the constable over with," she said, and Samuel understood the feeling.

CHAPTER TWENTY-FIVE

A S THEY APPROACHED the open door to the small salon, Clarice heard several voices coming from inside. Her whole body trembled, and she fought back the sudden sick feeling in her stomach. She needed to be brave. She needed to be strong. As much as she wanted to run away and hide from guilt and embarrassment for what her father had done, she would not. Ramsbury and Anna had nearly lost everything because of her father. Also because of her. If she hadn't come to Newmarket, none of this would be happening.

She had brought all this on them, and she didn't know how to make it right. Even if her father was arrested for this, he probably wouldn't receive any punishment whatsoever because of his title.

"Is everything all right?" Samuel asked as she stood outside the door. Samuel. Poor Samuel, who must also be battling guilt right now. Blaming himself, thinking that if he weren't staying here, Ramsbury and Anna's home wouldn't have been the target of a vengeful earl.

"It will be, in time." She forced one foot forward, then the other, until she found herself being introduced to Constable Everett. Once everyone was seated around Ramsbury and Anna on the settee, Ramsbury recounted the events of the night.

"I see," Constable Everett said. "I sent my deputy to the stables to fetch the boy and put him in my coach, then guard him.

I'll question him on the way back to town, make sure he agrees to name the Earl of Portsmouth as the one who hired him."

Samuel said, "I have a theory. A hunch, really, but the coincidence is too much to ignore."

He talked about the night Stanton Hall burned down, killing his family. Clarice's chest hurt so much she found it painful to breathe as she listened to Samuel, his voice sounding sad and strained as he expressed his thoughts. She'd never even considered that the fire that night could have been set. Oh God, had her father committed murder against his one-time best friend, his wife, and heir? She wiped her itchy cheeks with her fingers and was shocked to find her fingers wet from her tears.

Finally, Constable Everett stood and said, "I'll be on my way. I will send word in several hours after I have interrogated the lad. I will also send a letter to the Constable in Southampton, requesting that he do some digging into the burning of Stanton Hall."

After the constable took his leave, Ramsbury and Anna stood holding hands. "We're going to try and get some sleep. You two might want to do the same. I have footmen watching the outside of the house, so it should be safe to get some rest," Ramsbury said right before he and Anna made their exit.

After the baron and baroness left, Clarice turned to Samuel. "I think that exhaustion you mentioned has finally set in. Can we go to your room and try to get some rest?"

They entered the room Samuel was using, undressed, climbed under the coverlet, and fell fast asleep in each other's arms.

After they were rested, and in the days following the fire, there was much to be done. The friends of Ramsbury and Anna, along with Samuel's friends, Greyson and Hunter, came and assisted with cleaning up after the fire in any way they could. The parts of the house not damaged by the flames were scrubbed, cleaned, and aired out.

All the while, Clarice waited anxiously for word on her father.

Then the morning of the fourth day after the fire, while she and Samuel were having breakfast in the breakfast room alone, a footman entered and announced, "Constable Everett."

"Forgive me for stopping by unannounced and so early in the morning," the constable said as he bowed. "But I didn't want you to hear this from anyone other than me."

Samuel indicated a vacant chair. "Would you care to join us?"

"Thank you, Your Grace, but I must decline as I'm needed elsewhere as soon as I leave here."

"Then we won't keep you. Please tell us what news you have to share." Clarice said, feeling jittery all of a sudden.

"I'm sorry to have to tell you this, Lady Chesterfield, but your father has fled to France."

She gasped and covered her mouth in shock. She knew her father had many flaws, but she didn't think being a coward was one of them. And his fleeing to France was as good as him admitting his guilt in the deaths of Samuel's family and several servants. She tried to feel sad, happy, or anything, but when it came to the man who fathered her, she felt nothing at all.

"Thank you for coming and telling us," Samuel said, which was good because she didn't know what to say to the constable at all.

"I'm sorry for the bad news," the constable said. "I bid you good day." He turned on his heels and left, escorted by the footman.

When he was gone and they were once again alone, Samuel, apparently determined to change the subject, said, "Do you realize that the 1000 Guineas Stakes is tomorrow?"

"Yes. With everything that's happened, I'm surprised you remembered." She paused and took a sip of her tea. "There must be a ball tonight. Why haven't you mentioned it?"

"I didn't think you'd want to go."

"You thought correctly. Do you think we can go to the Red Lion Inn for my belongings? Anna must be tired of me wearing her old clothing when I have a perfectly good wardrobe full at the inn."

"We can do that, but first, I need to talk to Clover. She's probably nervous about the race tomorrow. This is her first real race."

Laughter escaped her as she asked, "You mean you are nervous?"

"As hell. Is it conceited of me to admit that I want to win again?"

"Not at all."

⸭

THE DAY OF the 1000 Guineas Stakes was upon them, and Clarice, once again, was sitting in Hunter's open-air barouche. Greyson, Lady Aurora, Lady Anastasia, and Letitia sat in Greyson's barouche. The crowd was larger than for the 2000 Guineas Stakes race, and she was just as nervous.

"There he is!" Greyson pointed. "Stanton, over here!" he yelled.

Clarice saw the moment Greyson called Samuel's name; the intense look on his face relaxed as he hurried toward them. "Perfect spot again," he said as he hopped into Hunter's carriage, curling his hand around hers. "I wish I could kiss you. But this will have to do." He raised her hand, turned her wrist over, and gently, sensuously, touched his lips to the pulse point where her short gloves met her wrist. Her blood hummed through her veins, fast and hot.

"Mmmm," she sighed. "That was nice."

"You two do realize you're not alone in this carriage? And that everyone who cares to look can see you two love birds steaming up the air."

Samuel burst out laughing. "Find yourself your own lady."

Now Hunter laughed. "I'm trying. She's being mighty stubborn."

"Oh my," Clarice said as she looked at him. "Who is it? I need to know."

The man blushed. "When I manage to convince her I'm the only gentleman for her, I'll let you know."

"I hope it's soon."

He huffed, "Me too."

"Bloody hell," Samuel barked out. "The race has started." He stood up and looked at the course. Clarice stood and, just like the last race, she felt and heard the thunder of horses' hooves before she saw them.

"Is that—?" Hunter yelled.

"It is," Samuel replied excitedly.

Clover led by a length and won the race easily. What were the chances that Samuel's Zeus and Clover would both win their first race? And as an owner, that he would have won his first two as well? Maybe their luck in everything was changing.

THE DAY AFTER Clover won the 1000 Guineas Stakes, as Samuel promised, the special license arrived via a footman. It had taken longer than expected, and he was beginning to panic, but it had finally arrived. Of course, with Portsmouth fleeing to France, like a coward, they could wait, post the banns and have a large church wedding and celebration if they wanted, but he was ready.

Standing in Clarice's room at the inn, he held up the parchment, worth far more than its weight in gold. "Last chance to change your mind and have the banns posted."

"Samuel," Clarice said as she approached from behind, wrapping her arms around his waist and resting her cheek on his back. "I don't want to wait even a day, much less four Sundays."

"Thank Christ, you haven't changed your mind." He turned around, cupped her cheeks, and kissed her deeply. "Will you make me the luckiest man alive and agree to marry me today?"

"Yes." She beamed, with all the love she had for him revealed on her beautiful face. "Can we go now? I have some ideas for tonight."

"You little devil, you." He chuckled.

She rested her head on his heart. "I'm serious, Samuel. I don't want to wait. What I want more than anything is for you and me to leave this inn right this minute, walk down the street hand in hand to the little white church at the end near the grove of trees, and say our vows with the vicar and his wife as witnesses. Swear our love and devotion to each other before God."

"What about our friends?"

"We will celebrate with them tomorrow. Let us make today about us and us alone. We have waited so long for this. Do you mind?"

"Do I mind?" he smiled, stroking her back. "Marrying you and becoming your husband today is everything I've ever wanted, and I'm so honored that you have chosen me."

⤞⤝

WITH HER HEAD resting on Samuel's chest, his heart pounding fast and steady, tears of joy rained down her cheeks, and her lips curved up into a smile. Today was the day she would marry the boy she'd once loved, who'd turned into the man she still loved with everything she had inside her.

He stepped back. "Do you need a minute to prepare?"

"I wore my prettiest and favorite day dress today, hoping for just this event. All I need is my bonnet, and we may go." She picked the bonnet up off the bed and placed it on her head, tying the ribbon beneath her chin. She held her hand out. "I'm ready."

They exited the room and the inn, surprisingly without seeing any of their friends, and walked hand in hand in the glorious sunshine down the street to the adorable, white-washed stone church, where, to her shock, the vicar and his wife greeted them at the doorway with smiles. "They were expecting us."

"Of course, my love."

"Welcome, Your Grace, Lady Chesterfield. I'm the vicar, Mr. Smythe, and this is my wife, Mrs. Smythe," the vicar said as he stepped aside. "Please come in. Everything is prepared. And may I say how honored I am to perform your marriage ceremony."

Once she stepped inside, Clarice's eyes widened. "Ohhh, the flowers, the altar, it is just as I imagined in my dreams."

"His Grace saw to it all," Mrs. Smythe said with pride.

"Samuel." She squeezed his hand. "It is like a fairytale. Thank you."

"Shall we proceed?" Mr. Smythe said. "Your Grace, please come with me to the altar. My wife will take care of Lady Chesterfield."

Clarice watched as Samuel, dressed in black riding clothes but looking more handsome than she'd ever seen him, walked up the short aisle to the altar overflowing with white flowers of every variety imaginable. And the scent in the air was divine.

"Let us step outside the doors, my lady. You should make an entrance," said Mrs. Smythe.

Once standing on the outside steps, Mrs. Smythe closed the double doors. "Oh, I forgot, these are for you." She handed Clarice a small bouquet of white roses, and she buried her face in them and inhaled the delicate scent. "His Grace thought of everything."

There were so many emotions hitting Clarice at once that tears pooled in her eyes. It all seemed like a dream, and she was afraid she would wake up at any moment and be alone.

"When I open the doors, I want you to slowly walk down the aisle and join hands with His Grace and face each other."

The doors swung open, and beautiful violin music drifted from a solo violinist. This time, tears streamed down her cheeks, her heart overflowing with love for her soon-to-be husband.

When she reached a smiling Samuel, who had tears in his eyes, they joined hands, and the vicar, with Mrs. Smythe by his side, married them.

"Congratulations, Your Graces, you are now married under God and in front of witnesses. May you have a long and fruitful life." He waved his arm out as if the church were full of people. "Let us welcome the Duke and Duchess of Stanton."

The door burst open, and their friends, Greyson, his sisters, Letitia, Hunter, Baron and Baroness Ramsbury, and Lord and Lady Kendall, all gathered in the church around them, wishing them well.

"Thank you, my husband. You made this day perfect. I love you."

"You have made my life perfect. I love you more, my beautiful duchess."

CHAPTER TWENTY-SIX

Five Months Later

"Are you ready, my love?"

"I believe I am," Clarice replied, leaning into Samuel's body for warmth, as autumn was upon them. And today, with the wind whipping, it was especially bone-chilling.

Clarice was ready to meet her son the day he was born. Now that she was close to seeing him—the son she had given birth to and thought she'd never see again—nerves and panic swirled inside her. It had taken months for the Bow Street Runner to track down the servants who had delivered her baby. Both women had changed their names to hide from her fury, knowing it was only a matter of time before she found them. At first, they'd refused to reveal their true identities, pretending they knew nothing of the Marquess and Marchioness of Chesterfield or any baby born on the wrong side of the blanket.

The Runner had made them see that if they were wise, they would also fear the Duke of Stanton. A duke of the realm was not someone you wanted to deceive. The women had finally admitted where their son was.

Over the past month, Clarice had been exchanging letters with her son's mother, Mrs. St. George. The son she never knew was named Reginald after his father, a local vicar in Northumberland.

Mrs. St. George had been cautious when she received

Clarice's letter, and she wasn't afraid to say so. Clarice still didn't know her well, other than through her letters, but she admired the woman. She had been unable to conceive. Mr. St. George was originally at a vicarage just outside London when Mrs. Fitzhugh brought Reginald to them—Mrs. St. George and Mrs. Fitzhugh were cousins. Chesterfield had apparently ordered her to kill the baby and toss him into the Thames. But though Mrs. Fitzhugh was an unkind woman, she was not a baby killer, so she brought the baby to her cousin, knowing she would take good care of him.

The vicar and Mrs. St. George, fearing Chesterfield, fled to the north, where the vicar was fortunate and received his own vicarage, as the previous vicar had recently succumbed to old age. It had been six years, and in that time she'd adopted two other children—a girl and a boy, Reginald's younger brother and sister. And Mrs. St. George assured Clarice in her letters that Reginald was an intelligent, smart, and kind boy.

Thinking about all this, Clarice wiped tears from her eyes with her gloved fingers. "You are so handsome, Samuel. I hope Reginald resembles you."

Chuckling filled the carriage. "Whether he does or not, I'm sure he is a handsome boy. And from reading Mrs. St. George's letters, he is a good boy and they love him and have provided for him, his every need." He paused, moved the curtain aside, and stared out the window. "We're coming into a small town. The vicarage should be nearby. I see an inn up ahead." He rapped the roof, and the carriage stopped. "I'll see about securing rooms for a few days."

Samuel disappeared and returned less than ten minutes later. "We have rooms listed under our last name of Radcliff. I'd rather no one know the Duke and Duchess of Stanton are in town until we know if the St. Georges plan to tell Reginald who we are."

"From what I gathered from Mrs. St. George's letters, they will tell Reginald when he is ten and can understand the circumstances of his birth," Clarice said.

"Regardless, during our time here, I need to speak with Mr. St. George to agree on the stipend amount to be sent to him monthly from my bank. Also, I want to inform him of a trust that has been set up, from which Reginald will begin receiving a portion upon turning twenty-one. I also want him to know that we will cover all his educational costs."

"Samuel, there will be time to discuss all of that. We don't want to insult the man, thinking he can't provide for his son. We should be thankful that we are finally getting to meet our child. And the time will come when we can acknowledge him, but we need to be patient and not compromise the wonderful job the St. Georges are doing raising Reginald. We will be introduced as friends from London for the time being."

Sighing, Samuel said, "I don't care who or what we are. I just want to see my son and know he is being cared for and is happy. I would never tear his young heart out and security apart by telling him the truth at his young age." He knocked on the roof and the carriage started going.

A short time later, the carriage came to a stop and Samuel said with a strained voice, "We're here." One of Stanton's footmen opened the door and flipped down the stairs. Samuel exited, leaned back in, and held out his hand to assist Clarice. When she exited and stood beside the coach, she swayed. As always, her husband steadied her by wrapping his arm around her back. Clarice's hand went immediately to her increasing stomach as the baby moved around. A little Stanton baby was due in roughly four months, and they were both elated.

"Mr. and Mrs. Radcliff." Mrs. St. George, a woman around forty, hurried over to them with Mr. St. George, two boys, and a girl following. Clarice couldn't take her eyes off the oldest boy, who did resemble Samuel. Blinking back tears, she forced herself to look away.

"Mrs. St. George, Mr. St. George," she said, briefly grasping Mrs. St. George's hands and meeting her kind, compassionate eyes. "It's so very good to see you both again. It's been too long."

Clarice went along with what the St. Georges had told their children. They needed to pretend they knew one another.

"Yes, it has," Samuel said as he stepped forward and shook Mr. St. George's hand. "And who are these fine children?"

Mrs. St. George's eyes shone with pride. The pride of a mother. "This is our eldest, Reginald, he's six. Richard is five, and Penelope, four."

Samuel held out his hand and shook each boy's hand, then bowed to Penelope, who giggled. "It is very nice to meet you. Your parents speak highly of you."

Clarice turned her back and quickly wiped away her tears from seeing Samuel shake his son's hand, before she pivoted and addressed the children. "I'm pleased to meet such well-behaved children." She curtsied, and little Penelope copied her while still giggling.

"Where are my manners?" Mrs. St. George said. "You must be tired from your long journey. Please come in. I had the cook prepare luncheon, hoping you'd arrive soon."

"Thank you. I hope it's not an imposition. We have taken rooms in town," Clarice said as they entered the square house built with cream-colored stone. It was larger inside than she had originally believed, comfortable and clean. The smells coming from the small kitchen she could see at the back of the house smelled divine. A nice place for Reginald to grow up in.

"No imposition at all." She pointed to a long rectangular table with eight chairs. "Please have a seat. Luncheon will be served."

"Thank you." Samuel met her eyes, hesitating on where to sit.

The vicar, noticing their hesitation, offered her a chair. "Please sit here, Mrs. Radcliff. Mr. Radcliff can sit beside you."

"Thank you," Clarice said as she sat down and Mr. St. George pushed her chair in. One servant served the food—a thick rabbit stew that smelled and tasted wonderful. Fresh bread and sweet cream, fruits, and nuts also accompanied the meal.

As the dishes were being cleared away, Clarice leaned toward

Samuel and whispered, "Would you please get the gifts from the coach? There are five of them."

Samuel stood up. "Please excuse me. I have some things to retrieve from the carriage."

Mrs. St. George said, "Reginald, why don't you go with Mr. Radcliff and help him?"

"Yes, Mama."

Clarice covered her mouth to hide her gasp. He even sounded like a young Samuel from when they were children playing together.

"Let us relax and talk in the drawing room," Mrs. St. George said as she led the way into the next room, which was bright with three large windows, two settees, and several chairs. "Sometimes the vicar entertains his parishioners here, so it's a little crowded with furniture."

"Not at all. It looks very cozy and welcoming."

"Please have a seat. You and Mr. Radcliff can take that settee, while the vicar and I will take this one."

"Thank you," she said as she sat down, hoping her nerves would settle and the awkwardness between them would fade. Meeting new people was always discomforting, but these were her son's family—people she could only acknowledge as Mr. and Mrs. St. George.

SAMUEL WALKED BESIDE Reginald toward the mews behind the house, which was right next to the small white stone church, with the burial ground on the other side. All the while, he tried to think of things to ask or say. His tongue and mouth wouldn't cooperate. Everything he wanted to say sounded wrong for a six-year-old.

He opened the door to the carriage, which was parked outside the stables, and motioned for Reginald to come closer.

"These two are for your parents. Take care with them."

"Yes, sir," he said with a nod as he held out his arms, and Samuel placed the packages in the boy's arms, one of which was quite heavy.

Samuel grabbed the three others, and they headed back to the house, his tongue still tied in knots. How could a six-year-old have him so nervous that he couldn't talk or think straight? *Because he's no ordinary six-year-old. He's your son.* All the more reason he should be able to speak to him.

"Mama!" Reginald exclaimed as he rushed into the room holding two presents. "They brought you and Papa presents." He handed one to his mother and one to his father.

Mrs. St. George's eyes sparkled with excitement. "Let the children open theirs first."

"We have presents, too?" Richard asked with wide, excited eyes.

"Of course," said Samuel as he handed them out. "We could hardly come visit our good friends without bearing gifts, could we?"

All three faces looked to their mother. "You may open," she said with laughter.

They tore through the wrapping, and the room's noise grew louder. "Look, Mama," Penelope said. "It's a dolly." She hugged the doll. "She is so pretty. Thank you, Mr. and Mrs.—what's their name, Mama?" she whispered, not very quietly. Samuel tried not to chuckle at the sweet little girl.

"Radcliff, my dear."

"Radcliff, thank you. She's pretty."

"I'm glad you like her," Clarice said, a tear falling down her cheek. His poor wife, overwhelmed by the emotions of carrying a child. Add the emotional overload from meeting their son, and he wondered why she was not sobbing into her handkerchief.

Richard opened his eyes and exclaimed, looking puzzled. "What is it, Papa?"

"It is backgammon. It's a game that I will teach you. You are still young, but you will learn quickly. Perhaps tonight I can teach you?"

"I would like that, Papa."

Reginald opened his present and shouted, "Look, Mama, Papa, it's my very own chess game. Now Papa won't be upset when I move his pieces around the board."

Samuel hadn't realized he'd been holding his breath while Reginald opened his present, and he inhaled deeply. His heart eased up on the pounding, and he noticed Clarice sighed and looked more relaxed.

"Now your turn, Mama and Papa," Reginald exclaimed with excitement.

Mrs. St. George opened her box and gasped as she dug through the paper wrapping. "It is lovely." She lifted out a wash basin and bowl decorated with blue and yellow flowers. "Thank you so much." She whipped a tear away, but others followed. "Your turn, vicar," his wife said with a beaming smile and tears streaming down her cheeks.

His eyes widened in surprise and elation when he saw what it was. Samuel and Clarice had hunted far and wide to find the beautifully illustrated Bible.

"Thank you," he said, hugging it to his chest. "It's the most beautiful Bible I've ever seen. I can't thank you enough."

Samuel nodded to him. "It is we who cannot thank you and Mrs. St. George enough. You have eased our troubled minds and hearts. There is no finer house than yours anywhere." When the vicar nodded, Samuel knew he understood. No finer house for their son to grow up in than theirs.

They spent nearly every moment of the next few days together until, teary-eyed, they had to say goodbye. Samuel and Clarice promised to visit at the same time next year.

EPILOGUE

THE SHARP PAINS stole her breath as they rolled over her stomach. Clarice wasn't frightened this time. She knew what to expect, unlike Reginald's delivery when nobody explained what happened in childbirth, and she thought her insides were being torn apart and she would die. She also had the support of a midwife and their family physician.

"Where's Samuel?" she asked Letitia. Another pain hit, and she moaned through it.

Letitia appeared worried. "I'll get him."

Clarice turned her head and watched Letitia open the door, gasp, and say, "You startled me. Clarice is asking for you."

A white-faced Samuel, the love of her life, stepped around Letitia and approached her bedside. "I'm here." One hand clasped hers while the other brushed her damp, sweaty hair back from her forehead. "I've been right outside, pacing the corridor, going crazy with worry." Concern radiated from his grey eyes. His mouth was tight, and his brows furrowed.

"Everything is progressing normally. Just as I remember it from before."

Bending down, he brushed his lips across hers. "I love you. Perhaps with the new baby, our life will settle down and become boring. I might enjoy boring for a while."

She laughed, then started to loudly groan. "Don't make me

laugh. It hurts. And boring? Samuel Radcliff, what would we do with boring?"

"I said for a spell. Not forever." He squeezed her hand. "Life with you will never be boring."

"Ouhhh,"

"I see the head," Miss Trumball said. "Next contraction, push hard and long until I say stop."

Clarice felt the urge to push, so she did, and moments later, she heard loud crying. "It's a healthy girl," Miss Trumball said as she passed the baby to Dr. Hughes. He cleaned her off, wrapped her in a blanket, and handed her to Clarice.

"Congratulations. You have a healthy baby girl, Your Graces," said Dr. Hughes.

"Look at her," Samuel said with a beaming smile. "She is beautiful. What shall we name her?"

"I was thinking Mary Elizabeth for my mother and yours."

He bent down and kissed first his lovely wife and then his daughter's forehead. "It's perfect. Our mothers would be honored."

Another wave of needing to push hit her. "Is that the afterbirth?" she asked through huffs of painful breaths.

"No."

Clarice tried to sit up and look, though she knew it wouldn't help—her stomach was still large and she couldn't see. "What is it then?"

"Another baby," Dr. Hughes said with a smile.

"Push," Miss Trumball said.

Clarice barely had time to push when she felt the baby slide out of her body, followed by more cries.

"It's a healthy boy," Dr. Hughes said as he cleaned the baby and wrapped him up, handing him to Samuel, whose mouth hung open in shock. "Congratulations, Your Graces. A girl and a boy. You have your heir."

Within thirty minutes, the room was cleaned, the bedding changed, Clarice was washed and changed into a nightgown, and the family of four was alone.

"Have you thought of a name for him?" She suspected Samuel would want to use either his father's or his brother's name. "Alexander Edward Radcliff. I think it's a fitting name for my heir."

"It is. I always loved the name Alexander."

He put his hand on his chest. "I'm wounded."

"Lean down so I can kiss you."

He did, and she did.

"I love Samuel, as well. The name and the man."

This time, he kissed her.

"Remember when you hoped for boring?" Clarice said as a baby suckled at each breast. "I have a feeling twins will be anything but boring."

Hearing her husband's laughter and having two babies to nurture and love brought tears to her eyes.

Tears of joy. Of rebirth and new beginnings.

THE END

About the Author

Christine Donovan is an International Bestselling Author who writes romance that touches the heart, soothes the soul and feeds the mind. In addition to writing historical romance set in the Regency era, she also writes contemporary romance.

When she landed her first job at sixteen as a cashier at a supermarket, the first thing she did each week on payday was stop at the local bookstore and buy the latest historical romance. It was a dream of hers back then to become a romance author.

She lives on the Southeast Coast of Massachusetts with her husband. She has four grown sons, two granddaughters, two cats, and a black lab named Luna. In her spare time, she can be found at the beach, reading, painting, or gardening. She loves to tackle DIY projects.

Website: authorchristinedonovan.com
Newletter: www.authorchristinedonovan.com/newsletter
Amazon: amazon.com/Christine-Donovan/e/B00APR743Y
Facebook: authorchristinedonovan
Instagram: christinedonovan6